I0681355

Someday Is Today

And Other Stories

An Anthology

by
Aaron Kemp

Order this book online at www.trafford.com
or email orders@trafford.com

Most Trafford titles are also available at major online book retailers.

Printed in Victoria, BC, Canada.

ISBN: 978-1-4269-3155-0 (sc)

ISBN: 978-1-4269-3156-7 (hc)

ISBN: 978-1-4269-3157-4 (e-book)

Library of Congress Control Number: 2010906371

*Our mission is to efficiently provide the world's finest, most comprehensive book publishing
service, enabling every author to experience success. To find out how to publish your book, your
way, and have it available worldwide, visit us online at www.trafford.com*

Trafford rev. 4/30/2010

 www.trafford.com

North America & international
toll-free: 1 888 232 4444 (USA & Canada)
phone: 250 383 6864 ♦ fax: 812 355 4082

Contents

Someday Is Today

Chapter One

Discontent sneaks through the cracks of a man's life at uncertain, unexpected times. A myriad of things bring on unwanted feelings of anxiety and restlessness that open the fissures. Perhaps they can be stuffed back or postponed, but the feelings can't be ignored for long. Discontent hangs on through every effort to end it with reason or judgment, growing worse with efforts to disengage it from consciousness. Frustration results from the attempts to avoid the discomfort that malcontentment causes.

Discontent shouldn't be confused with boredom, which, like guilt, is a manmade feeling. Boredom is the product of lack of imagination.

How many times had he found himself daydreaming about what he would do someday? When *was* someday, anyhow?

Dr. Mickovich, known to all as "Mick" or "Doc," was confused by his discontent. At sixty-two, Mick was a successful general surgeon and practitioner from a small, pleasant town in rural California. His twenty-one-year-old son lived with him when he wasn't away at college. He had a small but comfortable ranch in the foothills above Salinas, 125 acres of irrigated pasture, a few polled Hereford cows, and four nice Mustang-Arabian horses that Mick enjoyed riding, training, or just watching.

His practice was busy and successful. At sixty, he was excused from emergency-room calls, so his time was reasonably predictable. His office was open four days a week, and he did the surgeries that weren't too demanding and that interested him. He was financially secure, with stocks and annuities that guaranteed him more comfort than he dreamed of having when he was a young man just starting out.

Breast cancer took his wife of forty years only five years earlier. The hollow place left inside him when she died gradually filled with comfortable memories and hopeful anticipation of future happiness and purpose, though no matter how close those feelings came, they never fully moved in. Gradually, his optimism faded, and he became more matter-of-fact than he liked.

His two children were doing well. His daughter, Jean, finished teaching college, married well, and was expecting her second child. Clark, his son, was in his fourth year of pre-med. Despite a slow start and some wild times in early college, Clark's grades were good. He had an excellent chance of being accepted into medical school, even if it was in Mexico. Clark finally shaped up when Mick refused to give him any more money. He buckled down and worked his way through school as a deck hand on his Uncle Vito's fishing boat out of Pedro. Clark had a lot of pride, and Mick was proud of him. He told Clark he'd set aside money for his medical schooling, assuming he was accepted somewhere.

Mick had a close relationship with Linda for the previous three years, but he could hardly call it a romance, though she might. Weekends in Vegas and San Diego, a cruise through the Panama Canal, and two weeks in Tahiti solidified nothing. He wondered if he were capable of loving her the way she wanted. He had no one else, and he liked being with her and thought about her a lot, but he just wasn't sure.

The situation came to a head after Clark came home for winter quarter. He seemed pensive and preoccupied, which fit Mick's mood, too. After several abortive attempts to draw Mick out, Clark tearfully announced that he didn't know what he wanted to do. He wasn't returning to school for spring quarter. He wasn't happy with the prospect of medical school and the hours of dedicated study, and he wasn't sure he wanted to be a doctor.

"I don't know what I want, for Christ's sake," he said.

Mick understood, though he felt disappointed, too. "I'm sure you've given this a lot of thought. What have you come up with?" he asked in a fatherly way.

"I want to run Vito's boat. I got some ideas about going deeper and identifying different species before we set on them. We could go after Petrole sole instead of filling up with Dover or black cod, and yellow eye rather than rock cod, which are too small and getting smaller."

Clark fidgeted. "I wonder if you could see your way clear to give me the money you set aside for medical school to buy the gear?" A hint of pleading came to his eyes as he looked at his father. "I'll pay you back. Vita has already said he wants to give me the *Hooker.* Just give it to me! His girls don't want it, and his son's a busy lawyer who hates fishing."

Mick looked out the window, at the ceiling, the floor, his shoes, and his hands. "Just give it to you?"

"Yes, for one dollar." He paused. "There's something else, Dad. I want to write. I really want to be a writer." There was a long, uncomfortable pause. "I'll have lots of time with the boat on autopilot and the net out." He smiled, and Mick smiled back.

Mick stood, walked around the silent room, and turned to Clark, who looked apprehensive and tense. "All right. We'll do it."

"Don't you have to think about it, Dad? I mean, this is great, but...."

"Nope. It's on one condition."

"What?"

"I'm coming with you."

"You're going fishing?"

"Yes. We're going fishing on Vito's boat. Someday is today."

"What?"

"Never mind."

Chapter Two

Plans moved ahead rapidly. Mick, with Clark, arranged for a replacement to come to his office three days a week. His receptionist and billing clerk would stay on as long as they were needed. His office nurse was happy to work only three days a week.

Mick would be able to return to his office if he wanted or needed and take up where he left off. For the first time in a long while, he found himself humming, whistling, and singing out loud. He made a dinner date with Linda, eager to tell her and hoping she would share his enthusiasm.

The date didn't go very well. She was late, which was unusual, and she immediately ordered a Bloody Mary—also unusual. After planting a platonic kiss on the bald spot on Mick's head, she began small talk and pleasantries.

Finally, she looked at him with earnest restraint. "Mick, the bank wants to promote me to managing director. It's a vice-president's position."

"Well, that's wonderful, Linda."

She didn't seem pleased.

"Isn't it?" he asked.

"They'd have to transfer me to San Diego," she said flatly, her eyes searching his.

"Oh." He twisted his water glass in discomfort. When she didn't speak, he asked, "When?"

"Thirty days."

Anxiety tugged at him. So many things were changing. They ate lunch, but it was more like picking at their food in silence.

"I have some news, too," he said, looking at her over a forkful of fish and chips. He explained his plans, and she stared in disbelief.

"You're going commercial fishing? You're nuts," she declared.

The words, *Where does that leave us?* remained unsaid on her face. When she left, she went with barely a good-bye.

Troubled, he watched her go. She was fifty years old, intelligent, attractive, athletic, and had been divorced for a while. She had two grown sons who were married and living hundreds of miles away.

She'd be a great catch, he thought. *I don't want to lose her. I might even love her, but.... But what?*

"I don't know," he said softly. *Someday, maybe. Not today. Someday isn't today.*

Chapter Three

Red opened the sliding, sticky galley door and stepped into the deck, immediately feeling the breeze on his whiskered cheek, beet red and sensitive from the sun. Though slight, the breeze felt too cool. Rather than constant, it was intermittent, then turning brisk again a few seconds later.

He automatically scanned the horizon. It wasn't yet dusk, but sea birds winged toward shore and not in any formation. They weren't in a hurry, but they were flying at a constant rate without looking back or calling to each other. They kept the same altitude, not diving into the sea after bait fish or stopping to rest, bobbing on the incessant waves as they seemed to love.

In the warm, humid air, beads of sweat clung to Red's brow, and his shirt stuck to his back and underarms as he climbed the ladder to the bridge and into the wheelhouse.

He poked a finger repeatedly at the barometer glass, seeing the needle fall four units. He studied the horizon again, looking west. Five miles away, another vessel appeared and disappeared as if it were a magic trick.

Those shitheads, he thought. *They followed us out here, because we know where to fish.*

The thought brought some satisfaction. Those people followed only high-liners, not rust bucket half-assed scows. His brow wrinkled, as he squinted at the horizon. *The swell's building,* he realized.

Eight to ten miles west, he saw clouds gathering, with billowing fingers raised skyward—large, white thunderheads. With a gentle shove, he took the wheel from Ted, his son.

"Go down, get some dinner, and straighten up the galley," Red said. "We'll bring the net aboard soon."

Ted glanced at him inquisitively. "It's been only an hour, Dad."

Without looking at him, Red said matter-of-factly, "We're in for a blow. Get moving."

Ted looked at the horizon and saw the clouds in the west. "Yep." He left for the galley, feeling stupid for not noticing the change.

Ted and Steve, Red's sons, were good fishermen and sailors in their own right. They could navigate and steer with, against, or forty-five into a swell and hold a course within a few degrees, spinning or slowly moving the large wheel just enough each time. They were quick with mending nets and could splice line and cable using a marlinspike with skill and ease. They knew the names of the myriad fish species they caught and could calculate, within a penny, the going price per pound.

They were sailors who respected the ocean, weather, wind, sea, and their father.

Steve, the oldest at twenty-seven, quit school in the tenth grade when he was sixteen to fish full time with his father when he first acquired the *Charm.* Ted followed him two years later when he reached the same grade. They worked hard to refit, paint, repair, and refurnish the fifty-two-foot boat thought by many to be the best of its class in California. She could handle a storm, though a true sailor hated storms.

As Ted and Steve put away items in the galley, they felt apprehensive and carefully fastened all drawers and doors.

In less than thirty minutes, they were finished and stood on deck to gaze west. The boat rolled from port to starboard in an irregular rhythm that was difficult to anticipate or remain standing. A sailor on deck always stood with his legs wide while holding onto something stable. After many years of that, he did it on shore, too, out of habit. A sailor's knees were never locked but acted like automatic hinges, moving up and down with the roll of the sea. Consequently, his knees were always bent a few degrees.

Both men stood and held on, their legs broad-based, pulling on gear over their rubber boots.

Red slowed the boat to a two-knot crawl, keeping the bow forty-five degrees into the swell. "OK, start her in!" he called out the pilothouse door.

Steve pushed the big dog tender forward. With a soft moan of protest, the cable slowly came in, laid out in perfect rows by the level wind. It was nine-sixteenths stainless steel, capable of holding and pulling 30,000 pounds, painstakingly manufactured in Coos Bay, Oregon, where the magnificent winches were also made, the best and strongest available, used by fishing vessels around the world. When a wave struck the stern, the stretched cable sang like a banjo string. If it broke, it would send a man's head into the watch like a beach ball.

Fishing was dangerous work. The storm made it more so.

At first, the wind was just a little cooler than usual, but it soon turned cold and became a constant nine knots, with gusts up to twelve or fifteen. It whistled through the rigging, blowing the small flags into a flapping frenzy.

The clouds finished forming and covered the sky with gray, blowing amorphously west to east. The ceiling was no more than 700 feet. In the distance, sheets of dry lightning bit the sky.

The crew waited patiently for the huge doors to break the surface. Those were flat metal or heavy wood structures weighing 500 pounds or more, designed to hold the net mouth open and scoop in fish. When they were brought up from the depths, they swung to the side on additional cables supported and managed by large double blocks as they were shouldered into their rest positions on both sides of the stern. Heavy and difficult at the best of times, in rough seas, they were dangerous.

Finally, the two doors emerged from the stormy surface. The winches, lightened by the reduction in surface tension, turned faster, until the doors swung in the air.

The pull of the heavy net leveled the boat against the swell at first, then, with the storm held down, the bow swung from side to side in the waves. It was difficult for Red to maintain course, so he cursed as he fought the wheel.

The heavy doors came alongside, as the vessel pitched crazily. They came in unevenly, with the port three feet behind the starboard. The port side was left dangling on its cable as the port winch shut down, allowing the starboard one to catch up. Ted watched the starboard side over his shoulder as his own side was allowed to land.

"For God's sake, pull that port door up and make it fast!" he called.

The warning came too late. The boat lurched with the increased pull from the oncoming port sea. In an instant, the huge, heavy door came up over the gunnel and, with a sickening crunch, struck Ted's back under his arm. He was thrown across the deck like a rag doll and lay in a heap, moaning pitifully.

Red stared at the scene for a second. "For Christ's sake!" He turned on the autopilot and darted down the stairs to the deck. "Shut off that winch and help me over here!" he called to Steve.

Together, they wrestled the door around, backed the heavy cables, and lashed the door securely into place.

"Get the other one up," Red said.

"All right." Steve started the starboard winch again. When the door was alongside, they secured it, pulling and straining with the roll of the deck. Once that was finished, Steve started the net reel and wound the net aboard.

Ted hadn't moved. He lay with his face against the deck, breathing with difficulty, feeling apprehensive and in pain.

Red stood over him and lifted under his arms until Ted was on his feet. "You all right, Boy?"

"No." He coughed painfully. "My ribs are broken. I can fell them crunching. I'm hurt bad."

"Bullshit. Get up to the wheelhouse and keep her on course while we get the fucking cod in."

Ted held onto the bulkhead as he staggered to the ladder and crawled to the flying bridge. He was silent, though his face distorted and twisted with pain. With an effort, he slid open the door and fell into the wheelhouse, resting against the wheel.

The excruciating pain in his chest made him dizzy and nauseous. He stomach suddenly ached with a constant pain that was intermittently severe.

Nausea overcame him, and he vomited out the porthole. Staggering back, he slumped to the floor behind the wheel, unable to hold up his head as black fog settled over his eyes. Just before he fainted, an uncontrollable cough overcame him. Warm, frothy blood spewed between his lips and ran down his chin.

The net was reeled into the cod end, which was packed with 10,000 pounds of bottom fish. Working quickly, Steve and Red strapped the sack filled with fish aboard, spilling them into holders on the deck. With the net aboard, the boat floated more easily on the waves, rolling into the troughs between the swells.

Steve looked pleadingly at his angry, red-faced father, who stood on deck, his hands on his hips and up to his knees in fish.

"Ted's hurt bad, Dad," Steve said.

"Bullshit. He just cracked a rib."

Almost reluctantly, Red left the deck, climbed up to the flying bridge, and moved along the pitching deck to the wheelhouse. "What a hell of a mess," he muttered, shaking his head in resignation.

He wasn't prepared for what he found in the wheelhouse. Horrified, he saw Ted slumped on his side on the floor, with bloody sputum and dried vomit on his face. Ted was ashen and wet with sweat. Thinking his son was dead, Red felt his heart lurch.

"Steve!" He gently lifted Ted to the bunk on the wheelhouse's after wall.

Steve heard his father's desperate tone and ran to the wheelhouse as fast as he could. "Oh, God, Dad. What should we do?"

"Get on the horn and call the Coast Guard. Tell 'em we need a doctor fast!"

Steve took the mike in his trembling hand, flipped on the emergency channel, and said, "Calling the Coast Guard. Calling the Coast Guard. This is *M.V. Charm* calling Coast Guard. Mayday. Mayday."

The radio crackled, then a voice said, "This is the Coast Guard, Point Hieden back to the *Charm*. Please advise. Are you sinking and in immediate danger?"

"No. We have a severely injured man aboard. We need a doctor immediately."

"What's your position, *Charm?*"

"Loran lines 15796 and 60392."

"What are the weather conditions?"

"Twenty-foot seas, with ten- or fifteen-knot winds. It'll take us two or three hours to get to shore."

"We can't get a chopper out there now. There's a storm, and it's dark as hell. What's happening with the injured seaman? We'll ask a medic to advise you."

Red ran across the wheelhouse and grabbed the mike from Steve's hand. "Listen to me, You! It's my son, and he needs help! He was hit in the chest with a seven-cawl door. Do you know what that is? It weighs half a ton. He's coughing up blood. If he doesn't get help, he'll die. He's *not* a fucking seaman. He's my son. Now get a chopper out here!"

There was a pause, as the radio crackled.

"Stand by, *Charm.*"

"Stand by my ass!" Red shouted into the mike, dropping it and walking back to Ted. "Ted, open your eyes. Can you?"

Slowly, Ted's eyelids fluttered open. "Dad? Oh, God, Dad, my side and belly. I'm hurt. I'm dying. Help me."

Red wiped moisture from his cheeks and awkwardly placed a blanket over Ted. He felt for a pulse and found it was rapid and so weak he could barely feel it. Panic began to overtake his reasoning.

"How about that doctor on the *Rose*, Dad?" Steve asked.

Red stood slowly and moved stiffly toward the mike. "Calling the Coast Guard. *Charm.*"

"*Charm*, this is the Coast Guard, Medic Daniels speaking. Describe the patient's condition."

"Shit," Red said. "He's in terrible pain in his chest and belly. He almost hasn't got a pulse. He's puking and spitting up blood."

"Do you have a first-aid box?"

"Yeah, but all it has are some bandages and aspirin and shit."

"Don't give him any morphine. He's probably in shock."

"Morphine? I don't have any morphine."

"Have you got IV fluids?"

"What the hell are you talking about? I don't have anything like that."

"Keep him covered and as warm as possible. He's probably in shock."

"Covered and warm? Probably in shock? He's dying, you silly shit! Now get a chopper out here right now!"

There was another long pause.

"Weather conditions won't permit. With daylight...maybe a chance." Another pause followed. "Bad storm."

Ted moaned and coughed.

"Dad, he needs a doctor," Steve said firmly. "If you won't call the *Sea Rose*, I will."

Red stared at the radio. Steve reached for the mike, but his father pulled it away, dialed the selector knob to the hail channel, and spoke evenly. *"Sea Rose. Sea Rose. This is Charm."*

Ted coughed as they waited. Bloody spittle gathered on his lips.

"Sea Rose. Sea Rose. Sea Rose. This is Charm. Come in, please." Red closed his eyes and whispered, "Please, God."

"This is *Sea Rose,* back to call," a clear voice replied.

"Is the doctor aboard?" he pleaded.

"Yes, this is the doctor. Is there a problem? What's the matter?"

"Doc, my son.... He got hurt, hit by a door. Can you help me?"

There was another long pause. Red was ready to shout into the mike when Doc said, "What's happening with him? Where was he hit?"

"In the back on the left side. His ribs are broke. I can feel 'em move. He hurts like hell, and he coughs a lot. There's blood in his spit."

"Does he have abdominal pain?"

"What?"

"Does his belly hurt?"

"Yes, and it's swelling up. His pulse is really fast and weak, Doc."

"All right, *Charm*. I'm coming over. Did you call the Coast Guard?"

"Fuck, yes, but they can't help in this storm. Some shit-hell medic...."

"We're only a mile to your west. I can see your lights, I think.

Switch your mast light off and on. OK, *Charm,* I have you. Hold on."

Red dropped the mike and let it hang by its cord. "God, hurry."

The *Charm* pitched and rolled automatically to the swell trough. Red turned the bow into the waves and turned the engine up to 2700 RPMs, aiming for the lights to the west. Ted rolled slowly onto his left side, while Steve held his hand.

Aboard the *Sea Rose,* they just finished sorting their catch into the bins—only 2,000 pounds—when they heard the call. Clark, seasick almost to death, leaned over the rail, vomiting frequently. He was too sick to remove his oilskins and go below. His only comfort was the cool breeze on his cheeks.

"Someone's calling on the radio," Doc said, turning the bow toward the harbor.

After he finished the conversation, he set the autopilot and called to Clark, "Did you hear all that?"

"Yeah. You aren't going to help those assholes, are you? Fuck 'em."

"You get in here and take the wheel."

Clark didn't move.

"Now, Boy!" Doc said firmly.

Clark released the rail, scowled at his father, and reluctantly went into the wheelhouse.

"Head for that mast light," Doc said.

"God, it's rough. I feel awful."

Doc went into his stateroom and pulled out his emergency medical box from under his bunk, opening it to check the contents. There was a good supply of everything. He had three liters of normal saline, two vials of plasma, IV tubes, needles, and bottles of vosaxyl, morphine, Benadryl, and cortisone.

"Good," he said. "I'll need all of it." He closed the lid securely and took the large box onto the deck, fastening a cloverleaf around it with strong nylon line. "Then can swing their boom over to me, then they'll hoist this to their boat. How the hell will I get over, though?"

He looked at the ever-darkening sky and felt the first large, warm, soft, raindrops strike his cheeks. The *Sea Rose* cut through the swell easily, leaving a trail of singing foam in its wake.

He felt a moment of apprehension. *What if he's so injured, I can't help? God, I hope not, but I have to try. Jesus, how will I get to their boat in this swell and wind?* He looked into the sky and let rain fall softly on his face. "Jesus, be with us this night."

When the *Charm* came alongside, Red ran to the gunnels and shouted, "Keep about a fathom apart, so we won't bang into each other!"

Doc immediately took charge. "Loosen your boom, Red, and let it swing over my deck, so I can get my medical equipment over there."

Red appraised the situation for a moment, then silently released the guy lines on the boom. He expertly swung it toward the *Sea Rose*. While the boats pitched and tossed, nearly colliding more than once, Doc took the line from the end pulley of the boom and tied it to the four loops of the clover hitch on his medical box.

"Keep going straight ahead at three or four knots," he told Clark, who stood at the wheel. "You do the same, Red."

Red didn't reply, but his son called, "Gotcha!" and waved his arm out the wheelhouse window. With both vessels moving slowly at forty-five degrees to the waves, they were stable enough for Red to winch the boom back to his vessel and lower the bag safely to the deck.

"Good!" Doc shouted. "Now untie it and swing the boom back to me."

"Are you crazy, Dad?" Clark asked. "You're going to swing over there?"

"You got another idea? Should I jump?"

He flipped on the autopilot and moved aft.

"Damn you, get back in and steer!" Doc said.

The *Sea Rose* was lifted by an extralarge wave that sent it crashing into the side of the *Charm*. Doc watched his son race obediently back to the wheel and resume control of the boat.

Red swung the boom back over the *Rose's* deck. Doc hooked the line from the end black, pulled up some slack, and snapped it into a snug loop around his waist. He reached overhead and grasped the line tightly.

"Red," he shouted, "can you get me pulled up and over there? Can you hold me?"

"I can," Red called back.

With the strength of one powerful arm, Red pulled hard on his end of the line, lifting Doc one foot off the deck. With his other arm, he swung the boom back toward his vessel. It took a tremendous effort, but it was going well until Doc had one foot on the *Charm's* bulkhead.

Suddenly, both boats were hit by a large, rolling wave crested with windblown froth. The boats lurched and dodged crazily. Red held on with all his strength, sweat rolling down his face, eyes bulging with effort. All Doc could do was hang on, which he did until his hands ached from the strain.

He swung past three or four feet, then back, but he couldn't get over the side. His foot slipped off again, and he dangled precariously between the boats. An even bigger wave lifted the *Sea Rose* and slammed it hard into the *Charm*.

Red saw it coming and pulled Doc up as hard as he could. When the *Charm* rolled, Doc was finally over the deck. Red released the lines, and Doc crashed to the deck in a heap. Red grabbed Doc with both arms just as the wildly swinging boom came to the end of the line attached to Doc's waist. It pulled him to one side, and there was a momentary tug of war between Red and the boom, with Doc in the middle.

"Undo the damn line before it squeezes the shit out of me!" Doc said in quiet desperation.

Between them, they unfastened the swivel and released the line. They stood on the pitching deck, panting and relieved.

"If I knew you were going to drop me like that, I would've worn a parachute."

"Sorry, Man. You have to see my son quick. He's bad hurt."

Doc took one step toward the wheelhouse and fell forward on his hands as his ankle gave way with a nauseating surge of pain. He felt the grind of bone ends and stifled a cry. "I broke my ankle. Help me up the ladder."

Red looked at him, then at the ladder. With a grunt, he hoisted Doc to his shoulder and carried him up without any apparent effort.

They went across the bridge and into the wheelhouse, where he set Doc on the captain's chair.

Doc quickly took Ted's pulse. The young man didn't move and took short, painful breaths. His pulse was rapid and weak. Doc felt his cool, moist brow.

"He's shocky," Doc said. "Get that medicine box up here fast. Cover him with a blanket. Take off his boots and jacket first."

Red went back for the box, while Steve assisted Doc, rapidly removing each rubber boot and tossing them out of the way.

"Help me with his jacket," Doc said. "Lift easy."

Ted moaned and cried out as they removed his oilskin jacket. By the time Doc has his shirt unbuttoned, Steve tucked a blanket around his brother.

"Raise his legs up on something, too," Doc said. "What's your name?"

"Steve."

"Raise his legs into the air, Steve. Put those life jackets under them. We need to get them elevated."

Red returned, set the medical box on the deck, and opened the latches. Doc pulled out a plastic IV bottle of saline. Plugging in the IV tube, he let it fill, holding the bottle up with one hand. "Hold this, Steve."

Steve eagerly lifted it as high as he could reach.

"Not that high. Just hold it a moment." Doc took out an eighteen-gauge needle and attached it to the line, then he put a blood-pressure cuff on Ted's arm and pumped as he listened. He was barely able to hear the blood pressure. "Eighty over forty," he muttered.

"What does that mean?" Red asked apprehensively.

Doc didn't reply as he adjusted the blood-pressure cuff to fit so the veins would fill, then he took the IV bottle from Steve and held it below the patient while he punctured his antecubital vein at the elbow. When he saw blood enter the tube, he knew he'd hit the vein.

"Fasten the bottle on something high up," he said, deftly taping the needle into place. Taking a Velcro fastener IV board from the box, he attached it to Ted's outstretched arm.

"Good." He watched saline pour in and opened the valve all the way. Then he listened to Ted's chest. He heard air moving in and out on the right side, though Ted's breathing was labored. On the left, he heard ribs cracking together but no sound of moving air. The heartbeat had a strange slapping sound.

"He's got several broken ribs, and I think he's got a punctured lung." He listened intently at the apex of the lung. "He has a pneumothorax."

"Christ," Red said. "What's that?"

Doc listened, talking softly to himself, "He has a tension pneumo from the rib fracture puncturing the lung."

"Doc, what's happening?"

Doc looked up at Steve, who attached the IV bottle to the swinging chart light. "That's good. Start heading us in at a safe speed." He turned. "Red, do you have any medical equipment? There's no oxygen in this kit. Do you have an oxygen bottle?"

"Yes. There's a small one with the welder."

"Get it. Now."

Red raced out the door.

Ted looked better with the IV fluid, but he was still pale and seemed to struggle for air.

Doc, rummaging through his box, found an endotrachial tube, but there was no laryngoscope. He looked again without any success.

"There's no laryngoscope!"

"What?" Steve asked.

"I need a scope to put the endotracheal tube in his trachea. There's no fucking scope in this box!"

"What can we do?"

"We'll have to try something else." Doc thought hard. He had to release tension on Ted's left side. With each inhalation, air leaked between the lung and chest wall, not only slowly collapsing the lung from pressure but also forcing the heart and great vessels to the right, shifting the mediabtinum.

Doc moved the blood-pressure cuff to the other arm and read ninety over fifty. He glanced at the IV bottle, saw it was almost empty, and changed it once it went flat, letting it run directly in for a few minutes. Then he slowed it to a constant drip at about 200cc/minute.

"I'll just try to keep him at ninety systolic," he muttered.

Steve nodded, though he didn't know what that meant.

When Red returned with the oxygen bottle, Doc saw he'd cut the rubber tube, so it could be used to reach Ted.

"I brought a garbage bag, too," Red said, holding up the bag.

"What for?" Suddenly, he understood and slapped himself.

The two men opened the bag, punctured a hole in the bottom, and put the tube in. Masking tape helped seal the tube, as both men worked to fashion a makeshift oxygen tent. Red opened the valve on the bottom too fast at first, but Doc soon regulated it to a constant flow. They placed the bag over Ted's face and tucked it around the sides. He seemed more comfortable almost instantly, but his breathing was still labored and irregular.

Doc frowned as he touched Ted's trachea at the base of his neck. "He's got a tension pneumo, all right."

"Christ, Doc," Red said. "What does that mean?"

Doc explained how the leaking air was pushing Ted's lung sideways as it collapsed, like a low-pressure pump with a check valve, pumping air between the chest wall and the lung.

"I need some sort of one-way…. Wait. I've got an idea. Have you got any rubbers?"

"What? Rubbers?"

"Condoms. You got any?"

"Steve, you got any?" Red asked.

Steve hesitated. "Yeah, I have a couple in my wallet."

"Give 'em to him."

Steve fumbled in his back pocket, pulled out his wallet, and took out two blue-colored rubber condoms neatly placed in a folded sandwich bag. He handed them to Doc without a word, then turned to take over the wheel.

Doc found two number fourteen large-bore needles in his box. With many silk sutures, he tied the open end of the condoms over the connecting ends of the needles. With a scissors, he cut a small hole in the closed end. Knowing it would work, he felt some elation.

"I'm putting a hole in the cod end," he said, using a fishing term that referred to the bag at the end of the drag net that collected fish.

Steve and Red looked at him blankly.

"Never mind," Doc said, "though it *was* pretty funny."

He felt Ted's side and located the space between two broken ribs.

He pushed the needle through into his chest at an angle, slipping over the rib above. Ted winced and moaned.

"Hold still, Fella," Doc said. "This'll help you breathe better."

They all heard air escaping from the end of the condom as Ted took a breath. As he exhaled, the condom sucked shut against itself. A second needle-condom valve was deftly inserted into a space above and posterior to the first.

They worked. Each time Ted took a breath, his lung expanded against the air trapped in his chest, forcing it out the needle. When he exhaled, and the chest wall fell, air was kept from being sucked back in, because the condom collapsed, forming a shutter valve.

"Praise God," Doc said.

"What?" Red asked. "Will he be all right?"

"A wise friend of mine told me that good ideas come from God, so praise God."

"What?" Then Red realized the meaning of Doc's words and said, "Yes! Praise God, all right."

Ted became less restless, as his breathing eased. Doc felt his abdomen. It was firm and tender, slightly distended. He carefully pressed down a few inches under the ribcage on the left.

"Does this hurt here?" Doc asked.

"Yes," Ted said from under the oxygen tent. "A lot."

Doc pushed again and suddenly released pressure. Ted winced and moaned.

"He's got rebound," Doc said softly, placing his stethoscope on Ted's abdomen, where he heard loud, continuous bowel tones from the man's irritated intestines.

"I think he's got a ruptured spleen," Doc said. "There's blood in his belly. How long until we're ashore?"

"Two hours."

"Call the marine operator and contact the hospital. We need an ambulance waiting at the dock, with blood available."

While Red talked, Doc drew up some Demerol in a small syringe and administered it slowly into the IV tub. "This will help a lot," he told Ted. "Try to relax and breathe as deeply as you can. Things are all right. You're going to be fine." His confident tone was comforting to everyone, including himself.

"Can you get a bag of ice for my ankle?" Doc asked Steve. "It's killing me."

As soon as Steve brought the ice, Doc pulled off his boot and felt his own ankle. The bone on the outside moved under his finger, producing a sharp pain, making him gasp. He found an ace bandage and wrapped his ankle snugly, crossing over the joint. That felt better, then he placed a bag of ice over it.

"Is it bad, Doc?" Red asked in concern.

"No. I just broke my fibula."

"Oh." Red had no idea what that was.

Through the marine operator, they arranged to have an ambulance meet them at the dock. For two hours, they cruised toward shore with a following sea, pushing them forward with each wave. Every hour, Doc gave Ted a little more Demerol and kept the IV running at a constant rate, titrating it to maintain blood pressure of ninety. He also gave Ted two units of plasma via the IV. Occasionally, he looked up and was relieved to see the *Sea Rose* following them one hundred yards behind.

When they saw the flashing red light of the ambulance, as they turned around the jetty into the harbor, all that remained in the IV bottle was 100 ccs. Doc heard voices and the scuffing of feet as the ambulance crew came across the flying bridge into the pilothouse.

They skillfully and quickly appraised the situation, then one returned to the ambulance to bring in some O-negative blood in the plastic bottle, attaching it to the IV.

"How big's the needle?" he asked Doc.

"Eighteen gauge. It's in a big vein. Open it up. He's got a ruptured spleen."

"Are you a medic?"

"He's a doctor," Red said.

The driver looked inquisitively at Doc, taking in his scruffy beard and dirty clothes.

"I make house calls," Doc said matter-of-factly.

No one caught the joke.

When the blood was running satisfactorily, the medics carefully lifted Ted out the door and onto a stretcher.

"Be careful," Doc warned. "He's got needles in his left side."

The driver, looking under Ted's T-shirt, saw the needles with the condoms attached. "What the hell?"

"He has pneumo with tension," Doc explained. "Those are valves."

"Well, I'll be jiggered!"

"Call your hospital, and tell them to have the OR ready. He'll need a chest tube with suction, but he can't wait too long for that spleen to be taken care of. You hear?"

"Yes, Doctor. Will do." They carried Ted off the boat with obedient respect in their voices.

Doc sat alone in the wheelhouse. Red and Steve were in the ambulance, riding with Ted. Doc's ankle throbbed with so much pain, he felt ill, but he felt something else, too—elation and pride. He recalled feeling that kind of pride before, when he did well as a doctor, but he always pushed it out of his mind. That time, he let it remain.

"Sometimes, I can be a damn good doctor," he said pensively. "I wish I were the one removing that spleen."

Clark came to the wheelhouse door, deep concern on his face. "Are you all right, Dad?"

"No, I'm not. I broke my ankle." He grinned at his son. "Good job bringing in the boat. Now help me out of here. I have to get to the ER."

Clark lifted his dad to his feet and held onto his waist. "How's the hurt guy?"

"Pretty bad. He's got a punctured lung from broken ribs and a ruptured spleen." He paused. "He'll be all right, as long as the surgeon's any good. I want these stinking boots off."

Ritchie

Chapter One

For most kids, the thought of moving created apprehension and anxiety, even some fear of the unknown. For Ritchie, at age ten, it seemed like a great adventure was beginning. He lived in the city a few blocks from Greenlake. As long as he could remember, he always lived in a big house with a cherry tree in the yard, an empty garage, and an alley where he could play in the dirt. Harold, Ritchie's older brother, took over the garage and turned it into a clubhouse for his friends. Harold was mean and wouldn't let Ritchie or Arne, the other brother, go inside.

Arne was eighteen months older. Mother always called him, "The good boy." Ritchie was known as the clown, a mischievous actor who brought plenty of trouble to himself. He was the one who always got caught. Perhaps he was careless.

He was caught stealing oranges from the cart at the grocery store in Greenwood, and he received a spanking for it. He persuaded Arne to steal a box of wooden matches, so they could light a ball of paper on fire in the paperboy's shack down the street. That caused a lot of excitement. Both boys were spanked for that one, and Arne screamed all the while, "It was Ritchie's idea! He did it!"

When Ritchie was six years old, he crawled into a Model A parked on a slope, released the handbrake, and took a very short excursion into some garbage cans piled against a neighbor's building.

There was no spanking that time, because no harm was done. His father laughed and playfully punched his shoulder.

Then the family planned to move way out into the country, out where cows and horses lived, and there would be forests and streams. Ritchie was dizzy with the idea that he might someday own a horse, though it never happened.

They arrived at their new home near the end of the school year. Ritchie and Arne went into a classroom with other kids who already knew each other. The fourth and fifth grades were in the same room with Franny Burger, a sharp-tongued, round teacher who always seemed to sweat on her nose, making her constantly adjust her eyeglasses.

Most of the time, she was nice, but she was very blunt. She liked Arne, because he was polite, could read better than the others, and stayed out of trouble. She wasn't sure about Ritchie. She couldn't tell if he was bright and saw he was constantly daydreaming and not paying attention. He certainly didn't try very hard. Sometimes, his wisecracks seemed out of control, but he was funny enough that Franny often found herself laughing at him, much to his pleasure and her consternation, not to mention the class' disruption.

The boys tried fighting Ritchie on the playground a few times, but he knew how to fight back and was willing to bite, too, against the bigger boys. They soon left him alone—too much alone.

Arne had no such problem. The biggest kid in the class knocked Arne's books from his hand. Before they were on the floor, Arne punched him square in the nose and sent him crying to the boy's room with a bloody nose. Ritchie noted that Ms. Burger saw the whole thing and didn't say a word. Instead, she went from the hall into her classroom. That was pretty good.

They lived a long distance from the school and had to walk across a cow pasture, through some woods, and along a long, dusty road with a marsh on one side that filled with water when it rained. In the fall, green-headed mallard ducks with bright-red legs flew out of the weeds, honking their protests. In the spring, mother ducks skittered back and forth to their hidden nests. Soon, they were followed by trains of tiny little ducks, paddling desperately to keep up with mama.

Butterflies and brightly colored moths and bugs lived in the lacy, hanging bushes along the road, along with plenty of mosquitoes. Chinese ring-necked pheasants lived on the dry islands between patches of cattails. They were exciting to see walking on the road or taking flight, skimming the low trees and bushes on their way. They cackled wonderfully as they took off, perhaps protesting against whatever disturbed them. In the fall, they crowed and cackled every morning as if challenging the day.

Quail hippity-hopped along, darting into the blackberry bushes and peeking out their heads as people passed.

When the big blackberries were ripe and juicy in late summer, the air was filled with their sweet aroma. The sun-warmed berries were ready to be popped into a boy's mouth. Their fingers, lips, and cheeks became stained with juice, and their arms were scratched.

Ritchie always wondered why God put such awful thorns on blackberries. Maybe it was because they tasted so good. Good things were hard to get. It seemed a law of nature that good things had a price.

On the way to school, Ritchie passed a horse corral with two young horses and a burro. He began bringing sugar cubes and small carrots to feed them and longed to ride one. He liked their smell, the feel of their soft noses, and the breath from their nostrils on his neck and cheeks. They trotted to the fence, grabbed their treats, and ran around, kicking up dust. Ritchie wished he could become a cowboy.

One Saturday, Ritchie gobbled up his oatmeal and ran to the corral, slapping his hip in time with his footfalls to sound like a horse. He went between the rails and approached the docile little burro first. His heart pounding, he pulled himself onto its back.

It just stood there. Ritchie urged the burro forward with his knees and heels. Finally, totally bored, the burro walked slowly around.

That wasn't very exciting. Ritchie slid to the ground and stared at the burro for a moment, then began eyeing the horses. They weren't close enough to the fence for him to be able to mount one, but there was a tree with a good-sized branch at the correct level.

Ritchie climbed the tree and out onto the branch, jockeying his position until he legs dangled off one side. He waited a long time, until finally, the horse with the bald face walked into the right position, mindlessly eating.

"Now's my chance," he whispered.

He spread his legs, dropped onto the unsuspecting animal's back, grabbed its mane, and hung on. The horse took off at a dead run, its feet flying until it reached the fence, where it made a very agile right-hand turn. Ritchie flew over the rail and hit the rocky ground with his hands and face.

The wind was knocked from his lungs, and it was several seconds before he was able to yelp like a wounded animal, which he did very loudly. His hands were scratched, and a stone nicked his forehead, making it bleed.

Finally, when he realized no one was able to hear him, he shut up. Shoving his hands into his pockets, he trudged home. Disappointed, embarrassed, and alone, spitting dirt from his mouth, he vowed he would return someday.

Ritchie was alone that day, because Arne found some neighbor boys who were a year older than Arne. Unfortunately, they wanted nothing to do with his younger brother, so Ritchie couldn't play with them. He had friends at school, but he wasn't allowed to invite them to his house. His mother, who had six kids at home, didn't want any extras hanging around.

Ritchie, lonely and bored, met two kids in a pasture near his home. They seemed friendly until they talked him into peeing on the electric fence, which was a bad idea. When the joke ended, they tried tripping Ritchie. He bawled, saying he'd tell his big brother on them, and then they'd be sorry.

They threw dried horse manure at him, so he ran home.

Ritchie spent his time catching frogs by the hundreds and putting them in big jars with air holes punched in the lids. He wondered why they sometimes stuck together, belly to back. When he separated them, one always scampered to the other and leaped on its back again.

A boy at school who Ritchie played with during recess asked him to his house after school on Friday to spend two nights and attend church with him on Sunday, then his parents would take him home. Ritchie was happy to go and was given a note that he could ride home with his friend after school on the big yellow bus packed with other kids.

It looked like fun. Ritchie wished he were on the bus every day. The kids all knew each other, and, although there was a definite pecking order, at least there was contact. They called each other names, stuck out their tongues, and threw spitballs. They made a lot of noise until the driver made them shut up as best he could. Ritchie liked being with those kids and had no trouble joining in.

There were two separate districts at Lakeland school. One was people who lived in the countryside on stump farms, with doublewide trailers or humble houses, rusted car bodies, junk, and chicken coops in their yards. Ritchie's home had an old trailer house that was being used for a chicken coop. Its roof sagged, and the sides were moldy along the cracked, broken windows. Some of those homes still had outdoor toilets.

By contrast, David lived along Lake Washington, where people had nice homes, beach property with docks and boats, lawns with flowerbeds, and the children were well dressed on their bicycles and scooters. The neighborhood showed prosperity and contentment.

The visit went well at first. David had a large stuffed hobbyhorse in his basement, complete with saddle and bridle, and Ritchie had a fine time riding it, imagining wind on his face. They played with blocks designed to make houses, an electric train that ran around the room, over bridges, under tunnels, and through little towns and stations.

Ritchie stopped and started the train a dozen times, delighting in its whistle. He and David rode bikes up and down the street, with Ritchie riding David's sister's bike, because she wasn't home. Ritchie wondered why it had a curved bar in front of the seat, not a straight one like he was accustomed to. He'd banged himself on the bar at home several times, and it really hurt. There was no such danger with a girl's bike. He pledged that if he ever bought his own bike, he would get a girl's bike no matter what anyone said.

Eventually, Davy's mother called them in for supper. They put the bikes back in the garage and trudged up the kitchen stairs. Davy's mother wore a blue dress and white apron with flowers on it in the same blue shade. As she ordered the young men to wash their hands, she smiled.

When they returned to the dining room, David's father stood

waiting at one end of the table. He was a fat man with a big, red face and balding head. He looked friendly, though he seemed preoccupied.

"Joe, this is Ritchie," Davy's mother said. "What's your last name?"

"Pelton."

"Joe, this is Ritchie Pelton, Davy's little school friend."

Joe held out his hand. Ritchie never shook anyone's hand before, but he knew not to act too limp, so he squeezed hard and pumped the hand up and down. Joe looked startled, then grinned.

"Howdy-do, Ritchie Pelton. Joe Browne, here."

"Howdy-do, Mr. Browne."

"Let's eat."

They sat down. Ritchie sat, feeling strangely embarrassed, and pulled his napkin to his lap when he saw everyone else doing that. Then the three Brownes folded their hands in their laps and bowed their heads.

"Come, Lord Jesus, be our guest, so this food will all be blessed. Amen."

It was a nice dinner of roast beef, mashed potatoes, gravy, string beans, and little brown buns fresh from the oven. The salad contained celery, pickles, and black olives.

Ritchie, who was hungry, felt his self-consciousness vanish as he helped himself to the food in front of him, then more when it was passed his way. Seeing Mr. Browne filling Joey's plate, Ritchie thought that seemed odd.

He was full and satisfied when he looked across the table at David, who had a blank expression with tears in his eyes that were beginning to dribble down his cheeks. What was wrong?

"You eat everything on your plate, Boy," his father hissed under his breath. "You're going to clean your plate if you have to sit here all night, hear me?"

David began sniffling, and more silent tears fell. He shoved mashed potatoes and gravy into his mouth, looking like he wanted to gag, but he swallowed and kept eating until the food was gone. His mother sympathetically reached over his shoulder to cut his meat into small bites. Davy ate them one at a time until they were gone.

All that was left was a pile of string beans. David stared at them, and Ritchie stared, too, clutching his glass of milk and raising it to his mouth just to be doing something in the tense situation.

"I don't like string beans," the crestfallen boy said quietly.

"You can eat half of them," his mother said politely.

"He'll eat every goddamn one," his father snapped. "Clean up your plate."

David skewered half the string beans on his fork like a pitchfork lifting bay. In two loads, he stuffed all of them into his mouth, his cheeks bulging and his eyes watering. He chewed a few times, swallowed with a gasp, and washed them down with milk, some of which came out his nose.

His mother cleared the table humming, trying to be jovial.

Ritchie was confused. Why hadn't Davy eaten all that good food? It was fine. At his own house, with six kids in the family, they took what they could from each plate, or they didn't get to eat. If someone didn't like string beans, someone else would eat them. Why did Davy have to eat something he didn't like?

He was glad he liked everything—except for liver, of course.

Why was Davy's father so mean to him? Was he mad at him? Why had there been a contest at the table, which was supposed to be a happy place? He'd just witnessed a war, but he didn't know who won. It seemed more like a tie.

The boys went to David's room, which had two bunk beds with a bed stand between them. Davy even had his own radio. They listened to *The Shadow,* with Lamont Cranston, who could cloud men's minds to make himself invisible, to *The Lone Ranger,* which helped redefine the *William Tell Overture,* and to *I Have a Mystery.* On the following night, they heard Jack Benny and Red Skelton.

After they listened to the radio, David's mother poked her head in the room. "Get your pajamas on and come down for a piece of cake," she said.

Ritchie frowned. His sisters wore pajamas, but he slept naked.

David pulled on his pajamas, then Ritchie followed him to the kitchen, where two dishes with pieces of chocolate cake were waiting.

David's mother looked at the boys. "Did you forget pajamas, Ritchie?"

"Nope. I don't use them. I don't have any."

"Oh, my. Well, eat your cake, and we'll see what we can do."

After they finished their cake, which Davy ate without any trouble, they returned to his room.

"You boys take a shower bath now," his mom said. "I'll find some pajamas for Ritchie."

He didn't have a shower bath at his house, just a bathtub he used twice a week at most. It was a treat for him to stand under the sprinkler with an endless supply of warm water drenching his body and hair. That was fun. He smiled for the first time since their tense dinner.

Not only did Davy's mother find pajamas for him, she gathered all his clothes, including socks and underwear, and took them to the washing machine. Before leaving the room, she emptied the pockets and left them on the bedside dresser—two marbles, a large rubber band, twenty-five cents in change, a one-dollar bill, a pretty red rock, and a silver bottle cap with the writing worn off. A pair of pajamas were laid out on the bed, and, since Davy wasn't in the room, Ritchie supposed they must be for him.

Davy was a big boy, while Ritchie wasn't. The pajamas hung on him, making him feel like a clown. He stood beside the bed, looking at himself in the mirror and wondering if all rich kids had to wear clothes for sleeping.

Davy's mother bustled into the room with Davy right behind. "Don't you look nice?" she asked.

No, he thought.

"All clean and shiny. Dry your hair and come to the kitchen for some apple sauce."

More food? he wondered.

Davy pushed a toy truck with his foot and made automobile sounds while Ritchie vigorously rubbed his mop of hair with a towel. He didn't have a comb, so he ran his fingers through it to create some semblance of order, then followed Davy to the kitchen, where small bowls of applesauce were waiting, with gingersnaps still warm from the oven.

Eating went very well that time, too. Davy ate six gingersnaps and then ate his applesauce with a grin. He was rewarded with another scoop of applesauce and a small box of raisins.

Ritchie, who didn't like gingersnaps, ate one just to be polite. The applesauce, however, was very good, and he enjoyed slurping it from his spoon, though he stopped when Davy made a pig noise at him.

Going to bed with clothes on was a new experience. *I just sleep raw, like an Indian,* he thought.

The legs wadded up above his knees, and the crotch pinned his testicles, making him pull the cloth loose constantly. The shirt came up under his arms, and the buttons were hard against his skin.

When he awoke the following morning, he was naked. He would've slept better, but Davy snored like a moose.

Fat people snore, he thought, remembering his Uncle Oscar sleeping on the couch one night while visiting.

His clothes, freshly cleaned, appeared on the bed while he was in the bathroom using the toilet.

"Always wash your hands after going to the bathroom," Davy's mother called through the door.

"Uh-huh." He pulled on his clothes, still warm from the dryer. They smelled good and felt softer than at home, where they dried on a clothesline. "Nice," he said.

The day went well. They played by the lake, skipping rocks at ducks and wading up to their knees in cold water, mud squishing between their toes. They had a good time. Ritchie realized it was fun to have someone to play with.

The little public beach was beside a house built on the shore with a small dock. A boy their age came out and ignored them completely, climbing into a little rowboat, untying it, and rowing in zigzags and circles. He was very good and was clearly showing off while still ignoring the other boys.

"That's Gary," Davy said. "Nobody likes him. He goes to a private Catholic school. He's a snob."

Ritchie saw Gary glance at them occasionally. The look on his face seemed almost as if he were longing for something.

Snobs might just be boys who want to play but don't know how to join in, he thought. *Other kids have to invite them.*

He started to speak, but Davy threw a mud ball at him, so he had to throw one back.

Gary tied up his rowboat and went into his house without looking back.

Ritchie felt a tug of sympathy. *I wish I'd talked to him,* he thought.

After a lunch of hot soup and grilled-cheese sandwiches with cold milk, Davy's mother took them in her station wagon to drop them off at the show in Lake City. The Saturday matinee was a Hopalong Cassidy movie, accompanied by a Bugs Bunny cartoon and an Abbott and Costello movie about a haunted house.

While they waited in line for their tickets, where Davy paid for them both, because his mother told him to, even though Ritchie had a dollar to spend, Gary suddenly arrived behind them in line.

Without thinking, Ritchie turned and said, "I saw you rowing your boat. You're really good at it."

Gary sneered and didn't reply.

Asshole, Ritchie thought, following Davy into the theater.

After the show, Davy's mother picked them up and drove them to a store that had a lunch counter. They ate hamburgers, french fries, and malts for dinner, laughing as they recounted the Abbott and Costello movie, complete with sound effects. Davy's mother looked amused.

"Where's Dad?" Davy asked with more concern than seemed warranted.

"He won't be home until later," she said.

Davy became quiet, and the conversation died.

Joe wasn't home to take them to church the following morning, either. Davy didn't ask where he was and seemed resigned. Ritchie's father was away often, because he worked at a logging camp in North Bend. Sometimes, he wasn't able to come home even on weekends. When he arrived, the family was glad to see him, but no one seemed to miss him sometimes when he was away. Ritchie assumed that fathers sometimes didn't come home. They were different than mothers, who had to be there.

That night went better. Ritchie removed his silly pajamas and slept in his underpants, which had been washed and dried again, and he slept well. He dreamed of being in a rowboat, trying to row upstream, but he couldn't coordinate the oars.

He awoke in the middle of the night, aware that he wanted to go home, but he soon fell asleep again to the rhythmic honk of Davy's snoring.

Church was a new experience, too. Davy's mother wore a pretty blue dress with a high collar and ruffles on the sleeves. She smelled of lavender and left an air behind her as she left the room. Ritchie thought her very pretty. Her smile seemed a little fake, but she was still cheerful.

Davy wore corduroy pants and a white shirt. Ritchie had only the clothes he brought. He had no better ones. Davy's mother put a red sweater on him that was too big, but that helped.

They arrived in front of a small church that looked like it had been built from a converted schoolhouse. Ritchie would be taken home after church and could hardly wait.

Inside, he heard bellowing music, with blasting trumpets, loud drums, and a clanging piano. People muttered and shouted.

"Amen!"

"Praise the Lord!"

"Hallelujah!"

When he walked in, he saw people waving their arms in the air and singing, "He is moving. He is moving," repeatedly.

Terrified, he almost wet his pants. In his Christian Science church, people were quiet, dignified, and the whole place had an atmosphere of pleasant control. He never saw people act like that before. If he could've gotten away with it, he would've leaped out the window to escape. People hugged, wept, and some fell onto their knees, then to the floor, shrieking and moaning.

The preacher began a sermon that started out quietly but ended in gyrations and pleading supplication for poor, unforgiven sinners. Ritchie felt certain he was one of those, whatever they were. All he wanted was to get out. He learned that bad things happened even to good people.

When the action stopped with a final round of loud singing, applause, and a few more, "Hallelujah!" he ran out the door. Davy's mother, who'd been as wide-eyed as the rest during the service, looked normal again with her usual smile and calm manner.

No one mentioned the service as they got in the car. Ritchie was glad, because he didn't know what to say. It was as if nothing happened.

Davy's mother asked directions to take Ritchie home. It was an odd, quiet ride. Davy and Ritchie hardly looked at each other and said nothing the whole way.

The driveway leading to Ritchie's house was a quarter-mile long, just a dirt and gravel road leading through a swampy area. Ritchie asked her to stop on the main road, saying the mud and ruts made the driveway impassable. Really, he didn't want them to see his house, with all the junk in the yard and the decrepit travel trailer with sagging roof that was a chicken house. The regular house needed paint, and crude additions had been tacked onto it over the years. He didn't want them to see that.

Davy's mother got out of the car, opened the trunk, and handed him a large shopping bag. "Here, Ritchie. These are for you."

She seemed quite pleased, but he wasn't. Inside were clothes faded from long use and many washings. A pair of pajamas with little bears on them lay on top. Horrified, he managed to mumble, "Thank you for everything," before walking quickly down the driveway without looking back.

After hearing their car drive off, he found a big fir stump left from years earlier when the trees were logged. The center had rotted, leaving a large cavity. Ritchie pushed the bag all the way down until it was out of sight.

He ran to his house with a smile and light heart—something he hadn't felt for hours.

Ritchie and Davy played together at school every day, but Ritchie refused further invitations to Davy's house, and he never invited him to his.

A month later, Davy became quiet and sullen. He wasn't fun anymore, and he began biting his nails.

Finally, Ritchie asked, "What's the matter with you?"

Davy burst into tears and rubbed his eyes with pudgy fists. "My dad's gone for good! My mom and dad are getting a divorce."

"Oh." Ritchie didn't know what that meant, but he felt Davy's pain and insecurity.

"My mom and me will move to Spokane." He sat on the ground and rubbed his fists into his eyes harder.

Ritchie patted his back halfheartedly without a word, then he heard the school bell ringing and walked toward the building.

Davy didn't come in at all. A little while later, his mother arrived in class, gathered Davy's possessions, gave Ritchie a brief smile, and left with a shopping bag full of books, pencils, and crayons. She neglected to close the door on her way out. Ritchie noted the shopping bag was the same kind as the one he left in the stump—covered with colored stars. Sadness filled the room, but Ritchie knew that only he and Ms. Burger knew what just happened.

Ritchie found he missed the fat-faced boy he once spent recess with. At home, there was no one to play with. Big brother Arne was only one-and-a-half years older, but he was out playing with friends a year older than he was, and he didn't want Ritchie tagging along.

Ritchie was lonely. Money was scarce. His dad worked in North Bend and often came home only one weekend a month. He was surly and became more so after drinking beer. His parents fought and shouted a lot.

When his father left again, his mother was pouty, distracted, irritable, and angry. She showed no affection to her children. She spent hours mumbling over her Christian Science books. When disturbed, she raised her fist.

At other times, she flew into screaming fits for no apparent reason, then she wouldn't speak to anyone for days. Grandma and his sister looked after Ritchie. He knew to leave his mother alone at such times. If a divorce ever happened in his house, he hoped to go with his father.

In spring, it was pleasant walking three miles to school again. One day, a girl his age walked with him. He soon started talking with her.

"My name's Dora Mae." Her smile lit up her face like sunbeams on a pond. The dimples on her cheeks deepened. Her faded, light-blue dress had a funny, old-fashioned collar. Her not-quite-blonde hair hung straight to her shoulders, while her bangs were so perfectly even they looked like they'd been cut with a ruler.

To his surprise, she thrust out a hand to shake. Although thoroughly embarrassed, he shook it.

"I'm Ritchie," he said. "I'm sort of new here, too—nine months. What grade are you in? Who's your teacher?"

"Miss Walker. Where are you?"

"Same room as you, fifth grade. There's only one fifth grade."

"I know where you live. You're down that long driveway on Twenty-Sixth. I saw you walk down there once."

"Uh-huh."

"You know the big patch of woods on the other side of Twenty-Sixth? Right through there to Twenty-Fifth is where we live." She chuckled. "We're neighbors."

"Yeah," he said with a grin, "neighbors half a mile apart."

"We have a cow and a calf. My dad's a sheriff. He's going to get me a horse this weekend. Do you like horses?"

He unconsciously rubbed the old wound on his forehead. "Yes, I do. I wish I had one."

They met and walked to school together each day. Ritchie threw rocks at birds and kicked a can all the way to school one day. Dora walked along, looking amused, because she knew he was self-conscious and was trying to be male for her. Often, her subtle smile made her look like she had a sweet secret. She knew the names of several birds and called them out when she saw one.

"My mother's a birdwatcher," she said proudly.

One day, Dora said, "We don't have school Friday. Do you want to come over to my house?"

"OK," he said without hesitation.

They made plans. Ritchie walked through the woods to her house using a well-worn cow trail. He was anxious for Friday to come. When it did, he was up early and on his way by nine o'clock. Knowing it was early, he walked slowly, not wanting to seem too eager, though he was.

He stopped at the edge of the woods and looked at Dora Mae's white, freshly painted house with light-gray shutters. The small yard had a white picket fence around it with a gate on a spring. The walk to the front door was punctuated by flat stepping stones in alternate rows. Small flowers, or plants of some kind, struggled through the ground on either side of the path. A sheriff's patrol car was parked in the driveway.

With some hesitation, he walked to the door, opened the screen, and knocked softly. The door swung open quickly, and a woman looked down at him. Her smile of white teeth and freshly painted lips welcomed him. Ritchie immediately saw that she, too, had dimples.

"Is Dora home?" he asked.

"Sure is, Young Man. Are you Ritchie?"

"Yes, Ma'am."

"Dora Mae!" she called over her shoulder. "Your gentleman caller is here." She giggled and ushered him in, leaving the screen closed but the main door open.

Dora ran into the room, followed by a stringy little girl about five years old, with bony knees and elbows, who seemed curious and welcoming.

"Hi," Dora said. "My dad's asleep. This is my sister, Elizabeth Mae. We call her Liz, because she looks like a lizard."

"Dora Mae!" her mother said. "That's not nice!"

Dora reached over and hugged her sister. Ritchie realized there was a slight resemblance to a lizard.

"Come on," Dora said, pulling his sleeve. "Let me show you my horse." She ran out the door with Liz following right behind. Ritchie hurried to keep up on the way to the barn and surrounding corral behind the house.

There stood a typical stunted Mustang—a small black horse with a roman nose and hooves that were too large, a shaggy mane, and a long tail that touched the ground.

"He looks wild, but he's really tame and friendly," Dora said. "He was trained and broke, then he was turned loose for a year. My dad's having a cowboy come over to ride him a few times to make sure he's safe for me. He'll look better with his feet trimmed."

She held out a small apple and made a small sucking, hissing sound with her pursed lips. The pony, looking bored, walked over, accepted the apple, and chewed the entire thing, letting frothy juice drip to the ground.

"What's his name?" Ritchie asked.

"I haven't named him yet. What do you think?"

"Is he a boy or a girl?"

"Neither one, Dummy. Humans are boys and girls. Animals are males and females. He's a male, but his balls were cut off, so he's called a gelding." She said it without a hint of embarrassment.

"Oh." He tried to act wise, looking at the horse with deep, aching envy. When his family moved up from Seattle, his mother said they might someday have a horse. After a while, he realized that would never happen. Still, the desire was there, along with a kernel of hope.

Dora had a small playhouse under a big tree in the backyard. Inside was a lot of junk, including old magazines, newspapers, cracked and scratched forty-five RPM records, rags, and unidentifiable pieces of wire and metal. She also had derelict furniture, broken chairs, rotten pillows, and cracked lampshades.

"Daddy says if we clean this out, it's ours," Dora said. "Want to help?"

"Sure."

She ran into the house. Soon, her mother backed up a pickup truck to the playhouse.

"Don't hurt yourselves, Kids," she warned, returning to the house.

Ritchie lowered the tailgate on the old Plymouth pickup, and they began piling junk in the bed. Some, like a piece of old bed springs, required two to handle, with Dora on one side and Ritchie on the other. Liz always grabbed hold and groaned the loudest.

Ritchie felt a certain sense of satisfaction to work with Dora like that. He found himself patronizing Liz like an older brother or parent, which made Dora smile. He found himself looking forward to cleaning out the playhouse so he could move in.

At noon, Dora's mother called, "Come in for lunch!"

She shuttled the kids into the bathroom. "You're all grimy and dirty, like little gypsies. Wash your faces and hands with soap."

After they sat at the table that served for both the kitchen and dining room, Ritchie realized he felt very comfortable. Liz scampered around the table so she could sit beside him, her knobby knees banging into his as she squirmed into her seat. An adjoining door opened, and Dora's dad emerged from the bedroom, wiping his eyes and rubbing his chin.

He smiled at them as he sat down in his pajamas. Ritchie was shocked. He thought kids were the only ones who wore pajamas. *I'll be jiggered,* he thought.

"This is Ritchie, Paul," Dora's mom said. "He's Dora's friend."

"And mine," Liz interrupted.

"Yes, and Liz' friend, too." She winked at Ritchie. "He's our neighbor. He goes to school with Dora."

"I didn't think we had any neighbors," Paul said. "Where do you live?'

"On the other side of Twenty-Sixth."

"Where the long driveway is?"

"Yes."

"Well, Mr. Ritchie, what are your intentions with my daughter?"

"Paul!"

"Dad!"

Paul shrugged. "I'm hungry. Pass the biscuits to this poor, damn cop." He sniffed the steaming bowl in front of him. "Ah, rabbit stew."

"Paul, that's chicken stew," his wife said.

"Oh. I was hopin' it was bunny."

Everyone laughed, including Ritchie and Liz.

After lunch, Paul stood and scratched his belly. "I'll get dressed and help you guys clean out the playhouse. It needs painting." He went into the bedroom.

As was his custom at home, Ritchie picked up some dishes and carried them to the sink. "I'll wash. You girls can dry, because you know where to put things."

"Well, I'll be," Dora's mother said softly.

The two girls looked at each other, but, after a quick glance at their mother, they grabbed dishtowels.

Over the following weeks, the playhouse was cleaned out and painted the same color as the house. Sometimes after school and always on Saturdays, Ritchie spent time there with the girls. It was nice playing house. He was the daddy, Dora was the mama, and Liz was their daughter.

Dora started calling him, "Darling," and, "Honey." When their play ended, she kissed his cheek and sent him "off to work." Liz demanded a kiss from him, too. Like any good daddy, he kissed the top of her head.

That summer, they played almost every day at various games, but usually, they had the same roles.

The cowboy tamed the ugly little horse, and he was a wonderful pony. There was no saddle, so all the children became adept at grabbing his mane and swinging themselves up. Dora and Ritchie became good riders and soon learned how to gallop across the cow pasture and up and down the dusty road. One day, they rode to where he launched himself from the tree onto the surprised horse. He showed her his scar, and they laughed.

To begin, Dora rode in front, with Ritchie holding her waist, but, after a while, he began insisting he ride in front, saying, "That's where the man should be." Liz was left behind, waving at them from the barn with a blank smile.

Once when Paul was home, he ran out and said, "Hold up!" He lifted Liz to sit between them with a laugh.

The three of them laughed as they trotted across the pasture. It was impossible to hang on, because they bounced at different times until all three fell off in a tangle of arms and legs. The horse stepped away, looked at them in disgust, and ran back to the barn. That was fun.

Ritchie found himself thinking about Dora and her family a lot and wished he lived there. Love was scarce in his home with his father away most of the time. His siblings had their own lives, while his mother, with her mood swings from craziness to silent sullenness to wild temper tantrums, made him fear her. He spent as much time as he could with Dora, playing daddy sometimes and cowboy others.

A fair-sized creek passed through a big pasture with an orchard at one end. It was a great place to go fishing, made even more fun, because the lady who lived on the other side of the creek forbade trespassing, let alone fishing. If she saw kids out there, she ran out, threatening and yelling, waving her broom at them.

The kids soon learned to wait for her old Buick to pull out of the yard before going down the hill from the orchard to the creek. Their fishing poles were willow branches with a length of line tied to one end, six-inch nylon leaders, and hooks with wiggling worms on them.

They hooked many fish, but they caught only a few, which they kept in a plastic bread sack to take home. Sometimes, Dora's mother or father cooked them, but most of the time, they disappeared under the sink.

One bright day in August, Dora and Ritchie sneaked down to the creek and managed to lose their hooks on snags. Since those were their only hooks, they were done with fishing. Disappointed, they trudged up the hill in the sun and sat on the grass under an old, worn-out apple tree.

"Listen, Ritchie," she said quietly. "You can hear lots of things if you listen. Close your eyes."

He closed his eyes and listened intently. He heard grasshoppers rubbing their legs together, a tree frog cracking a song, birds fanning the air with newfound wings, and even the wings of a butterfly that flew close to his ear.

Down below, the creek laughed at the day as it splashed over rocks, making swirls of foam that sparkled in the sunlight. Birds chirped and whistled to each other. Ritchie and Dora kept their eyes closed for a long time, saying nothing, listening together with the sun on their cheeks.

He slowly took her hand. She gave a contented sigh, as she squeezed his fingers tightly. Then he leaned over and tried to kiss her mouth. She giggled and turned away from his bungling effort.

"Silly." She laughed.

He laughed, too, not knowing what else to do. He felt embarrassed and slightly disappointed.

She gave him a quizzical smile. "Look up there." She pointed at the top of the old tree, where one last apple hung on a limb by itself. "If you get me that apple, I'll kiss with you."

He slipped off his shoes, grabbed a low limb, and, using his toes and hands, pulled himself up branch by branch.

"Be careful," she said.

He reached the limb with the prized apple, wrapped himself around it, and crawled out until he could reach it. The old limb bent and split partway under him. He grabbed the fruit and climbed back to the trunk, holding the apple stem in his mouth. He smiled so hard, he almost dropped it.

On the ground, he presented the prize to her. It was red from the sun on one side and was nicely speckled on the other, and it was still warm from the sunlight. When Dora bit into the reddest part, juice flowed in abundance. She laughed as she wiped her chin and cheeks with the back of her hand.

"There." She held it out. He took a big bite and made a show of wiping away juice, too.

They finished the fruit until only the core, held delicately in her fingers, remained. She handed it to Ritchie, who threw it down the hill as hard as he could.

They stood for a moment, then Dora put both hands around the apprehensive boy's neck, pulled him gently to her, and kissed his lips, which he puckered for the occasion. When she pulled away, a soft smack sounded.

"Thanks for the apple."

"Thanks for the kiss."

He felt something subtle had changed between them. It made him a little anxious, but he didn't mind.

The Friday-evening show became an event he rarely missed. He hiked to Dora's house early in the evening, and either her mother or father drove them to the theater at Lake City. Liz usually accompanied them. At first, Ritchie hesitated to hold Dora's hand with Liz there, but, after a while, it didn't seem to matter, so he held her hand throughout most of the movie, usually between them. Their hands were in his lap.

Ritchie chewed a piece of old gum, trying to keep his confused mind on the show.

"Give me a piece of gum," she said.

"I don't have any more. There's only one piece."

"Yes, you do. I feel a package in your pocket."

She released his hand and quickly slid her hand into his front pocket, as he stiffened and wriggled. She grabbed, only to find it was definitely not gum!

She immediately released it, but she was slow to remove her hand from his pocket, hoping not to make a fuss. She giggled so hard she covered her mouth with her hand.

Ritchie slumped into his seat and tried to act nonchalant. His face was so red, he wondered if his ears glowed in the dark.

Fall passed into a wet winter. It was dark earlier, so he almost had to run through the pasture, down the trail through the woods, and down his long driveway through the swamp. He was a little afraid of the dark, though he didn't know why. It wasn't the dark itself. It was more that he couldn't see what was ahead. Sometimes, he talked aloud softly to himself.

"What am I afraid of? Am I big sissy? There are no wild animals going to jump out and get me. There ain't no bogeyman. That's kid's stuff. Anytime someone closes his eyes, it's dark. I wonder if everything is dark when you're dead?"

That last thought gave no comfort or courage. He forced himself to walk slowly, trudging along, peering into the trees and bushes he passed.

"I'm walking home," he said with conviction. "There's nothing to be scared of."

He heard somewhere that ghosts or spirits roamed during the night. Even if they did, why would they want to hurt anyone? Maybe they scared kids for the fun of it. The only dead person he knew was Grandma.

"She wouldn't want to harm me or even scare me." That made him feel a tiny bit better.

Forcing himself to walk slowly, he whistled tunelessly, wondering about dying. In Sunday school, he'd been taught not to fear death. "Jesus will come and pick you up and take you to a heavenly place in the sky somewhere, because He loves us and doesn't want us to be afraid. God is…."

A lone duck took off from the swamp beside the driveway. Ritchie ran home as fast as he could.

His days were usually the same. He went to Dora's house right after lunch. They climbed onto the ugly little horse and ran until he didn't want to run anymore and jogged along nicely. He seemed grateful when they turned toward the corral. Once they dismounted, the horse rolled, grunting and groaning, covering himself with dirt that eventually dried to a fine powder when they brushed him off before the next ride.

Dora beamed at him and said good-bye as they went to the playhouse. Liz usually came along. It wasn't like children playing house. They didn't even remember how the game began. Sometimes, they pretended to have a martial squabble, and they ended it when Ritchie received a kiss on his cheek to make up. They knew it was silly and childish, but somehow, neither wanted the game to stop. He liked swaggering around with his thumbs in his belt, while Dora fussed over him, and Liz looked on in approval.

They were happy, and they knew it.

One early Saturday, Ritchie went over, bringing two freshly cut willow fishing poles with string, leaders, and hooks attached. He carried a can of worms in his free hand.

Dora, looking pale and tired, came out when she saw him approaching. "I don't feel good, Honey." She usually only called him Honey when they played family. "I just want to lie down. My throat's really sore."

"That's all right, Dora. I'll come back tomorrow."

"OK." She turned toward the house, then stopped, paused, and went to kiss him. He felt her usually soft lips and realized they were dry and hot.

He walked home, not feeling like fishing anymore.

A few days later, with Dora absent from school all that time, a man came to the door with a uniformed sheriff. The man had signs that read, *Quarantine—No Passage.* The word *diphtheria* was printed along the bottom in big, red letters. A small paragraph of fine lettering spelled out legislation.

Ritchie's mother angrily opened the door. "What do you want here?"

The man with the necktie spoke courteously. "Ma'am, this place is under quarantine. It's the law. Your son's friends with the folks on the other side of the pasture and woods." He pointed across the road. "The Ross family. Your son's been exposed to diphtheria. You're not to leave the house, and no one can come here for two weeks. This is serious legal business." He gestured to the policeman.

"We don't believe in sickness in this house!" she screeched. "We're Christian Scientists, and you can go away!" She grabbed the paper from his hand, threw it down, and tried to slam the door, but the policeman stuck his foot in the way.

"Lady, we don't want any trouble," he said firmly but kindly. "This is bad enough as it is, for Christ's sake. You'll be posted and will obey the quarantine, or you'll go to jail."

She stood there, her eyes bulging in anger, while Ritchie listened from inside.

"Is Dora all right?" he squeaked.

The man in the tie knelt, his expression clouded. "Are you Richard?"

"Uh-huh."

"Are you sick, Son? Do you have a sore throat?"

"He isn't sick!" his mother said in a vitriolic tone.

"Let him answer, damn it!" the sheriff snapped.

"No, I'm not sick," Ritchie said. "How are Dora and Liz?"

The man rose. The words seemed to choke him. "Elizabeth's in the hospital. She's awfully sick." With hesitation and profound kindness, he added, "Dora died."

Ritchie went numb all over, as if he'd been hit by lightning. After the shock left, he felt nothing but numbness.

If he had cried, if he could've cared instead of feeling that frightful aching in his chest that immobilized him and made him stare blankly, things would've been different. That didn't mean better, just different.

The man nailed the signs to the door and left, glancing back as he did.

Ritchie folded himself into a heap on the dusty, smelly couch. It was hard to know what went through his mind. All his thoughts seemed senseless. No thought gave him any solace, though he yearned for some form of comfort.

His mother was schizophrenic. Her mood ranged from angry outbursts over nothing to periods of solemn silence. She gave her children wicked spankings or silent blubbering. It was no wonder his father didn't want to stay home. Luckily, she knew enough to leave Ritchie alone.

No one insisted that he eat or do anything. For two days, he lay around, his mind filled with disquieting, frightening thoughts. *I guess I'm next. I'm scared, but I don't care, either.*

A few days later, he found himself walking slowly up the long driveway, through the cow pasture and woods, past the corral and up to the door. He felt he was in a dream, locked in a stunted, uncomfortable state of separation from everything around him. Something had to give, but he didn't know what or how.

He knocked softly and heard soft rustling sounds inside. The door opened, and Mae, Dora's mother, looked at him with sad, hollow eyes.

"I want Dora." His voice came out in a high squeak that he didn't even recognize.

Her hand shot to her mouth, as she stifled a sob. Then she reached down and pulled him inside in an embrace. She sat in the big, overstuffed chair and took the sobbing boy in her lap. His face floated between her soft breasts as he snuggled against her, wetting her blouse with uncontrollable tears. Her chin rested on his hair, then her lips pressed against his cheek, as she began rocking back and forth. Together, they rocked into the long shadows of evening.

It was dark when car headlights lit the windows. When the engine stopped, footsteps came to the door, then it opened. The lights came on. Paul took in the scene with quizzical eyes and furrowed brow. Slowly, he walked toward them and took the boy from her limp arms.

"The boy has to go home now," he said, kissing his wife's wet face.

He lifted Ritchie to his shoulder and ducked out the door, as Ritchie held onto his whiskered cheeks. Through the forest and cow pasture, across the road, and down the long driveway, they walked.

Paul was sweating and panting a little as he set Ritchie down and knocked on the door. It immediately flew open, and his mother stared at them.

"Where have you been?" she demanded, grabbing his arm and pushing him inside.

Paul turned and walked away without a word.

"You!" his mother screeched.

"Leave him alone, Ma," Harold said.

His big sister came forward, pulling Ritchie close. "He's a good boy."

"Huh." Their mother walked into the kitchen and left them locked in a hug.

"I understand, Little Ritchie," his sister said quietly.

He went to bed and slept, curled under the covers, and dreamed of Dora's dimpled face laughing at him. He dreamed of the big, red apple and the kiss that thrilled him, of the rides on the horse and playing in the playhouse with Liz.

He dreamed a long time until he heard her say, "Don't cry, Honey. I'm all right. I'm safe here, and you can always remember me."

No thought from his own mind could've comforted him, yet those words did. He felt love fill him and empty out his grief, lifting the shadow from his heart and mind.

When the quarantine signs were taken down, Ritchie trudged back to school, into his classroom, and took his seat. Only once did he look at Dora's place, where another girl sat, fiddling with her pencils. He found he was able to think again, and he was glad.

That day at recess, he played baseball with the boys and hit a home run, which surprised everyone.

Despite the kiss from Dora, he never fell ill. People thought it was a miracle, and perhaps it was. His mother thought that was only to be expected from their religion.

Liz recovered, too. Somewhere, Ritchie learned that the poison from diphtheria had stopped Dora's heart.

Treasure of the Indios

Chapter One

The events didn't surprise Michael, just the timing. At four o'clock in the morning, Patricia came home with her clothing and hair rumpled and her lipstick kissed off. She walked into the bedroom, where he lay awake, turned on the room's indirect lighting system, and inadvertently turned on the CD sound system as well.

She fumbled, attempting to find the button to turn off the sound, then gave up and walked toward the bathroom in a rush.

Michael sat up in bed, lit a cigarette, and waited. When she came out, she didn't speak to him. Instead, she went to her side of the walk-in closet and lugged out a suitcase. He watched without surprise.

"Are you going somewhere?" he asked flatly.

"That's a stupid question," she answered matter-of-factly. "Why else would I be packing?"

"Where are you going?"

"None of your business. I'm leaving."

"I see. Are you mad at something?"

She stopped and stared at him. "Don't you get it? I'm leaving here—and you. I want out. I want a divorce."

"Patricia, mellow out. You're drunk."

"I am *not* drunk."

"Isn't this a hell of a time to just up and leave? Has something happened?"

"Yes, something has happened. I realized I don't love you now and probably never did." She continued packing.

"You tell me this at four in the morning after twelve years together?"

She stopped to glare at him. "We never should've gotten married in the first place. We couldn't get along even when we lived together. It's my fault, too," she said a little more kindly. "I don't know why we thought things would change by making it legal."

He looked down to put on his slippers. "I think I know who your lover is. You think Bob's your soul mate? He's been married twice before, you know. He has teenage kids, for Christ's sake."

"That's more than we have."

"Who the hell's fault is that?"

She didn't answer.

"Do you have a lawyer? I'm afraid that's another dumb question. Knowing you, I'll bet you do."

"No, I don't, damn it." She paused. "I have an appointment to talk to Harold on Friday."

"My golfing buddy? I'll be damned."

"His wife's my best friend."

"So what?" he exclaimed.

She placed toilet articles in a carry-on overnight bag.

"Why do you have to wait until Friday? That's a week away."

"He's in trial in Tacoma."

Michael got off the bed and started pacing, rubbing his face with his hands. "God, I don't want this."

"You think I did? I've given you twelve of the best years of my life."

"For the love of heaven! That sounds like a cliché from a soap opera. The best years of my life? Shit, oh, dear. Where was I in all that? How about *my* life?"

"You were in the school, while I marched my ass off. Then... then...." She paused. "All you did was work. You left me here alone all the time, looking for something to do with myself." She looked ready to cry but didn't. Instead, she looked as tough as leather. "No wonder...."

No wonder she found someone else, he thought. *That's what she meant to say,* he thought. "You're making a mistake, Pat. Bob's a womanizing asshole."

She closed her bags in a huff.

"He's about as sincere as a fucking.... I don't know what."

She pulled on her coat.

"Do you need help out with your bags?" he asked kindly.

"I'll manage," she replied with disdain, grabbing her bags and walking out without a backward glance. She slammed the door behind her with her foot, though she left the front door open. He watched her load her bags into the trunk of her Mercedes and pull away with tires squealing.

He stood and cried for a while, then anger took the place of disappointment.

Chapter Two

Saturday and Sunday passed at a snail's pace. He tried to drink, but that just made him feel worse. On Monday, he began planning.

He went to the bank where his credit card was issued and wrote a check for the maximum cash advance he could get--$12,000. *That's ironic,* he thought, surprised he didn't need her signature, too, because her name was also on the account. At another bank, he bought a safe deposit box and put $11,000 in there, keeping $1,000 for himself.

His assets were held by his professional service corporation, including his house, office, accounts receivable, his car, and his insurance. As a professional service corporation, his was the only signature required or that could be used.

It took two days to complete his transactions. He mortgaged his house and two cars to the max. His professional business line of credit was also maxed out. He borrowed against his insurance, reducing it to its base value. He sold all his stocks and borrowed the maximum allowed on his pension plan.

He sold his golf cart and pawned all the jewelry Patricia had been dumb enough to leave behind. He sold his furniture to a hustler and had it cleared out in a day, then he sold the riding lawnmower. Nothing much was left at home, just a bed, chaise longue from the yard, TV, refrigerator, and washer and dryer. His prized tool collection went into storage.

He changed the locks on the doors and garage, then took his monthly bills, including phone, utilities, gas, and electric, and shredded them, then he threw the shredder into the garage.

He told his office staff to cancel all surgeries and office visits and start looking for other jobs. They were shocked, but they did as they were told. He paid each of them one month in advance and told them to do something with the records, perhaps place them with a storage company that would return them with asked for a price that would include expenses and make a nice profit for copying, too.

All the money, totaling over three million dollars, went to an offshore numbered account in the Cayman Islands. He kept $12,000 cash in a lockbox for spending.

Friday, using the last of his MasterCard credit, he bought a one-way ticket to McAllen. Texas, and left with four large, new suitcases filled with clothes. During the plane trip, he was pensive. The bloody Mary he asked for tasted so good, he had another.

Am I vindictive? he wondered. "Hell, yes," he said under his breath. *If only she'd come to me and told me she was that unhappy.*

He knew something was wrong, but, as in the past, he waited until she came to him with her problems. He had planned to be understanding, then they'd make love and take a two-week vacation to Hawaii, Mexico, or the Bahamas, and everything would be fine again—for a time.

It wasn't to be. For three months, he heard her whispering on the phone, then she began coming home late at night saying she'd been "meeting the girls." She bought new clothes, purses, and shoes, which he gleefully took the Goodwill after she left.

Caller ID revealed who she was calling. Michael never liked or respected Bob, that good accountant boy. Then he despised him, but despising anyone was a waste of time. Michael knew the situation was partly his fault, too, though *fault* seemed like a hollow, meaningless concept.

People do what they have to do. Sometimes, they go along with something without considering the consequences, always looking for something new. When they are looking like that, they aren't acting normally. Reason and judgment flee with such discontent, then the conscience leaves, too, ushered in by recklessness. There comes a time when people have to stop, weigh the situation, judge themselves, and carry on while looking for forgiveness. Understanding isn't appropriate. Forgiveness is.

What's the greatest attribute a person can have? he wondered. *Someday, I'll know the answer to that. Self-sacrifice causes self-pity. Generosity seeks a reward. Honesty can be cruel, while deceit can be sparing. Religiosity is for those who are weakened by their need to control the universe and other people with senseless repetition and self-serving ritual.*

Under it all, I'm optimistic that people are generally good, and the world is filled with wonder. There is *a tomorrow. Next week, I'll be forty-five. That's still young. I'm healthy and adventurous, though the thought of adventure has been in the background for a while.*

He smiled as he mentally patted himself on the back. He came from a poor, horribly dysfunctional family, yet he became an MD and a surgeon, a fellow in the American College of Surgeons, and he made three million dollars.

I have lots of successes. It's too bad my major failure was as a husband. Stop! Don't blame yourself! You did the best you could. You did what you had to do. My God, maybe Patricia did the best she could, too. Under the circumstances, maybe she did what she had to do.

In his heart, he loved her and wished that things had been different, but Bob? He hated that nobody, a man he'd heard bragging about his conquests often enough. *Let him stick his dick in a pencil sharpener, that bean-counting fart. After his second divorce, he won't have much money left, what with alimony, child support, mortgages, and living expenses. He's in for a surprise. Michael Hart won't support any more lawyers.*

Am I vindictive? Maybe. Angry? Yes. Justified? No doubt.

As the plane landed in Texas, Michael reassessed. He hadn't read a word of *The Notebook,* the novel in his hands. It was time to look up his old college friend, Pablo Martinez.

As he gathered his luggage and had it sent to a taxi, he thought about Pablo. Michael handed the porter a twenty-dollar tip and had a good time trying to speak to the cabbie in his broken Spanish. He took

Spanish in college for three years, and it returned quickly. He always had a gift for language.

He found the name of his hotel in his shirt pocket—La Quinta on Palm Avenue. The heavily burdened cab took off with a fart of exhaust, and Michael found himself grinning.

Pablo would be surprised to hear from him. The little Mexican was five-feet-seven-inches tall and 170 pounds of pure, sinewy muscle. They'd last met two years earlier at a meeting in Albuquerque. Pablo was fifty years old, single—his wife died of ovarian cancer a few years earlier—and lived in McAllen, where he was surrounded by his siblings, four older brothers and three younger sisters.

The brothers ran the family grocery store, while one sister was a housewife, another was a successful real-estate executive in Tucson, and the youngest sister was getting her PhD in anthropology at the University of New Mexico. Michael had seen pictures of them all, and Rosa, the youngest, remained in his mind as a pretty, highly intelligent woman.

Pablo was a good GP with many interests that he always took time to pursue. An outstanding horseman who enjoyed polo, he was proud of the string of half-Arabian, half-Mustang horses he bred. He climbed mountains, sailed, and, most of all, liked to explore the backcountry of the Sonoran Desert on horseback, mule back, or on foot. He collected Native American artifacts, too, storing them lovingly in a special case at home, though he gave most of them to museums in Mexico and Texas.

Pablo loved to sing, dance, and play guitar with some of the mariachi bands with their blaring Spanish trumpets. He was a fine fellow most of the time, but sometimes, he seemed abrupt and rude and had no time for anyone. He was constantly moving and avoided eye contact. Not everyone liked Pablo, but Michael did. For some reason, those two opposite men became best friends during school.

One year before Michael's arrival, he accidentally met Pablo at a medical meeting in Santa Fe. They had a grand time drinking beer and going to sports bars to play pool, watch baseball, and flirt with the waitresses.

One night before closing, Pablo told him an interesting story. While exploring caves and climbing rocks in a desolate part of Old

Mexico, Pablo found a dinosaur graveyard. Preserved bones, bleached white by the sun, lay scattered on the ground, partially covered by dirt. Backbones and vertebrae of ancient animals protruded from the ground. Something had calcified those bones and preserved them like stones.

Pablo knew there were many small caves in the hills full of artifacts— small statues, flint arrowheads, stone knives, and small obsidian utensils that must've come from thousands of miles northward. Pablo's theory was the things had been brought there by the Native Americans as they passed through headed somewhere else. Small objects resembling buttons with holes, were inside some of the small jade statues. There was a lot of turquoise, too.

After Pablo told Michael the story, he fell silent. "If you come down to see me, don't tell anyone at all, you hear?" He took out a pen and card from a motel in McAllen and wrote a phone number on the back. "This is my very private cell phone. Show it to no one, not even your wife." He paused and looked at his friend. "It's very secret… private. *Sabe?*"

They dropped the subject and parted without speaking of it again.

Suddenly, Michael was in McAllen under strange circumstances himself. After checking into a modest hotel, he collapsed on the bed and slept for ten hours.

When he awoke, it was a quiet morning. He was still in his clothes. He felt groggy, as if he had a hangover. A shower and two aspirin helped him feel better. Hauntingly, he thought of Patricia, wondering where she was and what she was doing. As he wondered, he missed her so much he ached.

After a large breakfast of eggs and sausage, prepared Mexican style, plus a few cups of strong coffee, he contented himself with reading the newspaper until eight before returning to his room. Digging in his address book, he found Pablo's secret number and dialed it.

"Leave your name and number," a voice that wasn't Pablo's said.

Michael did and settled down to wait, with, of all things, a Gideon Bible opened to Timothy. He didn't have to wait long.

"Hello, Mike," Pablo said when he answered. "How the hell are you? What are you doing here?"

"Hey, *Hombre.* I came to see you and those dinosaurs of yours," he said eagerly.

There was a long pause. "Maybe, *Amigo.* I have to arrange. Go see the town or something. I'll call you at the hotel at eight o'clock sharp this evening. Be ready to move. I have a little trouble now." He didn't elaborate.

"All right. I'll be here."

"Adios." Pablo hung up.

Michael's day went well. He visited some Western clothing stores, a bookstore, and an art gallery. He had dinner at his hotel at six o'clock and went to his room to pack. He felt rested, though he was anxious to be doing something.

The phone rang promptly at eight.

"Hey, Mike, you all packed?" Pablo asked.

"Yes. Where am I going?"

"Listen carefully, but don't write this down anywhere. Go to the airport and buy a one-way ticket to San Antonio. Don't ask questions, OK? I'll get in touch. Get Southwest flight 731 that leaves at nine-thirty. Got it?"

"Yes. Sure."

"Hasta la vista."

Michael checked out, paying cash, caught a cab, and went to the airport. He bought a ticket and presented it to the counter when the boarding call came. He was given a red plastic card with the number seven on it.

The plane was a small turboprop that loaded directly off the tarmac. Michael fell into line, and a red-faced Mexican came to him.

"Michael, give me your boarding card. Thank you. Follow me."

They passed a man very near the line, and the Mexican handed him Michael's boarding pass. The man took Michael's place, while Michael was escorted through a small door, down a passageway, and, after three knocks on a second door, reentered the main terminal.

"OK, *Señor. Todo es bueno.* Go to the restroom to take a piss. Then go the street outside the Southwest baggage claim and wait on the sidewalk. Remember to wash your hands."

I don't know what's going on, he thought, his eyes wide. Then he shrugged. *Who cares?* He did as ordered and waited patiently on the sidewalk, smoking his first cigarette of the day.

Soon, a plain, green, new Suburban arrived. When the back door opened, Michael got in.

"Hey, old Mike!" Pablo said. "Good to see your shiny white face."

They exchanged a two-handed handshake, then Pablo gave Michael's head a playful slap. That was one reason some people didn't like him. It showed who was in charge and established the pecking order from the start.

"Why all the intrigue, Man?" Michael asked. "Don't get me wrong. I don't give a shit, but it's interesting."

"Then you don't have to know, do you? Hey, Felix," he told the driver, "take us to the whorehouse." He looked at Michael with a wry, charming grin. "Just kidding. Your dick would fall off around here. He's taking us to my nightclub."

"You have a nightclub?"

"*Si, Señor.* Just got it awhile ago. My apartment's upstairs, and my games are downstairs. Actually, it's my brother Paul's. You like to play Craps?"

"Sure, if the dice aren't loaded."

"Hell, the house doesn't have to load the dice to win. Could be done, but, if we loaded the dice, someone would squeal, and we'd be out of business in more ways than one. I forgot. How good is your Spanish?"

"I can read it pretty well, but my *Espanol* is *chistoso,* funny. I have a dictionary. Are we going to Old Mexico?"

Pablo suddenly became serious and nervous. "You are if you want. I can't quite yet. Rosa will take you there—the college teacher, you know? She's in anthropology and sociology. She's as tough as a mountain lion and smarter than a coyote. Watch out for her. She'll stomp you if you let her, and then she'll have no respect for you."

"My God. Do you like her?"

"She's my *hermana.* I love her." He lit a small black cigar and offered one to Michael, who accepted with a grin.

"Two doctors smoking," Michael said. "Are you still a sawbones?"

"Oh, yes, but only in Mexico. That's why I can't come with you right away. I have a clinic there in Mina for the poor. I'll be delayed, but I'll catch up when I can. I have some other—nasty—business that's rather pressing. I have to visit a guy named Oscar."

"Why are you hiding all this?"

"I'm not hiding me! I'm hiding you. Put it this way—there are some people who would really like to know where you're going and wouldn't want you to get there. *Entiendes?*"

"*Si. Bastante dices.*" He changed the subject. "When do I leave?"

"Early tomorrow."

Michael had the strong impression that Pablo didn't want him hanging around McAllen, but he couldn't tell why. He wasn't sure he wanted to know.

They had a drink of strong tequila at the bar. Pablo said that the drink cost $75 a fifth, but it burned just the same. With or without the lime, Pablo didn't know how to tell, because he hated tequila.

Felix showed Michael to his snug quarters, where a lot of outdoor gear was laid out on the bed and the chair. He saw cowboy boots that came to his knees, riding breeches of cotton twill, soft cotton flannel shirts, linen shirts, bandannas, and a straw sombrero with chinstrap. The belt that came with the outfit looked like the buckle was inlaid with green jade.

Felix stuffed all the items into a leather duffle bag, told Michael to pack his toiletries, underwear, and socks. He left out one outfit for Michael to wear. He noticed it had been washed to make it soft for riding.

When Felix told him, "Hide your ten thousand dollars," Michael was shocked. *How the hell did he know I have it?* he wondered. *Do I sleep that soundly? Not usually.*

Maybe that was why he felt so groggy when he awoke that morning—and why he needed aspirin. Then he remembered asking the skycap at the airport if he knew Pablo Martinez. That could explain the two-hour cab ride that should've taken forty-five minutes.

Felix showed him some ingenious hiding places in the sides and false bottom of the duffle bag. Michael wondered what he was getting himself into, but he felt more alive and excited than he'd been in a long time. When he thought of Patricia, he pushed her from his mind and fell asleep.

At four o'clock, Felix awoke him with a gentle shake and offered a cup of coffee. He smiled down at Michael like an old friend.

Michael felt fine and rested. He dressed quickly in his new duds and followed Felix downstairs, through the nightclub hall, and out the door to the waiting Suburban. Felix handed him a plastic plate of tamales with a plastic fork to one side. As Michael ate them, washing them down with warm orange juice from a can, they drove to a nearby border crossing.

"Where are we going?" he asked.

"Across the border," Felix replied. "First to the *clinica* for a day, then to the ranch of Homero, Pablo's *tio.*"

Chapter Three

The border crossing went without incident. Felix and the guard knew each other. They smiled knowingly as Michael presented his passport, quickly filling out a tourist card before they drove off. When they left, Michael wasn't given the tourist card.

Soon, they were in the heart of Old Mexico, doing sixty down roads that should've been taken at fifty, if that. When they turned west off the paved road onto a dirt road, it was still dark. The sun rose, painting the desert around them myriad shades of red, orange, and yellow. The distant hills were a constant, subtle, blue gray. They didn't seem to be getting any closer as they banged and bumped their way along.

Sometimes, they passed over and through creek beds, some with a small amount of water in them. Thick, gooey mud stuck to the tires and caked in the wheel beds, then dropped to the road in chunks.

The two men exchanged pleasantries in Spanish and English. Michael used his dictionary frequently but felt pleased by how much Spanish he remembered. Finally, they stopped at the side of the road to drink a bottle of cold water from the ice chest, eat a cold orange, smoke a cigarette, and pee.

"Lots to go," Felix said patiently. *"Vamos."* He ground out his cigarette butt in the dirt. *"Mucho lejos."*

"Hey, *Hombre,* can you tell me where we're going?" Michael asked as they drove off.

"To the foot of those mountains." He pointed with his chin. "About forty or fifty miles, as the road goes to the *clinica."*

Felix had the Suburban in four-wheel drive. They went over bumps and rocks, into ruts, into sand that made the wheels spin and engine whirl, then across small streams with a trickle of muddy water in them. Sometimes, he left the road entirely over the *cholla* to avoid an obstacle. Michael thought Felix had dropped his foot, the way he kept the accelerator down.

The air conditioner didn't work that well. When Felix lit one of his black cigars, Michael had to open a window, which mean dirt got in his face and mouth. If the big Mexican knew he was torturing Michael, he didn't seem to care. Felix didn't make much conversation, though he sang along continually to the merry Mexican music screeching over the radio.

When they reached the *clinica,* Michael was happy to leave the car despite the heat. He walked through dust to the front entrance. The clinic was an almost-new double-wide trailer with an air conditioner that choked on the heat and bounced so hard it seemed ready to fly off the roof.

Michael looked at Felix. "Tighten that thing down." He was accustomed to giving orders.

Felix looked up, nodded, and returned to the car for tools.

Inside, the clinic was pleasant, cool, and clean. The receptionist smiled at them and called to a nurse from inside the next room. A cute, small, fat Native American in green scrubs peered out at them.

"Dr. Michael," the receptionist told her.

"You're Dr. Michael?" she asked in perfect English without a trace of an accent. "Dr. Pablo will be out directly."

Michael stood and looked around. There were twenty people in the waiting room, and none of them was reading. All sat, waiting patiently.

In a few minutes, Pablo came through the door wearing scrubs and smiling broadly. "Michael, come in. Say hello to Sylvia and my little nurse, Frances."

The others smiled, nodded, and said, "Hello."

The rear of the clinic contained three exam rooms, a toilet, and a storage area. Everything seemed made of stainless steel. Each room had a stainless-steel cabinet with instruments, bandages, tape, syringes with needles, stethoscopes, and thermometers.

One room had disposable speculums and equipment for pap smears. All was neat, clean, shiny, efficient, and professional. Pablo was proud of the place. Across the hall, past a small pharmacy, was a closed operating room with lights, anesthesia machines, outside scrub sinks with water flow controlled by the knees, and two first-class operating tables. The walls were lined with glass cabinets containing surgical packs and IV equipment.

"You're ready to go," Michael said. "This is very well done."

"Thanks."

"Let me ask you some questions."

"Shoot."

"Electricity?"

"We have a top-of-the-line generator that runs by a combination of solar power and propane."

"Water?"

"It was a problem. I sank a thousand-foot well before hitting good water. Now we have plenty, and the Native Americans come to fill their barrels and jugs. We're getting more solar equipment. Eventually, the air-conditioning will be better."

"Tell me about your patients."

"These are Indio Indians. They speak their own language and most can't speak Spanish. They've never been to school. They were completely neglected—and still are—by the Mexican government. They had no medical care until I opened this place."

"Do you get paid?"

"I don't ask for pay. The government pays me pennies. Their story is that the Native Americans pay me. Some do, some don't. It has to do with where you're going in the foothills."

He led Michael to a small office, where they sat across from each other. Michael saw a small statue on the table made of coarse red clay, and he immediately saw it was pre-Columbian. It had big lips and eyes, and the fat, squat body sat cross-legged.

"The Indios," Pablo continued, "began bringing me small gold nuggets, silver teardrops, pieces of jade, arrowheads of all kinds, and some turquoise. What was really fascinating were the needles and pins made of ivory."

"My God! That's interesting."

"Everyone around here was sworn to secrecy, but still, word got out. Now I'm having a little problem with a *cavrone* named Oscar Gusman and his gang of thieves. He's a powerful crook with connections. He'll come down soon."

Michael didn't ask what that meant.

"The stinking, corrupt government hasn't learned about any of this yet, but I suppose they will. I want to be ready. They'll take everything and stomp the Native Americans into the dust.

A Native-American woman walked past the door and smiled at the men. Pablo stood and spoke, saying a few words Michael didn't understand.

"That woman saved me," he explained.

"Oh?"

"My mother was from around Mina, but she didn't have milk for me. Cresa nursed me for a year. What a story, eh? Needless to say, I take good care of her."

"You said you'd do a few operations." Pablo suddenly changed the subject.

"I did?"

"You said you'd help."

Michael paused for dramatic effect. "Of course I will."

Pablo led him to the restroom that doubled as a dressing room. Michael donned scrubs and walked to the operating room. On the table, a three-year-old boy lay quietly. A large umbilical hernia pushed his belly button out like a beer bottle.

"Pretty big," he said.

"Can you do it?"

"What do you mean, can I do it? Of course I can. Do you have any Morlex mesh?"

"As a matter of fact, we do. I brought it especially for you. Go scrub. Frances is your scrub nurse. She's ready."

"I'm always ready," Frances said haughtily.

Pablo slowly gave the boy Demerol and Xanax through the IV. He monitored his blood pressure and made sure the little guy snored blissfully under his face mask. Michael used Lidocaine 2% mixed half and half with Marcaine 5% to make a good regional block, then he reduced the hernia into the abdomen after dissecting it free from the apex. Luckily, it went in easily, so he didn't have to open the peritoneum.

He folded it inside, cleaned the edges of the rectus sheath, folded a square of Morlex, and sewed the rectus sheath over it. He trimmed off excess skin and closed the incision with the skin clips Frances provided.

As he placed the last clip, the boy stirred. Michael felt good. The operation went well, and he felt like the good surgeon he knew he was. He couldn't help thinking that the first surgery he ever did solo was an umbilical hernia that bled inside, and he had to go back in to repair it. He felt like quitting when that happened.

After a lunch of cold beans and soft tacos made with goat meat, washed down with water, Pablo presented Michael with other children with inguinal as well as umbilical hernias. All were repaired without a problem.

Then Pablo brought in a man of forty with both arms in splints. They met him in an examining room that had an X-ray screen. Pablo held the X-ray to the light, and Michael saw both the man's ulnas were broken. The bones were bent, fractured clear through and were touching the radius.

"My God!" Michael said. "Who did this? They must've used a crowbar. These are nightstick fractures."

He referred to fractures people received when they held their arms in front of their faces to keep from being hit by a policeman's nightstick.

"You're right," Pablo said. "He used a fucking crowbar. Wait till you see what he did to his daughter."

"Who did this?"

"Oscar's man."

"Why don't you call the police?"

"Are you kidding? They would never come to see an injured Native American. This is Mexico, remember?" Disgust sounded in his voice.

Pablo brought in a girl of twelve with an inch-long gash in her upper lip. She was tearful but quiet as Michael examined her.

"Her lip's split clear through," he said. "The teeth are loose but look all right." He pushed the three front teeth on the left side farther into their sockets. "When did this happen?"

"Same time as her father's arms, about ten days ago."

"What happened, for Christ's sake?"

"Oscar found out the guy gave me some gold nuggets. I'm not sure how, but I'll find out. He sent a man to get it out of the old man. He didn't know. His father or grandfather found them years earlier, and they were kept in a pot in his house. The Indios have been very careful to keep their secret. Most have a few nuggets hidden away. They say they don't know where they came from, and I believe them. At least, they won't tell me, and I know they trust me—as they should."

"Let's do the little girl first," Michael said.

Pablo brought her into OR, gave her some sedation, prepped her, and draped her mouth. Michael numbed her lip with xylocaine with epinephrine. He used acrylic dental glue to hold the loose teeth buttressed to the solid ones. With magnifying lenses on, he approximated the vermilion border. He closed the skin with very fine nylon sutures, taking care to trim away ragged edges. He used suture material called Monocryl on the inside of the lip, because it would be absorbed within weeks and wouldn't cause internal scarring.

He looked at his work and smiled. Frances and Pablo expressed their pleasure with praise that wasn't entirely spoken. Doing something well was its own reward, whether it was painting a picture, singing a song, or repairing a little girl's lip.

Gratitude is one thing that should never be expected, Michael thought.

Next, they brought in the man. The splints were removed, and both arms were scrubbed thoroughly and painted with Betadine iodine. Carefully feeling the ulnar bone, Michael drilled in above and below the fracture to thread wires, so the bones could be brought end-to-end and held with a plaster cast that incorporated the wire. They took X-rays to check the alignment.

Michael mentally patted himself on the back when he was done. Pablo did so physically.

"The ulna can't touch the radius at the fracture site," Michael explained, or the two bones will grow together. Then he'd never be able to turn his palm up or down. He needs to be in plaster for six week. He'll have permanent knobs on each side, but the bones will be stronger than ever in the long run." He looked at Pablo. "What happened to the bad guy?"

"I'll tell you, then you forget it, OK?"

"Sure."

Pablo led him to the waiting area, where a thirteen-year-old boy waited patiently. "Meet Louis."

"Hello, Louis," Michael said.

"Louis shot the son of a bitch between the eyes with his .22 rifle. They sent for me, and I beat it out there. We loaded the guy in his Jeep, which I drove to a deserted mineshaft. I parked the Jeep inside, then we used dynamite to blow the entrance shut. You ever use dynamite?"

"No."

"I can tell you that three sticks is a lot. We almost blew up the whole mountain. Two thousand years from now, some archeologist will dig up that Jeep and will write a paper on how aliens came from the center of the earth. That's it. Let's go, *Comer.*"

A large travel trailer was parked near the clinic, where Pablo and the nurses lived. Any patients or families were on their own. Some patients stayed in the infirmary overnight, but not often. There weren't any that night.

Michael, Frances, Sylvia, and Pablo had a roast chicken dinner with three bottles of Almo white wine. Despite Pablo's urging, Michael refused tequila.

"That stuff's fifty dollars in Mexico," Pablo said.

"Put it in your cigarette lighter."

"I can't. It would blow off my hand."

Exhausted, Michael crawled into the bed Pablo provided. The air conditioner was noisy, but he felt comfortable. He'd just fallen asleep when incredibly smooth legs against his skin woke him. Frances was there, beaming a smile he could barely see in the dim light. She wore only a scrub shirt.

"I brought you something, Gringo Doctor."

"What did you bring me?"

"A gift from Pablo."

"From Pablo? What?"

"A Mexican blow job."

She untied his scrub pants and pulled them off by tugging at his ankles. Michael didn't know what to do, so he didn't speak. She rubbed her hands, then spread creamy aftershave lotion on his scrotum.

"I always liked Mennen aftershave lotion," he whispered.

She left for a moment, then she returned with a mouthful of ice cubes. She opened her mouth and took him in slowly, gently, and repeatedly, using gentle suction and her tongue.

"I think I'm going to faint," he gasped.

"Not yet," she mumbled with her mouth full.

When his orgasm came, Frances barely got out of the way in time. The ice cubes fell from her mouth, and sperm was in her hair.

"You must've been storing that up for a while," she said.

"Uh...."

"Are you happy?"

"Yes, but I want to be inside you."

"No way. I'm Pablo's woman, and I'm faithful." She left the bed.

Two minutes later, Michael was asleep.

He awoke to the smell of sausage, eggs, and onions frying with sliced green peppers. His pants were on the floor, so he pulled them on over his semierect penis, which felt like greased summer sausage.

They ate breakfast together and drank coffee while chatting about the sun, dust, and cacti. Felix and his Suburban arrived. After handshakes and cheek kissing, Michael was driven away. He felt pretty good.

"Where are we headed now, *Hombre?*" Michael asked.

"Over there." He pointed to the blue hills in the distance, lighting one of his foul cigars and blowing blue smoke at the windshield.

"What's there?"

"One of Pablo's little ranchos. His uncle lives there and runs it.

Rosa, his sister, is there with the mules and some guys who work for Hamero, Pablo's uncle."

"Sister Rosa? Pablo's sister?"

"*Si. Es verdad.* She's there." His expression gave nothing away, but his tone showed respect and maybe something else.

Michael had seen a photograph of her when she was eighteen. She'd be in her early thirties then. He was glad he pawned his wedding ring and subconsciously touched his ring finger.

"Is she single?" he asked as casually as he could.

"I think so."

They bounced too quickly down the road, which, for some reason, was never straight for long. Felix said it as the way the stagecoach once ran to avoid side hills and gullies that were hard on the riders and the horses and coach. He made exaggerated humps up and down, like he was riding on an old stagecoach with leather straps for shock absorbers. With the road they were on, he didn't have to exaggerate much.

When they reached the rancho, nestled in a small canyon between rocks, with oak trees planted all around the house and an acre-sized yard, Michael was pleased to see green grass, too. The ample house had been recently restored, judging by the new paint and boardwalk leading to the porch surrounding what appeared to be an unused house.

Three men waited patiently as they walked up the steps, an older one in clean clothes and two cowboys in dirty clothes, with broad sombreros and high-heeled boots with spurs.

Introductions were made in Spanish. Only the older man stepped forward to shake hands. The cowboys nodded to Michael and lifted their hands to waist height in a polite wave.

The distinguished older man was Homero, while the cowboys were Luis and Rudolfo. Homero oversaw that ranch and another one thirty miles farther into the hills, adding that he managed Pablo's "other interests" in Old Mexico. He was charming, friendly, and considerate of Michael's stumbling Spanish, saying that his own English wasn't much better. Michael later learned he was being polite, because he was fluent in English.

Homero and Michael sat on the veranda, smiling and talking together in short sentences, while Felix went toward the barn and corral.

Presently, Michael heard female voices. The screen behind the door opened, and two women appeared carrying a pitcher and glasses on a tray. The older one, obviously Homero's wife, came forward to be introduced. She was round-faced, plump, and happy.

"Nice to meet Pablo's old friends," she said in broken English. "He speaks good things about you. He is so busy. He doesn't have many friends. *Mi casa es su casa.*"

"*Gracias, Señora. Muy amable.*"

Then Michael looked at the younger woman and saw she was Rosa, though she didn't seem particularly impressed by Michael, Dr. Hart, MD, Fellow of the American College of Surgeons, who had bestowed his presence on them. She seemed annoyed.

Michael spoke first, holding out his hand. "You're Rosa. I saw your picture when you were eighteen and just out of high school. Pablo was very proud of you and showed your picture to everyone. You were cute then, but you're beautiful now."

She shook his hand in a businesslike fashion. Her gaze seemed to look right through him. "Thank you for the compliment, Dr. Hart. Sit down. Have some rum and lemonade." She motioned him to a soft chair and put a glass in his hand that was filled with ice cubes.

"Ice! You must have a source of electricity," he said to Homero, though Rosa answered.

"We have solar panels that run our air conditioning as well as our generator. The generator has gas to keep the battery charged. Mexico is well ahead of the United States in solar energy, particularly the kind that is augmented by fuel."

"Like a hybrid car, a Toyota."

"We make Volkswagens in Mexico."

He felt put down and confused. An uncomfortable silence fell.

"*La cena* will be ready soon, Dr. Hart," the older woman said politely. "Rosa will show you to your room so you can wash yourself or...."

Everyone but Rosa smiled. She rolled her eyes. "Come on, Dr. Hart. Bring your drink." She walked into the house without looking back.

"Excuse me, Good People." He bowed and followed her in.

Rosa showed him a small but cool room at the rear of the house with an adjacent bathroom painted shiny white. Pictures of Mexican cowboys in various poses were painted on the walls.

Michael was enthralled. "Who painted these? They're very good. I know. I like to paint, but I couldn't do these."

Rosa suddenly smiled, showing beautiful white teeth outlined by full lips with a hint of pink lipstick on them. "I painted those and all the others you'll see in the house. You like them?"

"Yes, I do. Please show me the others."

She paused. "All right. I will, but after we eat. Once you finish washing yourself, come to the dining room at the end of the hall." She chuckled at the use of her aunt's phrase and smiled as she left, closing the door behind her.

Michael sat heavily on the bed, removing his sombrero and running his fingers through his shaggy hair. He thought of Patricia and how she didn't like his long haircuts.

"Piss on her." He drained the rum drink he brought with him.

He liked to shower before bed. He walked into the bathroom and saw the shower consisted of a plastic hose with spray attachment at one end. "Perfect. All the comforts of home."

Dinner was a pleasant affair. They ate grilled beef ribs smothered in salsa and smoked to perfection over a mesquite fire, coleslaw, sliced tomatoes, and wide slices of avocado marinated with onions in wine vinegar. The bread tasted like it came from the best French restaurant. There were also french-fried sweet potatoes salted and peppered with mild chili pepper powder, pieces of rubbery cheese like string cheese but tastier, and beer in frosty mugs from a freezer.

Michael made an effort to smile at Rosa and catch her eyes. Sometimes, he succeeded, and he saw her smile back like a little girl. He couldn't stop telling his hosts how he enjoyed the food and thanking them for their hospitality. Homero enjoyed his wife's pleasure at the compliments and attention.

After dinner, while the dishes were cleared away, Homero suggested they step onto the porch for a Cuban cigar.

"I have a date with Rosa," Michael replied politely, "but I'd like a cigar."

Rosa looked at him. "I was going to show him the artwork." She seemed a bit defensive over the word *date*. "I'll come for you after the dishes are done."

"That's fine with me." Michael followed Homero out the door.

They lit cigars and smoked contentedly for a while, then Homero eyed him seriously. "I have a letter for you from Pablo. He wanted to make sure you read it before you started off. There's some danger." His voice trailed off. "He also wants me to give you a pistol. I'll give you those later."

"Thank you, Sir." Michael felt bewildered.

"You leave tomorrow afternoon, after it cools down a bit. A breeze comes up each evening. You have to cross a desert, and that's best done at night. On the other side, the boys will ride north. Someone's been stealing horses up there. You and Rosa go south and west. Pay attention, use your compass, and take notes."

"I didn't bring…."

"I'll give you a special compass with range finder. Like I say, take notes. Rosa knows the way, but you won't survive alone if you become lost."

Michael nodded.

"There'll be a major surprise up there." He laughed.

"What?"

"If I told you, it wouldn't be a surprise. For one thing, there's a nice little cabin there with good water. It's near the bones and the caves." His eyes shone. "I wish I were going with you, but," he waved his hand, "business and cattle things."

They were silent awhile.

"Rosa's tough," Homero added. "She'll take care of you. Whatever you do, listen to her and do exactly what she says."

Finishing their cigars peacefully, they watched the sun set over the blue mountains. A red glow filled the sky for a long time. The last plaintive bird songs died out, and night sounds took over. In the hills, coyotes began yodeling to each other and the moon. To them, they were singing opera.

Michael recalled asking an old cowboy why coyotes howled and sang.

"Well, Boy, it's because they can," he said jovially.

People do things because they can. Michael used to think that, like monkeys doing things because they did them well, people did things because they could do them well, too. It wasn't exclusive. Many people did things because they hoped to do them well.

Michael played golf poorly and never improved, and his wife stuck with tennis although she didn't like getting sweaty and losing all the time. He once bought a banjo and pounded relentlessly on a piano, both of which gave him only pleasure, though they didn't do much for those forced to listen. He liked singing, because he knew he did that well, especially in the shower, which had better acoustics.

He chuckled at his thoughts, saluted the coyotes, said his leave to Homero, and walked into the house, passing Rita in the hall.

"Good night, *Señorita Linda*. I'm going to turn in."

"Good night," she said quietly.

He undressed, showered, and contemplated growing a beard but settled on a mustache, shaving all but his upper lip clean. Putting on clean underwear, he went to bed.

Thoughts of Patricia having sex with Bob came to mind and didn't go away until he slept. Something troubled him. He didn't care about her, but the insult was humiliating. Being insulted angered him.

Wait till she finds out she's broke and in debt to her tits, he thought. *I wish I could be there.*

No, he didn't. He felt saddened. At least he didn't have any more cigarettes. It was a good time to quit.

Chapter Four

He slept hard and was vaguely aware of dreaming. There was something about a bucking horse he couldn't control. His morning erection woke him, but he was aware of the bustle in the house and voices speaking in rapid Spanish. Glancing at his watch, he sat bolt upright.

My God! It's after nine! After a long urination, his penis returned to normal. He dressed rapidly and went to the dining room just as food was being set out—bowls of fruit, orange juice, coffee, and the ever-present breakfast tamales. He was hungry. After saying, "Thank you," and, "Good morning," in Spanish and English, he ate with relish. He tried small talk with Rosa, but she looked grumpy, so the conversation went nowhere.

After eating, they drank dark, rich coffee.

"Can we see your artwork now?" Michael asked.

""All right." Rosa stood from her seat.

"I have work to do in the barn," Homero said.

"I'll come and help if I can," Michael offered.

"After you see the art," Rosa said tartly.

They laughed at her tone.

Pictures hung on the walls of the house, carefully balanced for effect and continuity. All were at eye level for Michael's six-foot frame, and they were very good. Their colors were bright and cheerful. Red, yellow, orange, blue, green, subtle peach, and pale lavender blended in each one, creating beauty.

"These are beautiful," he said. "Why don't you sell them?"

"No one wants watercolors. Mexico's full of people who do those."

"But these are good. I know a little about art. These are sensitive and pretty."

"I wish the world was that pretty," she said softly.

"Rosa, don't you know that through your eyes, it is? The world *is* this pretty. Beauty goes into your eyes, to your brain and heart, then out your brush. In a way, you're a creator. In another way, you're a recorder. At any rate, you're an artist with all that means. What a gift. You do it, because you do it well," he finished softly.

"What?"

"Never mind. It's just more praise. Can we see your workshop? I know you make pottery, too."

"How do you know that?"

"You couldn't help it."

They went to the rear of the house, where a room with large windows and skylight contained a potter's wheel, kiln in the corner, and buckets of various colors of clay. On the bench were finished articles waiting for the kiln. Several more sat on the floor, fired and completed.

Michael studied the shapes. They were round, melon-like, and gourd-like, with curved handles, plain round handles on flowerpots, curved handles on water jugs, and bowls with lids. Some pots looked like old-fashioned chamber pots, while other pieces resembled large soup bowls. There were cups with thick, heavy handles. All the colors and designs were original and unique. Some contained sun faces. Others had deer heads, flowers, trees, horses, and burros.

"Did you create all of these? I've never seen anything like these colors."

"Most are natural colors. I use store-bought acrylics for the bright ones. I didn't make all of them. In fact, I made very few. My mother does them when she's here. Mostly, it's *mi tía*. You really like them, don't you? I think you're into color."

76

"That's true, but the designs…." He picked up a plain red statuette of an obviously pregnant woman with big lips and sagging breasts. "Where'd you get this? It looks old."

"You'll find out, *Gringo.* " She opened a big, heavy drawer on rollers, and Michael stared at gold nuggets the size of large peas and buttons of silver the same size. The rounded, green objects had to be jade. He saw shiny buttons and various-sized pieces of turquoise, all with creases of minerals in them.

"Where'd you get all these? What will you do with them?"

"*Gringo,* you'll see where they come from—if you're lucky." She closed the heavy drawer. "When I get enough, I'll make jewelry."

"Seems you have enough already."

"Not quite. There are some things I'm looking for, like garnets and…."

She's not telling me something, he thought.

"Let's go see the horses," she said suddenly.

They met at the corral and barn. Several nice horses milled around in the small enclosure.

Homero, a rope in his hand, cheerfully looked over the stock. "Which one do you like?"

"All of them," Michael said.

"Pick one." He stepped into the corral.

"I like the big black with the white blaze." He pointed to a horse in one corner.

"You pick a good one, *Señor*. He's very strong, with lots of spirit."

"That's what I like, *Señor*."

"You can ride?"

"Yes."

"Want to try him, or do you want to wait until evening?"

"It's hot. I'll wait, but let me handle him." He took a halter off a gate and approached the big, long-legged animal. The horse stood until he was four feet away, then bolted with a snort.

Michael followed him around the corral, careful to avoid his rear end and front feet. He talked quietly, never giving up. The black ran around the corral with Michael behind him.

After fifteen minutes, the hot, sweaty horse, stood still with wide eyes. Michael approached slowly, touched his neck and withers, then turned his back on him and stepped away. When the horse didn't move, he approached again, making noises with his lips. He touched him again and rubbed his chest.

The horse stepped away, then stopped and looked at him. Michael ignored him and walked a short distance away, turning his back, though he continued whispering and rattling his lips. The black stepped toward him, then came closer until he pushed his nose against Michael's shoulder.

"I'll be damned," Homero said.

The other cowboys stood and watched silently.

Michael reached around the horse's neck and put on the halter with slow, deliberate motions. "Let's be friends. *Amigos.*"

He led the horse to the gate. A cowboy ran up and opened it, then Michael led the black through, following him like a dog. He handled it all over, rubbing its chest and withers, lifting each leg to massage the muscles, and lifting its tail to pat its rump.

The horse never flinched. All quivering stopped. Michael removed his hat and patted the horse with it all over, then flapped it over his back. The horse trembled a bit, then calmed.

Michael pulled the horse's head down and blew softly in its nostrils. The horse pulled away, then stopped fussing as Michael breathed into its nostrils, allowing him to rub under its chin. When Michael turned his back and walked away, the black followed like a dog on a leash.

The cowboys were amazed, but Homero looked pleased by such a show of horse *sabe.* "You know horses, Doc. Let him put his nose under your arm. Here's an apple for him. See if he'll take it from you."

Michael bit off a chunk and pushed it into the rear of the horse's mouth. The surprised animal pulled away, tasted the apple, and began chewing. It nosed Michael for more, juice running from its lips.

"I have a friend." Michael smiled. "This fucker's broke, isn't he?"

Homero laughed. "Yes, Doctor. He's just a bit particular about who rides him."

"I don't think I want any spurs."

Homero translated that into Spanish, and the cowboys grinned and laughed.

"You don't know," Homero said. "All the ranch horses are ridden with spurs. That's how they're used."

"*Si, Señor. Ya entiendo.* We'll see."

Rosa, who'd been watching, smiled despite herself.

"*Venga aqui, Cabarello,*" the cowboys said.

Michael walked to Rosa, who stood by the gate.

"That's my horse," she said. "At least, he was. Now you have him. I'll ride a meaner one that's faster." Almost as an afterthought, she asked, "Can you ride?"

"Hell, yes. I was born on a horse. When I was born, my mother was riding a pregnant mare with bandits chasing us. She got off, had me, and the mare had its foal. She jumped back on the mare. I got the colt, and we escaped from those *banditos.*"

It took the others a few seconds to digest that. The cowboys read Michael's hand signs and expressions and didn't need any translation. They looked at each other approvingly and laughed.

Louis, one of the cowboys, took the halter, and Michael followed Rosa behind the barn, where a small hill afforded a backstop. Homero came, too. A few bottles and cans sat against the hill.

Rosa carried a Winchester model 94 .30-.30 carbine and a .22 Ruger pistol. She handed him the pistol.

"I'm not much good with a pistol," he said, shrugging.

He fired a few rounds and missed by several feet.

"If I may, *Señor* Doctor," Homero said. "You're very steady, but you make mistake. Look only at the target, not the sights or the barrel. Line them up in your—what you say?—your mind's eye."

Homero snapped off a shot, and a bottle exploded. He did it several more times until the pistol was empty, then he reloaded with .22 magnums and handed it to Michael butt-first.

Carefully, he did as he was told, and he came much closer. He fired again, and a bottle broke, then another. He fired four more times, and he hit a bottle each time.

"I'll be go to hell," Michael whispered.

"You're very steady."

"I'm a surgeon. We have steady hands."

"Bullshit," Rosa teased. "You were just lucky."

"Let me see you shoot."

She gave him a half-smile, raised her rifle, and shot the little pieces of glass lying on the ground.

"That was good, Rosa, but can you cook?" he asked.

"What?"

"Never mind."

Michael packed the compass with built-in range finder, tablet, and pencils, as well as his newly received pistol and ammunition in one side of his saddlebags while putting his shaving gear in the other, along with a package of Handiwipes to use as toilet paper. He tossed in his Spanish-English dictionary, a transistor radio that was also a walkie-talkie with a range of five miles.

He waited for Homero to give him the letter from Pablo. Finally, in early afternoon, when the horses and mules were being packed, he asked for it.

Homero pretended it slipped his mind, but Michael noticed that the envelope and been opened and clumsily resealed.

> *Amigo,*
> You're off on one hell of an adventure. I wish I could go with you, but business. You're under your sacred honor to keep the secrets of where you're going, understand? There are people after me I must warn you about. They're bandits and criminals, but they're powerful in Mexico and the US border.
> If anything happens, don't come back this way. Go north directly to the border, following the map I gave you. Follow the directions carefully. Use your compass and range finder to stay on the trail. Carry as much water as you can, and remember to have some for your horse.
> Go to the rancho marked on the

map. There, you'll find my cousin
Tony. Trust him, but not too much.
Don't trust the two guys who work
there. They have shifty eyes.

He'll get you across the border into
the US. Get to the hotel in McAllen.
I hope you don't mind the charade
at the airport, but believe me, I was
looking out for your ass.

Take care. See you soon.
Pablo

What the hell? Michael wondered. *I wanted adventure. I guess I'm getting one.*

He didn't think of Patricia all day, though he wondered what his friends, associates, and family would think. He told no one he was leaving or where he might go.

After an early dinner of *pallo mallo,* rice and beans, all was ready. The pack animals stood in a row, waiting patiently head to tail. Rosa would ride a big, heavy palomino that acted a bit nervous, chomping at the bit. Michael's horse, the black Barb, was fitted with a bosal around its muzzle, not a bit. He looked dangerous but quiet. Horses like that often exploded into action.

Michael checked the girth, making sure the saddle was tight, then sprang on and waited. The horse bolted forward, then reared, and Michael checked him with the bosal. It crow hopped in circles, then took off in a fast trot away from the direction they were supposed to go. Michael looked good in the saddle and knew it. He also knew the cowboys and Rosa were watching.

"Easy," he said. "Easy. Whoa. Down." He touched the horse's neck and pulled him to a jerky walk, noting the approval from the cowboys and nonchalant acceptance from Rosa.

"You should've given me that plow horse you're riding," he told Rosa.

"He's not a plow horse. He's big and strong for roping cattle." She nudged the palomino, and it broke into a dead run. She ran him in a fifty-yard circle, returning with figure eights, always in control.

"That's a good horse," he said. "How much do you want for him?"

"He's not for sale. You think you can buy anything?"

"I haven't got a place to keep him, anyway."

Their friendly exchange began their night-long ride like a pleasant jaunt.

Michael kept careful track of where they went. He tried to mark landmarks, but there weren't any. All he saw was rocks, cactus, mesquite, and greasewood. He kept track of his position by the mountain to his right.

Rosa, who was ahead of him, slowed until she was alongside. The horses, accustomed to walking in a line, fussed a little at first. "Where'd you learn horses, *Gringo?*"

"I don't know why you're calling me *Gringo*. Call me Mike. I think *Gringo* might be a subtle insult."

"In this instance, it's not. It can be, though. So all right, *Gringo,* I'll call you Mike. How'd you get good with horses?"

"Well, Rosie, if you must know, I spent my teenage years in a reformatory, a place for bad kids. I wasn't that bad. I just stole some cars, got in street fights, and burgled a few houses. Nothing that bad. I didn't kill anyone.

"Anyway, they sent me to a boy's ranch. Actually, it was a reformatory in Oregon. Chasing cattle on half-wild ranch ponies took care of whatever was wrong with me. I even got baptized and learned to say my prayers." He laughed, though his expression was serious. "I caught up on my schoolwork and found out I liked to study and learn. I even took correspondence courses in the winter when there wasn't much else to do."

"Like what?"

"Literature, psychology, sociology. I don't remember all of them."

"How about your parents?"

"My father, a merchant seaman, was away all the time. My mother had all she could do with eight kids and almost went nuts. My big sister looked after me, but none of them could control me. I had a lot of rebellion in me. I was one angry guy."

"You're still angry."

"How do you know?"

"I know."

There was a lull in the conversation.

"That's quite a story," Rosa said. "You should be proud of all you've accomplished."

"Thank you. I had a lot of help. I feel appreciative and grateful more than proud."

"I think you should me more proud, too."

He didn't reply.

They rode through the bright, moonlit night, stopping only for an occasional drink of water. Nighthawks whistled past, and owls appeared out of nowhere to circle overhead. A light, pleasantly warm breeze touched their faces. Around them, coyotes sang to the moon, and once they heard a rabbit's piercing squeak as a bobcat caught it. Trees, bushes, and bugs contributed to the night noises. If he listened carefully, he could hear a bug hop from branch to branch or perched birds moving from foot to foot.

The plop, plop of the horses' feet kept time with the orchestra of night noises like a metronome. Moon shadows from giant saguaro cactus were like ghosts. They were spectacular. Saguaros had to survive for seventy-five years before they could send out a branch, living in the most-miserable climate in creation.

During rain, a cactus could suck up and store a ton of water. Birds pecked holes in them to live in and ate the center of the cactus without seeming to compromise the plant's health. In spring, under the right conditions, flowers appeared on the arm tips, followed by fruit. People made jelly from the fruit, but some thought it tasted hideous.

The cactus could be squeezed for its juice to make pulque beer and distilled for tequila. Its spirit, some said, held the blazing, unforgiving heat of the sun.

The mescal cactus, with its saber-like arms, was eaten for centuries and was a favorite with the Apaches. The base of the arms were like artichokes, soft after being baked in the ground for a day, very nutritious, and rich in vitamins. Peyote cactus, the size of golf balls, was dried and chewed allegedly for ceremonial purposes, but modern people took it recreationally, giving a pleasant high. It was also a powerful aphrodisiac. Michael heard of a man who was so aroused after eating peyote, he tried to have sex with a pine tree. He wondered what it would be like combined with Viagra.

Desert flowers were rare and didn't last long. Some indentations in the ground allowed them to grow. They smelled sweet in the night breeze. In the morning light, they were the purple sage mentioned in song and story. Under them, rabbits hid. Rattlesnakes waited for small rodents and ground lizards. Such patches were few, and men knew they should be left alone.

Around midnight, they reached a true desert of sand and rock, devoid of plant growth for miles. Unbearably hot in the daytime, it was icy cold at night. There is no chill like the desert at night.

The sand still retained some of the day's warmth, and the air was still. At the edge of the sand, a trickle of water had been extracted from deep in the earth by a large windmill built with imported timber. The trickle fed a partially full trough. Each horse was brought to drink. Soon, the trough was empty. The animals, knowing the trail, understood that water would be scarce for a while.

The riders checked their cinches and made sure none of the animals had sore spots from rubbing. After a brief rest, while they, too drank some water, they mounted and set off.

It took four hours to trudge through the soft sand. The absence of desert sound was marked by a strange margin of yellow grass growing in clumps. They rested again, allowing the tired horses to forage a bit. Michael's mount was as quiet as the others. He blew softly into its nostrils, and it allowed the gesture without protest.

"This is where we part company with the boys." Rosa waved her hand northward. "We each have a pack mule with gear. You take the ugly black bastard, because it matches Diablo. I'll take the beautiful red one."

"The horse's name is Diablo?"

"Yes." She snickered. "The mule is Matador. Don't ever get behind him."

"*Matador* means killer."

"That's right, *Gringo.*"

"Now you tell me."

"You didn't ask. Let's go. We have a full day ahead."

They rode off leading their respective mules, waving good-bye to the cowboys and the cows moving the other direction. The cowboys waved half-heartedly back.

Chapter Five

At five o'clock that morning, the sun was just touching the sky. There was no breeze, and it would become hot very soon. They still had four hours' ride to water and six to their destination.

Michael, feeling hungry, said nothing. He knew Rosa was hungry, too, because he watched her tighten her belt.

My God, her waist is slim already, he thought, tightening his own belt.

Later, when the temperature grew hot, he saw Rosa unbutton all but the last buttons on her shirt and pull it from her waist. He copied her, feeling air circulate. When intermittent puffs of breeze sprang up, their shirts billowed a little.

Rosa rode in the lead, and it took him a while to get a look at her shirt. Her beasts were plump, smooth, and pointed just right, with natural roundness and erect nipples.

What am I doing? he wondered. *I've seen plenty of boobs and even did surgery on a few dozen.* Feeling like a teenager, he adjusted his riding position.

Michael was careful to mark his map every mile or so if their direction changed. The range finder was useless in estimating distances to landmarks, because its range was only 500 yards. He soon learned to judge landmarks that were only a third or a fourth of the way, then multiply 500 by that number. It wasn't that accurate, but it was better than nothing.

When they reached the water, it was almost dry, nothing more than a mud hole. They moved their animals back and forth through the mud, an old Native American trick to bring water to the surface, and let the impatient animals drink in fifteen-minute intervals.

It was noon when they crawled back into the saddle with a couple strips of jerky and another bottle of water. When they dismounted at the watering hole, Rosa buttoned her shirt before getting down. He cursed mentally, glad that she unbuttoned it again when they rode off.

She caught him looking but ignored him. Without facing him, she said, "You have more hair on your chest than a monkey."

"What do you have on your chest?"

"I know what I have."

"So do I."

"*Gringo travieso.*" She wagged her finger at him like a schoolteacher.

He pulled out his dictionary and discovered the word meant *naughty.*

"I'll be dipped," he said softly.

They faced the low mountains ahead, Michael noting the change on his map, and rode for four more hours before the ground began to change. He saw clumps of yellow-green grass appear, then they passed an oak tree. Ahead he saw cottonwoods, which took a lot of water to survive.

They crested a rise and saw below them a cabin with separate barn, a large water tank, and a secure corral of five-foot octo cactus surrounding the barn, making a fence. The animals walked in automatically and waited, sighing.

The source of the water was a small, clear creek coming off the facing hill. A flume of rough boards could be pushed under the flow to allow water to enter the watering trough, made of rock and hard mud, called *calice,* that dried like concrete.

By the time the trough was full enough to spill over the top,

Michael and Rosa unsaddled and unharnessed the pack horses. He was surprised to see them roll before heading toward the water.

When the creek flowed freely, it filled grooves cut into the corral floor for irrigation. Egyptians and Mayans used the same method for thousands of years, as had the Incas and Aztecs. The thick grass was almost waist high.

"They graze only an hour, then we put them in the barn," Rosa said. "Otherwise, they eat everything in a day and trample the rest."

She went to the flume. "Help me, *Gringo.*"

Together, they pushed it to the big, round water tank made from wood like a huge barrel that was five feet tall and twelve in diameter. Small leaks appeared in places, but Michael assumed that once the wood became wet, it would swell and close the cracks. He was partially right. Some places were stuffed with wool cord that hung in the barn, which made excellent caulk. Slowly, the tank began to fill.

Michael carried the heavy provisions into the cabin. Rosa made several trips with lighter items. They brought the saddles to the porch and slung them over the rail built for that purpose. Both of them left their shirts open.

He finally removed his shirt and soaked it in the water before putting it on. Rosa looked at him, then did the same, keeping her back to him as he pretended to try to see around her.

"*Tonto,*" she said, buttoning her shirt again.

The cabin was built against the rock face in the hill. A fireplace afforded cooking with a swinging arm above a flat grill. A crudely made plank table sat in the center of the room with four chairs. Utensils hung on the wall—a couple of pans, a Dutch oven, a huge frying pan, and a coffee pot.

"Leave our stuff in the panniers," she told him. "We'll take out what we need. Push them under the *cama.*"

He noted there was only one bed with a rolled-up sheepskin mattress over leather straps.

"Are you rested, *Gringo?*"

"Why?"

"Do you want to go for a walk? You'll see something I'll bet you never heard of."

"As long as I don't have to ride anymore, I'll be fine. My butt has so many blisters, I'm sitting tall in the saddle. How far?"

"About a mile, but it's hot. Put the horses in the barn, will you? I need to put on something more comfortable."

He laughed as he went to do his chore. When he returned, she was placing perishable in a sack. She wore a shirt, khaki shorts with plenty of pockets, and tennis shoes.

Under the bed, Michael saw a pair of sandals with thick leather straps and soles made from old tires. "These will feel better than walking in high-heeled cowboy boots." He removed his boots and slid his feet into the sandals. "They feel just right. Who left them here?"

"No one. I brought them."

"Thank you. Now, if I only had shorts instead of jeans…. Hey, I do." He unbuckled his pants and peeled out of them, wearing boxer shorts like the Navy issued, except his were blue and white. Rosa seemed entirely unaffected.

"Do you have a safety pin?" he asked. "I could use two to prevent fallout."

Rosa stood for a moment. "As a matter of fact, I do." He rustled in a pouch in one of her saddlebags and brought out two safety pins. "Do you want me to pin them on for you?"

"That would be nice."

"Do it yourself, *Gringo.* Grab that bag, and let's go."

He pretended to stick himself as he fastened the fly closed. "Do you have a Band-Aid you could put on me?"

She walked out without replying. Michael was right behind her and soon began sweating in the afternoon son. He couldn't help looking at her, seeing her brown face shiny with perspiration. She was beautiful.

They walked down a faint trail until they reached a gash in the earth that dropped precariously for one hundred feet. It was rough going. As the passage narrowed, he saw soft, thin mud on the ground, and the air became cooler. Farther down, the passage ended in a wider area.

Rosa grabbed a small camp shovel that had been left by someone before them and scraped away a foot of loose dirt from the walls near the floor. "Look. Feel."

He felt the cavity with surprise. "Ice crystals? I'll be damned. I never heard of such a thing. The ice must've been left here when the plates shifted in the last ice age. For God's sake, ten-million-year-old ice? I knew there was a place like this in Oregon, near the Dalles, but in the desert? That's something."

"You may not know it, but we're at ten thousand feet."

"No wonder I'm short of breath."

"You get used to it in three days or so. Look around and see what you can find."

Under a pile of dirt, Michael discovered small, old-fashioned Mexican beer bottles with faded, warped labels. "I'll be double damned. These have been here a long time."

"Yes, at least from the thirties, when the cabin was built."

"Let's have one."

"Let's split one for a taste. There aren't many."

"Well, we can leave them. I don't have an opener in my pockets, anyway."

"You don't have any pockets."

"That's my point." He replaced the bottles and covered them carefully.

Rosa dug a bigger hole with plenty of ice crystals and placed the bag of perishables in it. "Our refrigerator. I'm getting chilly. Let's go back into the sun."

"Yeah. My nipples are like frozen peas."

"*Tonto.* Idiot."

He chuckled at the expression. Whoever wrote the Lone Ranger pulled a good one with that word. *Tonto* meant *idiot*, while *Kemo sabe* meant *know nothing*.

By the time they reached the cabin, they were sweating profusely. Michael was a bit out of breath, but not Rosa.

"Let's check the swimming pool." She peered over the edge and saw it was almost full of water. He splashed her with it, pleased at the temperature.

"It must come from the ice," he mused, scrambling up the rock above the pool, kicking off his sandals, and jumping in with a yell and a splash. "Man, this is unbelievably nice!"

"Wait for me." She laughed, ran into the cabin, and reappeared carrying a bottle of shampoo and wearing a large T-shirt that hung to her knees. She scrambled up on the rock, using small steps that were cut there, kicked off her shoes, and jumped in with a shriek. Her T-shirt went up to her neck, and she clutched it furiously while Michael laughed.

"That was cute," he said.

"*Tonto!*" She shared the shampoo with him and lathered up, ducking her head a few times to rinse off.

"This is the best damn bath I ever had," he said.

"Don't look when I climb out of here," she warned.

"I won't," he lied.

She stepped up the ladder but had to reach for the last step. Her shirt rose, and so did part of Michael.

"Are you coming out?" she asked.

He looked up and smiled. "I'm afraid I can't right now."

She looked at him with understanding. "Pervert." Her T-shirt clung beautifully, draping her pointed breasts, as she pulled on a pair of red shorts.

When Michael left the pool, he was almost under control again. Inside the cabin, he saw she'd made a small fire with mesquite chips. The frying pan and a small pot were over the grill, and soon, the cabin filled with the smell of onions and beans. When the frying pan was hot, two large rib steaks seasoned with salt, pepper, garlic salt, and a fine sprinkling of chili powder were set to sizzling in the pan.

"How do you like your steak, *Gringo?*"

"Anything but raw or well done. I ain't that picky."

"You ain't? Look what I got." She held up a box of mountain burgundy.

He poured two glasses. "Here's to ice caves, ancient beer, swims at ten thousand feet, and flying T-shirts."

Her expression was priceless. She didn't know what to say, so she sat at the table and ate. Steak, fried beans, sliced tomatoes, and tortillas disappeared.

It was getting dark when they washed their few dishes with water from the tank. Rosa lit two large candles, and they sat on the porch, sipping wine and gazing at the desert, lost in their thoughts. Any thoughts of Patricia or surgery left Michael's mind.

Finally, Rosa asked quietly, "Are you married, Mike?"

"I'm not." It was technically a lie, but he didn't feel the subtle discomfort that bordered on guilt. Was it a half-truth? A half-truth was usually a lie and a lot more, because there was an extra measure of deceit. He felt comfortable with his answer. "How about you, Little Sister?"

"I'm not your sister."

"I'm glad."

There was comfortable silence.

"I have a sort of fiancé," she said, embarrassed.

"How do you have a *sort of* fiancé?"

"I haven't told him for sure. There's no date."

"How long have you been *sort of* engaged?"

"About four years."

"You aren't engaged, Rosa. Love doesn't wait that long. Do you love him?"

The silence became awkward.

"I don't know," she whispered.

"If you don't know if you love someone, then you don't. Maybe you want to, but you don't."

She looked away. "Give me another glass." She held out her mug.

Michael filled both mugs and was about to speak when she spoke again.

"How do you know if you love someone?"

He stroked his chin like a wise, old man. *Me, giving love advice?* he wondered. *Boy, that's ironic.*

"Well, Girl," he said in a fatherly tone, "romantic love has indefinable attraction. That's true physically and otherwise. The attraction can be based on beauty, sex, or lots of other things."

"Like what?"

"Need, acceptance, loneliness, social pressure to conform, pride of having a trophy mate, envy of others, and happy mothers." He stopped. "Love like we're trying to get at has something about it that's hard to express. It means you want to be with the person, you want to share things about living with him, babies, adventures, experience, companionship, even jokes. The bottom line is that you're more concerned about that person's happiness than your own."

"You sound like a shrink, *Gringo.*"

"I read a lot, but I'm afraid I haven't lived much of it. I always thought that unless I could be the best in every way, I wouldn't be good enough for someone else. That's respect, I guess—self and otherwise."

"You always thought? What do you think now?"

"I don't know. Trying to possess another is a big factor. That can't possibly work."

"Why not, if he or she possesses you, too?"

He laughed. "Don't confuse me, for Christ's sake. My mind's crystal clear."

They laughed and drank some more. Michael sang some show tunes. He had a good voice and knew it, a beautiful lyric baritone that could reach the tenor range on some songs.

Rosa listened, encouraged him, and smiled, as he sang, *I've Grown Accustomed to Your Face, The Girl that I Marry, Younger than Springtime,* and *Until There Was You.* He had fun.

"You're a big, soft romantic," she said when he finished. "Do you know that, Mike?"

"I am not. I'm a tough cowboy."

They talked about the stars. Finally, when a shooting star appeared, they stopped talking.

They sipped red wine in a silence that felt awkward to them both until the wine warmed them. Another shooting star streaked across the sky.

"You know what?" he asked. "When I was a teenager, when a guy sat with his girl, and they saw a falling star, that meant he could kiss her."

"How quaint," she said sarcastically.

"I always thought it should be permission for them to kiss each other."

"Permission from whom?"

"I don't know, but permission for both. Who would want to kiss someone, if she didn't want to kiss him back? You'd kiss me back, wouldn't you?"

"Stay away from me, *Gringo.*" She squirmed away from him on the bench with exaggerated motions.

"Well, maybe if we were teenagers…."

"We're not."

"I know. That's the only reason I wish we were."

"What are you talking about?"

"Kissing because we saw a falling star."

"Do you know you're nuts?"

"Yes, but God, I'm a romantic nut. It's funny, but I thought that part of me was gone."

"Which part, the nuts or the romance? What kind of funny— laughing or peculiar?"

"A little of both."

"Don't be wishy-washy."

"I haven't got a wishy-washy bone in my body. I'm a tender, soft, emotionally charged, hopeless romantic."

"I'm not."

"Yes, you are. I can tell underneath."

She didn't reply.

"You know what, Rosa? The things waiting to be found, statues or maybe even dinosaur bones, are the same age as that shooting star. It was light years away. I can't remember the speed of light. Anyhow, it's fast."

"186,000 miles per second."

"Smarty. Anyway, when the star blew up, it was 5,000 years ago, and the light's just now reaching us on earth. That's about the time those statues were made."

"How do you know?"

"You told me."

"I lied. They're between one and two thousand years old, if that. I always exaggerate to make a point. It's more fun."

"That's not very scientific for an archeologist."

"Some things aren't scientific." Her double meaning hung in the air.

They felt warm and comfortable with each other as they perused the sky for more dancing stars.

Rosa got up and quietly entered the cabin with Michael close behind. They rolled out the thick sheepskin over the strap bed together without speaking. Michael blew out the candle, and moonlight through the open door gave the room a yellow glow.

His arms found her waist, and he pulled her gently to him. Her face turned up to his six-foot height, her moist eyes sparkling in the moonlight as if she were almost crying. Without speaking, his lips found her warm, plump, soft ones. She tenderly returned the kiss.

"Oh, Mike," she whispered. "You're the prettiest *gringo* I ever saw. Make love to me."

On the soft sheepskin, his hands found the bottom of her shirt. She wiggled out of it and her red shorts. Michael's hands, tongue, and lips were all over her, moving slowly and deliberately. He loved her silky wetness, her taste, smell, hair, and lips.

"I can't stop kissing you," he said.

"I don't want you to stop."

With a long kiss that neither of them wanted to stop, her legs opened wider, and he found his way inside her soft walls. Gentle, slow, rhythmic pauses and restarts ended in gasps, whispered breaths, and many deep kisses.

They held each other through the night, locked together like spoons in a drawer. They slept soundly and peacefully until the sun rose through the door to wake them.

Rosa looked a bit self-conscious as she grabbed her clothes and went out the door without a word. His morning erection vanished once he had the chance to urinate behind the cabin. He came around the big rock, climbed up, and jumped into the pool to join Rosa, who was already splashing about.

"Did you pee in my pool?" he asked in mock sternness.

"Yes."

"Good." He jumped in beside her. They kissed and held each other like they couldn't believe their good fortune.

Michael let the horses out to graze in the enclosure, and he and Rosa ate cold tamales with mugs of hot coffee.

"I didn't bring you all this way just to seduce you," Rosa said, laughing. "Let's go exploring. Bring just a couple water bottles."

"Do we walk?"

"Yes."

"Good."

"There was nothing wrong with you last night."

"That's because of all the wine you gave me—forced me, actually."

"Tonto!"

The brought the animals back to the barn and trudged off toward the south until they reached a small field turned bare by sun and wind. Michael looked around and saw dozens of dinosaur bones. Some were backbones poking through the earth, their spines pointing skyward.

Rosa hadn't been there before, and they were like two excited teens, brushing off bones and looking further. She found a small petrified dinosaur egg, the shape unmistakable.

"I want to keep this." She dropped it into her sack.

They spent a long time looking, exploring, kicking clumps of dirt, and studying bleached, white bones.

"How old, Doctor?" she asked.

"I don't know, but at least ten million years."

"Amazing!"

They drank a bottle of water. Rosa studied a notebook-sized piece of paper that appeared to be a crude map. "This way." She pointed. "Up into those side hills. At least they aren't that high."

"Rosa?"

"Yes?"

"Any rattlesnakes up there?"

"I don't think so. I read somewhere that they don't live above 10,000 feet."

"I hope you're right," he gasped.

It was rough going. They hadn't walked more than 200 yards before they found their first cave. There were several, no more than six feet deep, with openings two feet square that must've been dug when the earth was softer. The first four contained only pieces of broken pottery.

The fifth, behind a bush, must've been overlooked by casual explorers. Inside were three statuettes of red clay, coarsely made from solid clay and very pretty. All the figures were female, with baggy breasts and enlarged abdomens, similar to the one Rosa had back at Homero's ranch.

"Let's leave them," she said. "They meant something to the Native Americans who left them here. They're prayer symbols, asking for fertility. They aren't Aztec or Mayan. The local Native Americans, like the Anasazi, did them."

"How can you tell?"

"I'm an archeologist, you know. Let's go farther around the hill."

They walked slowly and awkwardly over loose, crumbling rock until they came to a shallow gorge they had to climb and crawl into. They were rewarded by finding two adjacent caves.

Inside the first was a treasure. Arrowheads lay on the ground, all half an inch long, very fine, made of obsidian. There were also several statues, some a foot tall, which were different from the others. They'd been made by artistic hands at least 2,000 years earlier. There were three females and one obvious male with a large penis out of proportion to his body. He had a leering smile on his round face.

"Looks like me," Michael said.

Rosa glanced at him without speaking, then put the arrowheads into her canvas bag. "These are perfect bird points. They're beautiful. Do you know that the obsidian had to come from at least 2,000 miles north of here? Native people migrating through probably brought them. There were trade routes even then, quite extensive and more efficient than we imagine."

"Migrating from where?"

"From Asia, across the Bering shelf. That really happened. The Athabascan Native Americans along the Bering Sea speak a language that can be understood by a Navajo in Arizona or a tribe in British Columbia or Oregon." Her animation and interest were contagious.

"I read that when they came to the southwest," he said, "they found other people already here."

"That's right. The little cliff dwellers were here. There were regular-sized people, too. The San Joaquin man was 50,000 years ago. A jawbone dated by carbon fourteen confirmed that and turned many theories upside down. Other finds have documented previous people. Clovis points found in Washington state, Nevada, and Texas, are 10,000 years old. Human footprints found in Texas could be as much as one million years old."

"That's hard to believe."

She ignored him. "Here are some flint arrowheads, later ones. How'd they get here?" She lifted one of the foot-high statues, but she could barely get it off the ground, so she shifted position to lift it carefully. A clay plug was in the bottom, made of another kind of clay that hadn't been fired with the rest of the piece.

She took out a pocket knife with leather punch and worked out the plug. When she held up the statue, bean-sized pieces of bright or dull-yellow nuggets spilled out in a pile, followed by flecks of silver and yellow-green jade and turquoise.

"My God!" he gasped.

"Put this in your bag, Mike. All I want is the statue. It's very interesting, because it's not Aztec. I think it's Mayan. They opened others and found the same thing—gold nuggets, silver teardrops, and pieces of jade with occasional silver nuggets."

Michael filled his bag while Rosa selected statues that interested her and left the others empty but in their places.

They looked in several other caves. Many of the statues were hollow but empty, though others held treasure, mostly the large, shiny, well-made ones.

Rose was very businesslike as she put selected statues in her pack, padded with dried grass. She seemed a bit more reserved than their find deserved.

"Didn't you find what you were looking for?"

"Yes and no."

They walked back toward the cabin without speaking.

"I noticed you didn't take the statue with the big *pene,*" he teased.

"I prefer real ones," she shot back.

Chapter Six

When they returned to the cabin, the afternoon sun was very hot. They peeled off their clothes with abandon and jumped in the overflowing tank, where they kissed, fondled, and teased, splashing and laughing. That evening, they drank more burgundy, eating a hastily prepared *cena* of beans and fried, shredded meat with onions and tomatoes.

They sat on the porch awhile, contemplating their amazing day and listening to the night as they watched for shooting stars. They made athletic love on the sheepskin, desperate and quick, with Rosa in command on top. Then, as they fell back, love became gentle and caring, with caresses and long kisses.

Early the following morning, they were back on the trail. When they reached the dinosaur field, Rosa paused and looked at the hills.

"I have an idea," she said.

"Alert the media! What is it?"

"Never mind. *Tonto, Gringo.*" She walked more toward the south than the previous day. "Let's see what's on the other side of this hill, OK?"

She trudged off without waiting for an answer. By the time they reached the other side, each of them drank a bottle of water. Their shirts were open, and they shone with perspiration.

What they saw was startling. There, on a wide, flat shelf, were granite statue heads a foot in diameter. They inspected them with awe.

"Look at these, Rosie!" he said. "They have helmets with spikes on top. Look at the mustaches and slanted eyes. My God! They're Chinese! The Chinese visited central Mexico 1,000 years ago!"

She dropped her bag and sat panting on a rock. "Let's find a cave."

They found one under an overhanging rock that hid the entrance. Inside were well-made, polished statues of blue as well as red clay. Some were heavy and yielded gold and a few garnets. Others were empty. Rosa chose one, and Michael gathered the treasure.

"Let's go farther up the hill," Rosa said, leading the way.

Fifty yards up, they found a large cave and went in. The statues were very different. Made of red or blue clay, some were painted yellow. The men had large penises, while the women squatted, babies' heads protruding from between their legs. Rosa took a good sample of each. Luckily, they didn't weigh much.

They found heavier ones in the rear of the cave. The statues had plain heads and bodies with feathers scratched on them, painted in various earth tones.

"Michael," she held up one, "these are Inca, from South America."

"Are you sure?"

"I'm sure."

"Well, if they could come from China, they could go to Easter Island, they could come here, but why?"

"I haven't got a clue," she whispered.

Then they opened one that surrendered its treasure reluctantly. Michael shook it gently. The gold was shiny, not dull, and the balls were purified gold the size of marbles. Then out came dull, opaque stones, like glass, some with a light-pink color.

"These are diamonds," she said.

"I'll be."

"They're unpolished diamonds, and they're found only in South America, Brazil and Venezuela. In Peru, there's a diamond the size of a walnut with a hole in it that hangs around the neck of a priestess. There's no known way to make a hole in diamonds. I just remembered, there's a place in Arkansas somewhere that has diamonds."

"Clinton wasn't one of them."

"What? You talk funny, *Tonto.*" Three of the diamonds went into her sack.

Looking further, they found a dozen more coarse diamonds, some pieces of polished jade that were perfectly square with holes in the center, and those, along with a handful of garnets, went into her sack, along with many of the shiny gold marbles.

They found no more caves in the area. Satisfied, with a promise to return someday, they left with a look behind them, as they touched each other happily,.

The next day, they slept late, draped around each other's naked bodies. They teased each other until they got up and bathed, then they ate breakfast and went out to practice shooting the pistol and Rosa's .22 automatic rifle.

They ran around naked in the sunshine, made love several times, bathed again, ate the last of the food, drank the wine, and packed their gear to depart in the morning.

They fell asleep with the thought of the long trail back.

In the morning, they ate cold beans and tamales and packed two apples each with some trail mix.

The horses and mules were glad to head home. Michael studied the map he made and led the way, but Rosa trotted past him.

"I'll lead, *Gringo.* You'll get us lost, and we'll die out here stuck together someplace."

"What a way to go."

"*Tonto.*"

Down the trail, Michael suddenly saw a flash in the distance to one side. It looked like shiny metal or a mirror. He looked through his monocular telescope in his range finder and saw a horseman disappear behind a rock.

"Rosa, did you see that?"

"Yes. I think we have company."

"They appear to be staying away from us."

"For now, maybe. Load your pistol."

"It's loaded."

"Is it a .22 or a .22 magnum?"

"It's a .22 long."

"Change to magnum and load it."

He obeyed without question, keeping the pistol ready in his lap. "Oscar?" he asked.

She looked at him in surprise, then nodded. "Oscar."

He remained vigilant the rest of the day. Across an open field up ahead, he noticed a very large boulder. As he studied it with his scope, a flock of desert doves took off.

"They aren't our friends, *Gringo.* They want to kill us for what's in your bag. They've been spying on us. I hope they didn't see us playing naked Native Americans."

"What should we do?"

The change in her attitude was remarkable. Suddenly, she was hard and commanding. "We kill them first," she said matter-of-factly. "Angle to the left and follow me, so they can't see us if they're just watching the trail."

He followed her until she was fifty yards from the boulder. She dismounted and motioned him to do the same, as calm as a gunnery sergeant. They tied their animals and approached the boulder from the opposite side of the trail, moving quietly and as quickly as they could, bent over at the waist.

They reached the back side of the rock without being detected and moved around it quietly. Rosa had her rifle at the ready, and Michael's pistol was cocked. Just ahead, three men squatted with rifles in their hands, staring at the trail, while their horses were ground-staked right behind them.

Rosa stood. "Drop the rifles, *Cavrones!*"

The men were startled, but they had no intention of dropping anything and spun around, hoping to shoot. Rosa's gun spoke twice, and two of the men fell with bullets in their brains. Michael kept his gun aimed at a man who stumbled. When he came up, Michael chose his target and squeezed his index finger. The man dropped his rifle as he fell on his face with a bullet in his heart.

Rosa walked forward rapidly, her rifle ready, but she didn't need to use it. All three were dead. She walked to the horses and spoke calmly to them.

"These are Homero's horses," she announced. "Bring the rifles. They're brand new .30-.30s."

She slipped a rifle into its scabbard, removed the bridles, and tied them tightly to the horns by the reins. She slipped off the rope halters the horses had been staked with and shouted while waving her arms.

"They'll find their way back to Homero," she said. "He takes good care of his horses."

She wasn't shaking and didn't seem nervous at all. Michael felt weak-kneed and trembling.

Suddenly, she looked at him. "I think I'm going to faint." She slid to the ground.

Michael sat beside her, holding her hand, until both were ready to move. They didn't glance toward the bodies as they walked to their mounts. When they rode off, he was pleased to find she let him lead.

It was evening when they reached the watering hole beside the sandy stretch of desolate desert. It had almost a foot of water in it. They let the horses and mules drink for a few minutes at a time to avoid colic. The animals ate all the grass growing nearby in less than an hour.

"Mike, you have a map from Pablo?"

"Yes. It's right here. Are we going to his cousin's ranch on the border? What's his name?"

"Antonio."

"Yeah, Antonio. It must be eighteen hours from here."

"We aren't going, Mike. You are."

"What?"

"Mike, I have to take these findings to Monterey and ship them to the Museum of Anthropology in Mexico City. Do you understand? I must. It's my duty."

"God, Rosa. I don't want to leave you."

"I'll be all right."

"That's not what I meant. I want to be…to be with you."

"I want to be with you, too."

"I could, well, I could love you." He removed his hat. "I mean, really love you."

"I could love you, too." She put her arm around his shoulders and kissed the top of his head, which was bent with defeat. "Where are you going, Bandito, when you leave Mexico?"

"I don't know. Can I come to Albuquerque where you are?"

"Yes, Mike. Forever."

They made tender love on their saddle blankets. Both of them cried. They planned for him to meet her at the university library in two weeks. It seemed she had one too many people in her apartment.

Without looking back, Rosa rode across the desert sands, while Michael turned north to follow the map.

Chapter Seven

It was pitch black, and he was ready to give up, when he saw a dim light ahead. Checking his map carefully, he thought it had to be Antonio's ranch. He worried about approaching it without being shot, so he rode slowly, calling, *"Hola!"* from a good distance.

Finally, someone shouted back. Michael rode up and saw a suspicious man in the middle of the yard with a child's baseball bat.

"Buenos noches," he said. *"Eres Antonio?"*

"No Antonio fui ayer."

"Mi nombre es Michael. Pablo me manolo."

"Si? El gringo. El amigo de Pablo."

"Si. Es mi. Habla ested Ingles?"

"Some."

"Can we take care of my animals?" he asked before dismounting.

"Yes." The man walked forward to help.

He's the most shifty-eyed son of a bitch I ever saw, Michael thought. *He looks like a rattlesnake ready to strike. He was waiting for me like those bastards behind the rock.*

He trusted his instincts. After they unpacked and unsaddled, Michael watched his leather duffle and canvas sack. Then he noticed that Antonio had picked up his club. When the man came up to him from behind, Michael was ready.

He turned, grabbing the man with his left hand and placing his right under his descending arm. He bent and threw in one motion, but, unlike his karate practice, he didn't let go as the man went over. Michael heard the arm pop like a broken limb. He screamed and lay writhing on the ground.

Out of the darkness, a familiar figure came forward carrying a pistol the size of an anvil.

"Pablo!" Michael said.

"Hi, Mike."

"You were there all the time?"

"I wouldn't let him hurt you. My God, you were fast. I almost shot you by accident." He studied the man writhing on the ground, his right arm flopping crazily when he tried to move it. "Gastone, I didn't think you were the one working for that fucking Oscar. I would've sworn it was Paul. Sometimes, I'm wrong. Didn't I treat you good, Gastone? Didn't I take care of you and watch out for your family? Then you sold out to Oscar."

"Please!"

Pablo blew off his head with his .757 magnum. "You know what, Michael? I still don't trust Paul. We have to be cautious."

"Where's this Paul guy?"

"A good question. He appears to be talking on a radio." He held up a small RDF, radio direction finder. Suddenly, the light stopped blinking.

A few minutes later, a blond, blue-eyed, dirty man in jeans and a T-shirt charged from the house with a pistol in his hand. Pablo yelled at him to stop, saying he was Pablo.

The man approached cautiously. Even in the dark, he looked shifty-eyed and ill at ease.

"Give me that damn pistol, you idiot!" Pablo barked, snatching the gun from his hand. "I told you not to have any weapons unless I gave them to you."

"Why?" Paul stammered, his blond ponytail flopping halfway down his back.

"Because I say so. For one thing, if the *Federals* catch you with it, you'll never get out of jail." His tone changed. "This is Michael Hart. He's the one I want safely across the river tonight."

Paul nodded but didn't speak or offer his hand.

"Go get the canoe ready. I want him across by midnight."

As Paul left, Pablo turned to Michael and said, "You have a bus to catch. Let's see what's in the bag, *Hombre.*"

"It was an experience. Let me show you." He took the thirty-pound bag and spread out a sample of the contents on a workbench.

Pablo fingered them, looking pleased without being surprised. "There's at least thirty pounds of gold alone."

They brushed the nuggets into the sack, then Michael handed it to Pablo.

"What are you doing?" Paul asked, grinning.

"These are yours."

"You got them, Man."

"Don't argue, *Amigo.* I owe you."

"You owe me nothing." Still, he kept the sack.

"Take the bag, Pablo."

He took it and looked at Michael with respect. "Thank you, Michael. It's a good thing you do. This all goes to the clinic and back to the Native Americans. It's a very good thing."

After a long pause, Pablo asked, "What are you running from, Michael? Can I ask as your *amigo?*"

"You can ask. I'm running from a lot of things. Mostly, it's from a flat, disappointing marriage, betrayal, infidelity, and things that just went wrong. I run away from love to anger and hurt, if that makes sense."

"it does, but it's always best to run toward something, not away. When you run toward something, you can and must leave something behind and take what you want with you. You must take what is valuable and makes you feel like yourself. Take what makes you *love* yourself.

"Know that someday, you can look back and see some good things and good times. Then the pain will be gone. So, *Amigo,* be ready to look back when the time comes and don't be afraid. Always be two things—tough and hell and as kind and fair as the world will let you."

Michael looked pensively at the stored supplies. "Like medicine and surgery."

"What?"

"Can I come back to the clinic and help out?"

"You can live there if you want."

"If I do, I'll end up taking Frances from you."

"Not a chance, *Gringo*. She said you have a cute little dink. It's just like a real one, only smaller."

"You're bad!"

They sat in silence, puffing on Cuban cigars.

"It sounds like you've thought about these things a lot," Michael said. "Are you religious?"

"After my wife died, I thought about a lot of things. A man must fight against the injustices of the world that can be fought and do his best to accept the rest. Some people must be shot between the others. Others must be kissed on the cheek."

Michael didn't comment on that.

"About religion, well, I hate religiosity. Look at our heritage. The Spaniards gave the Aztecs a great choice. 'Become Christian and hang, or don't be Christians and get skinned alive.' Whole generations were branded and forced to live in mines the rest of their lives for the hideous Catholic church of their day. Little boys were castrated to sing soprano in the choir. Look at the Spanish Inquisition."

"That was a long time ago."

"It goes on today. Priests molest little boys under the protection of bishops in the United States. If it goes on there, where we wash our dirty linen for the world to see, what the hell must be happening in Europe and elsewhere?

"The church punished Galileo for saying the earth rotated around the sun. They locked him up for it. Now the president stabs science in the ass to protect embryos from stem-cell research, because it conflicts with his religiosity. The Protestants and the Catholics are fighting in Ireland. Mormon offshoots have polygamy and child rape. In the name of religiosity, women are stoned, their genitals hacked off. They're killed for family honor and burned alive, while their husbands live. Shall I continue?"

"No."

"I get carried away."

"You always did."

"I know."

"Well, Pablo, do you believe in God?"

"Hell, yes, and Jesus, too. Do you think I'm an atheist?"

"No. It's time for me to get across the river. First, I want to know something. When I came here, that dead guy paid a lot of attention to my duffle, like he knew what was in it. He couldn't take his eyes off it. That's what warned me. Only certain people know about the money in there. Could it be that the one carrying the tale is the same one who tipped Oscar's boys about the gold nuggets?"

"Could be."

"Felix."

"Yeah, Felix."

"Did you kill him?"

"No. I sent him away to Guatemala. I got him a job in a mine. Actually, it's a private prison."

"I'd rather be dead."

"So would he."

"I owe you for the adventure by itself. There's one thing I'd like to have out of here." He felt in a deep corner of the sack and took out a diamond the size of a lima bean. "I'd like to keep this one."

Pablo's eyes bulged.

"Rosa has more," Michael said. "I'd like to tell you what else we found. There are Chinese granite heads and pieces of jade, arrowheads so perfect and sharp, you cut your finger holding them, made from obsidian for shooting birds. My God, there's that ice cave in the desert! We ran into some bad dudes, too, Pablo. There was a little gun fight."

"I know about that. They were Oscar's men. They didn't know he was dead, but I doubt that would've changed their minds."

"You say he's dead?"

"Yes. The poor son of a bitch died out in the desert. His car ran out of gas, and he didn't have any water. Can you believe it? There was no radio or cell phone, either. Tsk, tsk. It's funny. He was barefoot, too. Do you have the pistol we gave you?"

"Sure." He pulled it from his baggy pocket and handed it to Pablo, who made a show of deftly spinning the cylinder. "One round's been shot."

Pablo took a piece of pencil lead that looked like a fishing weight from his shirt pocket and crammed it down the length of the barrel, twisting it and pushing it out of sight with a leather punch on his pocket knife.

He handed it to Michael. "I want you to give this to Paul. Tell him it's a gift for helping you."

Paul came into view along the trail leading to the river.

"All right, Pablo. It's time to tell me about this fucking Oscar."

"Why do you have to know?"

"I don't have to know anything except how to get out of here with my ass intact, but he tried to kill me, *Hombre*. I deserve to know something about what's coming down."

"All right, my friend." He sat quietly on a bale of alfalfa. "Don't you smoke anymore?"

"No. I quit. Stop trying to change the subject."

"I do." He took out a small black cigarette and lit it, blowing pungent smoke from his nose. "Oscar Gusman, may he not rest in peace."

Michael waited.

"Five years ago, I started a clinic for the poor people. They were most Native Americans, Gespe Indians, forgotten by time and certainly by the Mexican government. They were hostile and resentful for a while, suspicious as hell. Their bright-eyed children, with round faces and bright teeth, were like angels. The men were skinny and tired. The women were worn thin and burdened with more children than they had any reason for. They ran things, a matriarchal society like the *Novekas*.

"When they began to trust us, it was good. I came to the clinic for four days at a time, once or twice a month, and they would be waiting. It was like seeing my family. It was a good thing.

"They started bringing me things, though we never asked for pay. You know what they brought, *Hombre?* Gold nuggets, sometimes pieces of jade. There were flakes of silver and the biggest garnets you ever saw. It wasn't possible to find out where they got them. I never really did, but I had a good idea from the old line-shock watering hole you went to. I guess I was right. Anyway, it's from around there. Did you see the dinosaur bones?"

Michael nodded.

"And the ice cave or whatever it is?"

"Yes. That's the damnedest thing I ever saw. There's beer in there if you go back someday—beer on ice."

"What?"

"Go see for yourself."

"I probably will, but you asked about Oscar. He's an asshole we call a coyote. He smuggles people across the border into the States. I should say he *did* smuggle, along with pot and cocaine. He was a bigshot son of a bitch in south Texas and northern Mexico. He paid off a lot of the Mexican authorities, which, as you know, is easy. It's not as easy in the States, but he got to the border patrol around McAllen.

"When they caught some guys trying to escape Oscar's goons, they found gold nuggets on them from you know where. Oscar's goons beat it out of them. They said they got it from the Native Americans. Some of the people around Oscar, who are my friends, said he lit up like a pinball machine.

"He was a bad man surrounded by bad men before that. The illegals he was supposed to get across the border ended up cooked to death in the freight yards or dead of thirst in the desert. It was men, women, and children, always with empty pockets. The girls were raped, the men were beat up, and the children were left on their own.

"One of the kids who survived told me about it. I tried to talk to the law in both countries, but all I got was threats and deaf ears. It really stinks."

Besides being angry, Pablo was sad and close enough to tears to embarrass both men.

"Sometimes, *Señor,* men have to take the law and punishment into their own hands. It makes our hands bloody, but it's the price we must pay." He looked thoughtfully at his hands.

"As I was saying, Oscar tried to find the source of the nuggets. He tried using force, but that didn't work. His men were ambushed if they entered the hills and asked too many questions. His men beat up some of my patients and terrorized a few families I was close to.

"Oscar lived in McAllen or across the border in Reynosa. I thought it would be nice to take him for a ride into the desert. Somehow, we forgot water. Can you believe it? A nail poked through his gas tank. Sancho said Oscar owed him a pair of shoes, so he took them. He left Oscar with a bottle of tequila in trade. Dying from tequila in the desert sun is probably more than you understand. It turns a man inside out."

"You're a hard man, Pablo."

"No, I'm not. I'm a soft man who's been pushed too far by people who make me ashamed of being Mexican or even part of the human race."

"It's not hard to see why you did it. Just don't become too much like the people you hate."

"Only as much as I hate to, *Amigo.*"

"I'm ready," Michael said, not looking at anyone.

Pablo shook his hand, then he suddenly hugged the taller man. *"Adios."*

"Adios, Cuidadoso. Just a minute. I have to say good-bye to Matador and Diablo." He hugged each animal's neck.

Michael lifted his leather duffle and followed Paul to the river, where he got into a canoe painted black. *For night work,* he thought, chuckling, as Paul untied the bow and jockeyed the canoe around.

"I sure appreciate your help, Paul," Michael said. "Let me give you something." He handed the pistol to the surprised man, spinning the cylinder like Pablo and pushing out the empty shell, lining up the cylinder so the hammer would fall on a live bullet.

"Thanks." He tucked it into his belt.

Paul worked carefully at just the right angle to bring the canoe across the river. He nudged it against the bank upstream from a large branch.

Maybe not, Michael thought, reaching for his duffle.

"Leave the bag, Man."

Michael turned and saw Paul had the pistol aimed at his stomach. "No. I'm taking my bag."

"You ain't goin' nowhere."

"Oh. Did you know that Pablo's on to you and that Oscar is dead?"

"Bullshit."

"It's not bullshit. I'm leaving." He reached for his bag.

Paul raised the gun and fired. It exploded and took his hand with it. An artery pumped bright blood from the stump, and Paul screamed in horror, trying to stop the flow by squeezing what was left of his wrist.

Michael stared at the man, who held out his arm as if asking for help. He tossed his duffle on the bank. With the canoe wedged against the current, he tied the end of the bow rope around Paul's forearm as a tourniquet. He tossed away the paddle, scrambled up the bank, and kicked the canoe into the current.

As it drifted away, he said, "*Adios, Shithead.*"

He blubbering man crouching in the canoe didn't reply.

Chapter Eight

Michael found a path through the woods that led to a road. He'd been told to turn right until he came to a gas station that was also a quick-stop grocery store. Walking inside, he learned that the bus to McAllen was due at any minute.

He waited outside and boarded the bus, paying with a handful of change. He felt drained. Just before he fell asleep, he saw a border patrol car pull out from a driveway and follow the bus.

He awoke with a start at the downtown bus station, grabbed his duffle bag from between his knee, and got out. Border patrol guards were waiting.

"What's your name?" a small Hispanic man with a mustache demanded.

"Who wants to know?"

"Sergeant Alvary, United States Border Patrol."

"In that case, I'm Michael Hart, MD, an American citizen and registered voter."

"Come with us," the younger man said.

"Do you have a warrant?"

"We don't need a warrant to question you about immigration and travel violations." He led Michael into the station to a brightly lit, closed cubicle with the words *US Customs* on the door.

"I'm going to search your bag," he announced.

"Not without a warrant, Officer," a pleasant voice said behind them.

A man in his late twenties stood there, wearing a sharp suit, shiny boots, and carrying a briefcase.

"Who the hell are you?" Alvary demanded.

The well-manicured man produced a card from his vest pocket. "Pablo Martinez. As you can see, I'm an attorney at law. Dr. Hart's my client."

They looked abashed and defenseless.

"What do you wish to ask him, *Muchachos?*"

They glared at him for calling them boys.

"Were you in Mexico?"

"What kind of question is that? Were you in Mexico> I'm sure he's been in Mexico at some time. When, for Christ's sake?" Disrespect dripped from the lawyer's voice.

"In the last two weeks."

"No," Martinez said.

"Let him answer his own questions!"

"No way. I'm his attorney, and I'll answer for him unless he's ordered to answer by a judge. If you don't know the rules, I suggest you learn how the game is played. We want to go, unless you're charging him? *Habeas corpus.* You have no proof or suspicion of a crime."

Michael decided it was time to speak. "Let them search my bag, Counselor. I give my permission."

"Against advice, Michael."

Michael winked. "It's OK. There's nothing in there but filthy underwear and socks."

The agents were rattled. Michael knew that the compartments that held his cash were so well hidden, he had trouble finding them himself. Those clowns wouldn't be able to find an Easter egg.

He unzipped the bag and showed them his round-trip plane ticket to San Antonio. "You can check with the airline and this hotel in San Antonio, if you wish."

The agents looked surprised. The situation wasn't what they'd been told to expect. They quickly searched the bag, then Michael took it back.

"Why do you guys look so surprised?" Michael demanded. "You know I don't like the Mexican desert that well. People go crazy out there. They found some barefoot geezer named Oscar out in the desert recently. He didn't have any water and died of thirst."

The agents glanced at each other, then looked away.

"I'm sure the Mexican and American authorities will work on that case together," Martinez said. "They have many documents concerning shady deals that imitate law enforcement. If I were working with Oscar on anything, I'd hightail it out of here."

He picked up Michael's duffle bag and nodded him to follow. Once outside, he looked at Martinez sincerely.

"It's very nice meeting you, Mr. Martinez," he said. "Thank you very much for showing up like that."

"Call me Simon, doc. Pablo's my uncle. I'd do anything for him. It was a last-minute call. I was just going to bed—not by myself, either. Pablo sent me through college and law school. He managed to straighten out a street kid nobody else liked."

"By God, I like you, Simon."

"I'll drop you at your hotel."

Chapter Nine

After sleeping ten hours straight, Michael awoke the following day and felt his curiosity overcome him. He called his accountant in Tacoma, who worked in the same firm as Patricia's lover.

"Hey, Lou," Michael said. "It's Michael Hart. I'm calling from a pay phone in New Orleans. How are things?"

Lou paused, then asked softly, "Where's the money?"

"Fort Knox. I know you'll have a lot of shit to contend with—a lot."

"You're right about that!"

He couldn't stand it and finally asked, "How's Patricia taking it?"

"She's a hysterical mess. She spent two days in a soft, rubber room before she found out she couldn't pay for it." His tone was serious.

"How's Bobby boy taking it?"

Suddenly, Lou laughed. "He's worse. We haven't seen him this week."

"I just want you to know that I'll pay you. I can send you a retainer."

"I trust you, Doc."

"That's fine, but I'm shipping five grand in cash in a plain, brown wrapper to your home. It'll arrive from Texas or Arizona."

"Hey, Doc?"

"Yeah?"

"Good luck, and be careful."

Using a Cayman Island contact, Michael was able to find a diamond-processing center in Amsterdam, where he sent the yellow-tinged diamond for cutting and finishing.

He had two weeks to wait, but he didn't want to hang around McAllen, so he booked a flight to Albuquerque. *I can wait in the library,* he thought.

Chapter Ten

He spent ten long days in Albuquerque, sitting near the library door each day at closing time, sometimes for as long as two hours. He joined a health club and spent his time working out and practicing karate with people he met. He rarely thought of Patricia, and, if she came to mind, he roughly shoved her from his thoughts. He realized their marriage had been over for at least two years before the divorce. Both of them must've known it.

It's too bad people can't be more honest with each other, he thought, *and themselves.* By then, his anger was gone. *My God, revenge sure is therapeutic.*

He set down his book and walked out the heavy swinging doors into the dim evening.

"Hey, *Gringo.*"

He saw her standing beside a fountain, and his heart leaped in his chest. He walked over nonchalantly and gazed into her big, brown, sparkling eyes and admired her plump lips with a hint of pink lipstick. One hand felt for the ring in his pocket he'd received from Amsterdam.

"Nice fountain," he said, glancing at the little waterfall. "Want to go for a swim?"

"*Tonto!*" She laughed.

"I missed you, Rosa. I mean, I really missed you. I wasn't sure you'd come."

"I missed you, too, very much. I wasn't sure you'd be here, but I knew you'd come if you could."

He took her into his arms and kissed her tenderly. They gazed into each other's eyes.

"So, Rosa, we missed each other. Where do we go from here?"

"Wherever you want to take me, *Gringo Tonto.*"

Grabbin' Chickens

Chapter One

I first met Anton Christensen when I was fourteen. As I rode my bike in Spring Lake, he pulled up beside me in his big, red, diesel truck with *AC Chicken Farm* on the doors. People called him Grumpy, but for no good reason. He was anything but. Maybe the name came from *Snow White and the Seven Dwarves.* He ran a chicken farm where Spring Creek flowed into the lake. He also raised some cattle, a couple goats, and a few sheep. There were always hides stretched out in his barn.

Everyone knew he was a moonshiner who made good whiskey, the black stuff, cured in charred-oak barrels. He sold it for top dollar, because it was good quality, made the way people in his home state of Tennessee did it.

He also raised hound dogs, crossbred from black and tan to Plotz and blue tic. He loved chasing coons and bobcats with a whiskey jug tucked under his arm. The best part of my life was when I went with him.

He put on barbecues of chicken legs—no other part—for a fair or for picnics for clubs, the local union, and the sheriff's department. He once told me, under his breath, that the sheriff's department was his best customer for skee.

When he pulled up beside me, I hadn't met him yet, but I knew a lot about him. Locally, he was famous.

"You want a job, Kid?" he asked.

"A job?"

"Yeah. Grabbing chickens."

"Grabbing chickens?"

"You catch them and put them in cages in the truck for market. I pay $1.25 an hour."

That seemed like a good wage for a kid my age. "All right."

"You know where I'm at?"

"Yes, Sir."

"Come to the chicken barn at seven. You'll work all night, no overtime. Wear sneakers and a long-sleeved shirt. I furnish gloves and lunch. I ain't no sir. See ya there."

"Yes, Sir."

"What's your name?"

"Robert Abbott."

"My name's Anton, not Grumpy or Sir." He drove off.

I was so eager to start my new job, I pedaled to his place right after dinner.

I soon learned about chicken grabbing. All the chickens lived in one big, open room. Continuous feed trays lined the sides. The tops of their beaks were burned off, so they couldn't peck each other. If a chicken had a bloody spot, the others would attack it and tear it to pieces. I never liked chickens, but, after that night, I hated them. The wooden floor was covered in a layer of sawdust thick with chicken shit, which made it a slippery, slimy, hazardous surface.

When it got dark, the only light in the place came from a few blue bulbs. The idea was to grab the chickens by their legs and put them in a wire cage by the door, which could be picked up by a forklift once it was very full, set on the truck, and shipped off to the butcher shop in downtown Kent.

Three other kids were there. Anton showed us how to grab the chickens by taking three of them by their legs in each hand and setting them in the wire cages.

"They can't see the blue light," he said. "They're asleep."

Yes, they can, I thought. *No, they're not.*

There were 2,000 chickens in that room. When I grabbed one, it spurred me with its claw and shit on my arm up to the elbow. I slid on the slippery floor, and the chicken ran off protesting with such zeal, the others were immediately alarmed. I couldn't get the sawdust off my pants. It was glued on. No one laughed, though, not even Anton.

By morning, I was pretty good at it, though I wasn't as good as Anton, who was a whiz. At two o'clock that morning, two of the boys quit. Maybe the other boy and I were too dumb to quit. I slipped and fell several times, but the other kid fell even more. Anton never fell.

The chickens were collected into an increasingly smaller area. Finally at 5:30 that morning, they were rounded up, grabbed, and loaded. My pants were ruined.

My new tennis shoes were a mess, I had chicken manure on my arms and in my hair, and I was totally exhausted.

"You did good, Bobby," Anton said. "Those other galoots lasted until two o'clock. That's better than usual. Come on. Let's wash up for breakfast."

I looked around, but the other kid wasn't there. I hadn't noticed when he left.

"I paid him off," Anton said. "I didn't like his attitude."

We washed in a horse trough. I threw my shirt in a burn barrel and took a standing birdbath with Ivory soap. The towel he handed me was previously used.

"You're a good boy, Bobby. Come with me while I haul these birds to the butcher shop."

"I don't have a shirt."

"I'll get you one. Come in. Let's eat."

I followed him onto the porch, where I saw a table outside the kitchen. He brought me a yellow-gray T-shirt that had once been white, but it was clean and smelled like Ivory soap, too.

Then we had breakfast—warm milk fresh from a cow, burned toast fresh from an incinerator, and a not-too-fresh barbecued chicken leg from a barbecue a few days earlier. I never had fresh milk like that before. It tasted good. I ate the burned toast with plenty of homemade butter without salt. That wasn't bad, either. I couldn't eat the chicken leg, though.

As we bounced down the road toward the butcher's shop, Anton smiled. "I'm always glad when a job's done. New chicks arrive tomorrow. We have to clean up and spray the chicken house and put down fresh sawdust. Did you know that chicken manure's the best fertilizer there is?"

I was tired and sleepy. I signed on to grab chickens. I didn't give a whit about fertilizer. *What does he mean we?* I wondered.

On the way back from the butcher's shop, I fell asleep in the truck, grateful for the smell of Ivory soap.

That was how I came to work for Anton Grumpy Christensen. After that, he gave me a job feeding, cleaning up, and helping make whiskey mash. We fed the used mash to his pigs, and they seemed to like it. I thought they got hangovers, though, because they lay around all day.

When it was time, the mash was mixed with water for a couple days, and the almost-brown liquid was put in barrels that were burned to charcoal on the inside. He stored the barrels and siphoned the contents into jugs once a year.

Siphoning was a fun day. He sang songs about loggers and waitresses, crazy horses and hound dogs. My job was to put in the corks and sock 'em in place with a large wooden mallet. He called me a "corksocker" with the damnedest grin when he said it. It took a long time for me, a naïve guy, to catch the joke.

He became my friend and taught me to train dogs, shoot a rifle, and run a barbecue cooker. One day, I asked if he'd ever been married.

"Yep. She ran off with the chicken-feed salesman. My daughter went back to Tennessee when she was eighteen and got married. She writes all the time and calls on the phone. She has two little girls and plans to come out to see me next summer. We need to get their rooms up and painted. I think I need to buy a little horse, too."

"I guess."

Sometimes, he paid me $1.25 an hour, sometimes not.

My father was David Abbott. He came from a small town north of Spokane where he and his family lived on the homestead that my grandfather and mother's family settled. They worked a logging operation that consisted of my grandfather, my uncle, and my dad. They were doing fine, with good horses and big wagons, until tractors and logging trucks came. They were the first to buy those. My father had good aptitude and ran everything first and best. He was only eighteen when he married my mother, who had just turned sixteen.

In general, they were doing all right, but not that well, when the Great Depression arrived. Times got hard, and they finally lost their lease on the timberland. The equipment sat idle. Cut logs were piled up, because the sawmill closed. Oscar and my dad, two defeated brothers, left, leaving his older brother the whole mess.

They came to Seattle to find work. Somehow, they survived until my father learned about a construction project on Snoqualmie Pass to create an eight-lane highway. He hitchhiked his way up there, fearing to take his Model A. That was back in 1938, and the world was staggering and confused by economics. He sought out the foreman of the project.

"My name's Abbott. I understand you may be hiring."

"Maybe." He looked my dad over. "You ain't very big."

"I can run equipment."

"What kind?"

"Dozers, loaders, scrapers, crushers, trucks—anything."

"How'd you learn all that?"

"Some of it, I learned logging. Some of it, I just knew."

"You just knew?"

"Yes. I can figure out how to run anything right off."

"Well, I'll be damned. You sure got nerve. I'll hand you that." He laughed. My father was easy to like.

"Yes, Sir."

"See that dozer over there?" He pointed. "See if you can get it started and push those rocks over the edge."

It was a new bulldozer at that time, and the blade lifts were made of cables. The hydraulics were the push-pull type, off-on with no stat control. It was all or nothing and very tricky to run. There was no way to control the blade's angle, either. It was either up or down.

My father, an eager, confident young man, opened the dozer's hood to check the oil, then he checked the fuel. He made sure the fuel filter contained a full load of gasoline, which was used to start the diesel engine.

The foreman watched and was pleased. My dad climbed aboard

and studied the controls, then he tapped the gas pedal a few times with his foot, made sure the transmission was in neutral, and advanced the spark. The engine caught on the first turn.

"I'll be damned," the foreman muttered. "He's good."

Dad moved all the controls—blade up and down, right and left tracks, then reverse. When he inched forward, he looked in perfect control, but his heart was pounding, and he was sweating, though his hands remained steady.

"Don't over control!" the foreman called. "Just use your fingers."

Dad nodded and pushed the rocks into the gulch below. All four bashed their way down with a loud rumble. He left the engine running as he walked back to the foreman.

"They don't start very well when they're hot," he explained, "so I left it running."

"You're hired. I'm Barney Hull."

They shook hands and went to the construction shack to sign Dad up. He felt like he could fly back to Seattle. It was Friday. By Saturday, he and my mom moved to North Bend, a small town at the bottom of the pass on the west side. Monday, Dad started work. One week later, my older brother Otis started work, too.

Dad did his job well. He was well liked, and he worked his engines with concentration and care. Whenever a new, bigger, improved dozer, loader, or grazer was brought in, he was given the task of learning how to run it. He was talented at running equipment and took great pride in it. He also took correspondence courses from Central Washington College for something to do in the bunkhouse at night when he couldn't get home, which was often. Sometimes, the men worked through the weekend and didn't return home for twelve days at a time.

I was born in 1939, a year and a half after my brother. My little sister was born two years later. Our lives were going well.

Then the Japanese bombed Pearl Harbor. Two weeks later, we were at war with Germany, too. My dad came home and said he would enlist in the Army Air Corps. My mother said little about it. The money they saved for a new house would be used for her living expenses. She was an accepting woman, though perhaps complacent would've been a better word.

My father had a bit more than two years of college through his correspondence courses, which gave him an associate degree. I doubted the service even knew what that was, but it was a degree, so, after boot camp, he was selected for OCS and flying school. His same talents applied, because he was a successful pilot and was soon asked to fly the *big ones.* In nine months, he was a copilot of a B-29 bomber. After a two-week furlough, he was on his way to England with one hundred brave, very young men.

After the war, he was back with big D-9s, bulldozers with hydraulic controls, fancy angling blades, and nonslip tracks.

He said nothing about the war until on Saturday when two men came to the house and introduced themselves as representatives of a new airline forming in Seattle. They carried a lot of papers, which they laid out on the table, while my brother and I stayed in the room. As long as we were quiet, we could stay to watch.

"Colonel Abbott," the man in the blue suit began.

I noticed the other man wore the uniform of an airline with three stripes on the sleeve.

"I'm not a colonel anymore. I'm a civilian."

"Sir, with great respect, you'll always be a colonel."

"OK."

"You flew missions from England."

"Yes. B-29s."

"You were the pilot?"

"After a while. At first, I was copilot."

"You had a distinguished record."

A page was open, and I saw certificates of merit as the man turned pages one after the other. There was a Distinguished Flying Cross, a Golden Eagle, and a letter signed by Winston Churchill on behalf of England. There was also a letter of recognition from Dwight D. Eisenhower, praising Dad for things I couldn't read, though I saw the words, *fortitude and bravery above and beyond....*

"This is a fine record, Sir," the man said.

"Where'd you get it?" Dad asked irritably.

"From the War Department, the United States Army Air Corps. It's public information."

"I want it kept confidential."

"Yes, Sir. Of course."

"What brings you men out here?" he asked impatiently.

The man in the pilot's uniform spoke. "Sir, it's a great honor to meet you," he paused, "and offer you a position as pilot with our airline. You'll find our salary and benefits are very generous. We'd like you to consider...."

Dad cut him off. "No, thank you. I don't fly airplanes anymore. On my last mission, I made an agreement with God. We had only two engines left, and one of those was smoking. Four of my crew were dead." He looked up at the ceiling. "I asked God to get us down, and I never wanted to fly again." He paused. "I fly big bulldozers now."

The men stood in silence. The man in the suit opened his mouth, but he didn't say anything. He put away the papers in disbelief, but he knew better than to argue or attempt persuasion.

"Thank you for your time. This is a great opportunity, you know."

"You're most welcome. Thank you for considering me."

They left in a hurry. The pilot stopped at the door, turned, and saluted. Dad smiled and waved his hand.

"You know what, Boys? The B-29's a great airplane. It's easier to fly than a D-10 dozer, and I can rake the leaves off your lawn with one of those."

The man smiled and left without looking back.

Around midnight, the phone rang. Somehow, I knew it was for me. Dad reached the phone just as I did.

"Hello," I said. "This is Bobby. All right, I'll come right over." I hung up.

"Who was that?" Dad asked.

"That was Anton."

"What did he want?"

"He makes whiskey at his chicken ranch, you know."

"Yeah. Everybody knows."

"He just got a call. Someone told him the Feds, the revenue guys, will raid him in the morning. He needs help cleaning out his place."

"Let's go," Dad said with an urgent grin.

We dressed, climbed into our pickup truck, and drove away.

Anton opened the gate for us as we arrived. We piled out of the truck, looking for something to do.

"Thanks for coming," he said. "Mr. Abbott, will…?"

"My name's Dave," Dad said.

"Thanks. Can you drive a bulldozer, by any chance?"

I almost said, "That's his job," but Dad beat me to it.

"I can muddle through," Dad said.

Anton had an antique dozer with cable lifts and a flexible blade. "I'll get it started."

He pulled off the air filter, poured a little gas in the carburetor, while Dad pressed the starter. The engine coughed pathetically, then ran.

"We got to get rid of the mash. Damn. That's good mash, just about done cookin'." Anton looked sad.

"I'll bury it," Dad said.

"Where?" he shouted over the engine, which, without a muffler, was very loud.

"Right here." He pointed at the manure pile.

Anton grinned.

Dad planned to push the manure pile aside, scrape out a hole, put in the mash, and cover it with manure again.

"Makes me cry," Anton said. "That was good mash."

A couple tough-looking guys I didn't know came and watched.

"What now?" someone asked.

"I got six months' shipment we got to dump," Anton said.

"Where?"

"We'll pour it in the river and fill the jugs with river water."

A pickup backed to the storage shed, where an empty still with propane tank sat idle in the rear. We filled that pickup with jugs of brew and drove to the creek, 500 yards away at the corner of the property.

Dad filled his pickup, too. I climbed in beside him, and we rattled and bumped across the field to the creek. Dad laughed like a teenager pulling a naughty prank. It was great. God, I loved being with him like that.

He backed up so close to the creek, we almost went in. We jumped out, pulling corks and lids before pouring the jugs into the stream. Then we refilled them with creek water.

"What a ghastly shame," Dad, my partner in crime, said, sampling a bit of a jug before tossing it out. He smacked his lips and wiped his mouth. "Good skee." He smiled.

I sipped, too. At first, it burned like fury, and the fumes came out my nose. After a while, I liked the taste and the fumes. The skee warmed my stomach.

Most of all, I liked working with my dad. I seldom called him that. We banged shoulders together, bumping into each other, sipping and laughing as we dumped the aromatic black liquid out and replaced it with creek water.

We stumbled around in water up to our ankles, inevitably slipping and falling ass-first into the freeze water. We were a little drunk, laughing like hell, and unable to help each other up.

"Damn," he said, "I wasn't supposed to take a bath till Saturday. Too much bathin' weakens a man."

I laughed and hiccupped.

"Ho, ho, yourself!"

When the jugs were finished, we hauled them back to the storage shed and stacked them in neat rows. The other guys seemed as happy as we were.

"This will be good," a logger said.

A few jugs had been hidden for ready access, and the men accessed them several times as we waited.

At dawn, the federal men arrived. We waited, trying unsuccessfully not to grin too much.

Anton opened the gate for them with a wave and a bow. Two sheriff's cars with four deputies in each one came in, along with a car labeled *Marshal's Office for Official Use.* Then came a fourth car with men who looked like FBI agents. Finally, a TV camera truck rolled up.

"You stay out," Anton said, smiling as he locked the gate.

"Hey!" the driver yelled.

"Hey, Yourself, Asshole." Anton gave him the finger. "Now, then. What do you guys want?"

"Here's a warrant." The head sheriff handed a piece of paper to Anton.

"My, my. A search warrant. Go to it."

"Over here!" a deputy said, opening the storage shed.

"You're in a heap of trouble, Mr. Christensen," the sheriff said, reaching for his handcuffs.

"Now, Mr. Sheriff, why would that be?"

"Look at all that whiskey."

"What whiskey? That's river water for my chickens. The tap water has chlorine in it, and I can't distill it out." He pointed at the still in the shed. "That's what I have that for." He grinned.

The pot-bellied sheriff ran up and opened several jugs, sniffing and tasting. He became wild-eyed and hyperactive. Sweat broke out on his forehead, and spittle gathered at the corners of his mouth.

"Where's the damn whiskey?" he shouted.

"You need a drink, Sheriff?" Dad asked. "I got an unopened bottle of Jim Beam in the truck. You'll have to drink it all, you guys." He nodded at the deputies, paying special attention to the men in suits. "I can't have an open bottle in my vehicle. It's against the law, you know."

It was hard, but we didn't laugh. The sheriff stared blankly into space.

I thought Dad was wonderful. I saw one of the sheriffs turn around and his shoulders shake with laughter. Maybe he'd been the one who warned Anton. Anton said he never knew, but maybe he did. Suddenly, a deputy leaped forward and pointed at a wooden barrel.

"Look!" he said with a knowing sneer.

Anton explained it was a big pickle barrel, because he cooked chicken at fairs and picnics.

"False bottom!" the man said, poking around with a small crowbar.

"Hey, you cockroach," Anton said. "Those are my pickles."

The man kept pounding a hole in the lid. He rolled up his sleeve to the elbow, plunged in his hand, and groped around. Dad came up beside him, pretended to stumble and hit the man hard enough to send him into the barrel up past his shoulders.

"Oops," Dad said.

"Shit!" the man shouted.

The sheriff stared in disbelief. "Get out of here, Rupert. Get in your squad car and get the hell out of here!"

Rupert did as he was told. The others stood around, shuffling their feet.

"Anyone want a barbecue?" Anton offered. "I can have some barbecued chicken legs ready in a jiffy."

The deputies looked at the sheriff for permission, but it wasn't forthcoming. The men in suits left without a word. The TV truck crew filmed it all from beyond the gate. As people left, a few waved. Finally, only Dad and I were left with Anton.

"Kind of lonesome here," Anton said, taking a jug from a sack of chicken feed.

We all had a drink, though I only sipped mine.

"Thanks, Davey Jones," he told my dad.

"You're most welcome, Antonovich Christenovich."

I wondered where he got that name. We staggered to our truck. Dad leaned on me so hard, I wobbled.

"Bobby, do you know how to drive?" he asked.

"Yes," I lied.

"You'd better drive us home."

Wow! I released the clutch, and we leaped forward as if pulled by a bungee cord.

"Good boy," Dad said. "I used to fly airplanes."

Somehow, we got home. Dad slept all morning, but, before he fell asleep, I said, "I love you, Dad."

"Yeah, me, too. Right back at ya." He hiccupped.

Chapter Two

When Dad came home from working at Snoqualmie Pass, it was always a good time. He brought deer ribs, which we cooked in the oven and ate. Sometimes, Uncle Oscar came, too. I liked him. He treated us kids well, bringing candy or comic books.

Once, Uncle Oscar asked Otis and me if we'd like to go elk hunting with him and a couple cowboys he knew. That meant riding horses and staying at a hunting camp. I really wanted to go, but Otis had baseball. I knew he didn't like hunting.

Dates were set, and we made arrangements to pick me up. I was excited and told Anton.

"Going elk hunting, eh?" he asked.

"Yeah, with my uncle and his cowboy friends."

"Where you going?"

"Up White Pass in Yakima."

"Good place. What kind of rifle do you have?"

"My dad's .30-.30 Winchester carbine."

"That's no good for elk. Let me show you something."

He came onto the porch a moment later—he never invited me into his house—and showed me a new rifle still sealed in its box, a

.22mm magnum Wetherby with a beautiful blond stock and four-power scope made by Weaver.

"You can use this," he said. "I'll sight it for you at 200 yards." He seemed proud of the rifle.

"Gosh, Mr. Christensen. I can't take that."

"Why not? I've had it for ten years and never even fired it."

"Why?"

"I don't know. Mostly, it's because my hunting partner died. I felt awful bad. I never found another one."

I didn't know what to say.

A couple days later, the rifle was sighted. The first time I fired it, I aimed at a cracked jug and blew it apart, then I shot the pieces.

"You can shoot, Bobby."

"Yes, I can. With that scope, I don't need my glasses." I slipped on my wire-rims and grinned.

"Good."

"This is a fine rifle." I patted it.

"Beautiful, isn't it?"

That hunting trip was the most fun I ever had. The men gave me a good horse with saddle and scabbard for my rifle. We rode into the hills for four hours. At a higher altitude, the forest gave way from thick, red-barked Ponderosa pine and Douglas fir to open fields filled with meadow grass just turning yellow from the autumn chill. As we emerged into the sunlight, fields filled with red, yellow, purple, and blue mountain flowers greeted us. Some were tall, others short, with green or straw-yellow leaves. Bushes were orange and yellow with splatters of red and green. I saw firewood, lupine, Indian paintbrush, and others I didn't recognize.

The blue sky had only a few puffs of white cloud that didn't move, as if they'd been painted in place. Grasshoppers flew everywhere, while talkative jays followed us.

We pitched camp in the shadows of the trees along the edge of the meadow. Nearby, a small stream burbled across shiny rocks, providing water for the horses and ourselves. We let the horses graze with hobbles while we erected tents, built a fire pit, and dug a latrine one hundred yards away. After allowing the horses two hours to graze, we brought them into a rope corral.

That night, we ate steaks roasted over an open fire, beans from a big pot, steamed cornbread cooked in a Dutch oven, and canned peaches for dessert. I slept dreamlessly, warm and comfortable in my down bag.

The following morning, we started off with hot coffee and a couple of biscuits, returned to camp by eleven o'clock for brunch and a nap, then took off again in the afternoon.

One cowboy named Red took me under his wing, probably because I had red hair, too, or maybe it was because he admired my rifle. He was a good guy. We stayed in touch for years after that trip. He made me check my compass often, then he quizzed me about my direction.

We spent each day like that. Most of the time, we were on foot. Some days, we rode our horses over the hills. Those were the best. We brought lunch in our saddlebags, stopping in a sunny spot to eat peanut butter and jelly sandwiches and apples, drink little cans of orange juice, and have a candy bar for dessert.

The sun felt wonderful on my face and back. I smelled the mountains around us, and all of us were seduced into pleasant drowsiness and restful meditation. I never wanted to leave.

We saw deer immediately, skipping over the grass and darting into the brush, but no elk until the second-to-last day. Around four o'clock that afternoon, Red and I saw a herd of twelve elk on the side of a hill, with one big bull, three longhorn spikes, and a two pointer. The shadows were growing, and the evening breeze shook the leaves. We watched for a while, seeing some fat beauties in that group.

"They eat at night," he said softly. "They must've been traveling to eat here now. With luck, this is where they'll feed tonight and will still be here in the morning."

We went back to camp. No one else had spotted any elk. The others became excited and planned an Indian sneak on the elk for the early morning.

We were up an hour before sunrise and met on a grassy hill to plan the sneak. They sent me to climb a rocky hill overlooking a slot in the rocks where the others thought the elk might run. It was loose shale, hard to climb quietly, but I did my best and reached the top, waiting in the dark.

At daylight, one shot came, then another. I heard hooves pounding and earth flying. My heart raced as I climbed around the shale, and suddenly, the rocks slid out from under me. The rifle flew from my hand and scraped down the rocks.

The elk ran another way out. I dragged my bruised body down the hill, slipping and sliding until I retrieved the rifle, only to see a large gouge in the stock. I sat down and cried. How would I return the rifle to Anton in that condition? He was so proud of it. I hated myself.

I was still there when Red found me. He looked at the rifle and immediately understood. As he sat down, shaking his head, he didn't speak for a moment.

"Bobby." He spoke kindly. "Things happen. It's no one's fault. These rocks are slippery and loose."

"I should've been more careful."

"Careful ain't all, Man. Accidents happen whether you're careful or not. This was just a shitty accident."

"Shitty is right."

We sat there awhile.

"Oscar got an elk."

"He did?"

"Yeah, a big spike. Right at daylight." He paused.

"All right."

I was one sad guy as we rode away from camp. Oscar was happy when he dropped me off at home. Dad wasn't home, so Oscar drove away. I lugged my gear to the porch, went in without turning on a light, and went to bed.

The following morning, I tied the rifle, rolled up in part of a blanket, to the handlebars on my bike and pedaled to the chicken ranch to see Anton. He met me on the porch as I slowly rode up.

"Well, Bobby Boone, how'd you do?"

I didn't answer.

"What's wrong?" He came down from the porch.

I started blubbering quietly.

"Are you hurt?" he asked.

"No. It's the rifle, Anton."

I untied the rifle and unwrapped it, handing it to him. "God. I'm so damn sorry."

He looked at the stock, and his face fell for a moment, then he chuckled. "Bobby, I see you feel right bad. You fell on a rockslide or got knocked off your horse?"

"I fell on loose rock."

"It happens, Boy. Accidents happen. This gun will shoot just fine. A damn little scratch don't matter none."

"It's a big scratch."

"It don't matter none." He patted my back.

That was the first time he ever touched me. Feeling like someone lifted a weight off my chest, I smiled for the first time in days.

My mother was a fine, loving woman, an intelligent person who read constantly and studied what she read. She had to help on her family farm, so she never progressed beyond the fourth grade in school. That familiar story, however, wasn't true.

The real reason was, her family didn't value education. Because they lived far from town, they wouldn't go out of their way to help her learn, which was a shame. Aside from being smart, she was wise. When my parents could afford one, Dad bought her a $25 piano, which she taught herself to play.

She always seemed melancholy to me. Maybe that was because Dad was away a lot, and she felt she left a lot behind.

Otis was an athlete. He played baseball, football, and basketball equally well. Though he was one year ahead of me in school, I helped him with his studies. I didn't mind. I liked it, and I always had plenty of time for my own schoolwork.

Mother was apple pie, bread baked from an oven, venison stew, and corn on the cob. I wished she smiled more. One day, she returned from the doctor's office in Seattle and stopped smiling forever.

It didn't do any good cutting off her breast. She died six months later with my father's hands on her cheeks and us kids crying in the hall in a place people called a nursing home.

Dad lost his spark and became a little too quiet, but he got over it.

I never did.

Chapter Three

We never know what's in store. I prefer that idea to the one that God has everything planned for us, as well as the nonsense that God will never give us anything we can't understand. Maybe he wouldn't do that. I prefer to believe He wouldn't, but something can and does. Accidents happen. Children are burned, and little girls are raped and strangled. Babies are born with two heads and joined at the hip and spine. Those things can't be from divine intervention. They're accidents. That's all.

Once my dad brought a big tractor-trailer home. He had to take a dozer to Everett, so he stopped at home for the night before going up the hill in the morning to work.

Barbie, Otis, and I were outside playing around. Dad started backing the trailer out of the driveway, showing off by going fast. Otis rode his bicycle and held onto the big fender, laughing hysterically. He hit a tetherball Barbie threw at him, and his bike tipped over. He went under the big wheel behind him and thumped like a rag doll.

I couldn't scream, but Barbie did. Dad looked through the side mirror and stopped. He came running with an expression of horrified disbelief. Otis gasped, his chest crushed, and died within a minute. Something died in Dad too. He was never the same again.

I noticed little things in him at first that insidiously progressed during my high-school years and first year of college. Sometimes, out of nowhere, Dad began crying. Sometimes, he was too jovial. Sometimes, he called me Otis.

Oscar, Dad's brother, Barbie, and I decided Dad needed to be cared for. Oscar's wife was a nurse and social worker. Through the Veteran's Administration, Dad was put in the VA home in Orting. He seemed eager to go and made no fuss about it. They said he had pre-senile dementia. I thought it was a broken heart and ruptured spirit that sabotaged his brain to spare him more pain than he could face.

I went to Washington State to study English. I had a half-assed scholarship that paid only for tuition and books, so I had to work. I wanted a PhD and to become an English professor, though I didn't understand why. When I came home on school breaks, I always had a job waiting for me at Anton's place. He paid me well and slipped me extra money, too.

"Why don't you take some skee to college and sell it?" he offered.

That seemed like a good idea, so I did.

Anton became ill soon after that and sold the chicken business. He still made whiskey but with less enthusiasm. He coughed more and began losing weight. He told me the thing he hated most was giving up the chicken-leg barbecues.

He got me a summer job with a friend of his, cooking, of all things, on a salmon seiner in Puget Sound. The job was OK at first, but we never made much money, and I grew to hate it. All my college acquaintances were having Pepsi parties on the beach, while I was wet, covered in scales, and tired constantly. That was a lousy time of my life.

Just before I graduated, I went home to see Dad like usual. He slept in a corner, as always, and I nudged him awake. He looked like he returned from far away, though he was excited and happy to see me.

"It's my boy!" he shouted. "It's my boy, come to see his old man!"

"Pop, do you remember when the revenuers came to Anton's place, and we helped him take care of his stuff?"

"Yeah. Wasn't that a hell of a time?" He laughed, slapping his knee. "My God, the looks on their faces when they couldn't find anything!"

I laughed with him. "Remember pushing that dude into the pickle barrel?"

"Boy, do I!" He laughed again.

"Do you remember when we were down at the creek together, dumping out whiskey and filling jugs with water?"

"I sure do. That was some kind of job, wasn't it? We sampled a fair amount, and you had to drive the old man home. I thought you'd snap my head off."

"That was sure some night, eh, Pop?"

"Sure was, Otis. Too bad Bobby couldn't have been there."

"Yeah, Pop. Too bad."

Chapter Four

When I graduated from Washington State, Uncle Oscar and his wife, Aunt Sue, along with Barbie and her latest boyfriend, came. The other one who came really touched me. It was Anton Christensen, looking as flamboyant as a used-car salesman. He wore a double-breasted suit that was obvious secondhand, because it looked like it had been draped on him from three feet away. No one on earth could've smiled broader.

"Congratulations, Bobby," he said. "I guess you won't be grabbing any more chickens."

"No, I won't, or cooking on a fishing boat, either."

"Here." He shoved an object into my hands that I immediately recognized. "Your graduation present."

I unrolled the 7mm Wetherby and saw the scratch was still on the stock.

"You fixed the damn gouge," he said.

I hugged him fiercely. He patted my head and coughed many times.

On the way to Seattle and graduate school, I stopped to see him, and his daughter, Karen, was there. She was attractive, in a plain-Jane way, very nice and likable. I said hello to Anton, who looked terrible, coughing deeply without producing anything. Small talk seemed senseless, because he kept nodding off. Karen asked to talk to me outside.

"He looked a lot better a few weeks ago," I told her.

"Bobby, he was holding himself together to watch you graduate and give you that present. He's dying."

"I see that."

"He says he has no pain."

"I don't think he'd tell you if he did. My God," I said into my hands as I sat down hard. "He's the best friend I ever had. I love him."

"He feels the same about you. How can I reach you?"

"I don't know yet. I'll call as soon as I have a phone."

"OK."

After saying good-bye to my friend, I left.

A couple days later, I called Karen with my new number. "What sort of disease is it?"

"Some kind of fungus from chickens."

"Is there a cure?"

"There isn't even a treatment."

Anton left instructions for immediate cremation with no ceremony.

Six months later, Karen called. "Bobby? This is Karen, Anton's daughter."

"Hello, Karen. How are you doing?"

"I'm fine. I have some things to tell you. Can we meet somewhere?" she asked earnestly.

We agree on a small café in Kent the following afternoon.

"Would you like to eat?" I asked after we sat down.

"No, just a Coke."

I ordered two from the waitress. When she left Karen spoke immediately.

"You know Anton owned all the property on the lake with the stream frontage going through?" she asked.

"Yes."

"It's very valuable, you know, with all the growth in the area."

"I guess so. I never thought about it."

"He left it to both of us—fifty-fifty."

"He did?"

"Yes."

"I'll be dipped in...."

"There's a little problem, Bobby."

"What?"

"Are you in school?"

"Yes, in grad school."

"You can't have your half until you finish school. It's spelled out as plain as day."

"Oh."

"When?" she asked.

"At least three years, maybe four."

"What do you want me to do?"

"Let me think."

We sat in silence.

Finally, I said, "Karen, I turn over complete decision-making and management to you. You can give me an accounting when I'm done with school. Is that all right?"

"Yes, but are you sure you want to do that? That entails an awful lot of trust."

"You're Anton's daughter. I trust you."

"As a matter of fact, my husband has an idea how to develop the property. If you sign control to me, we can get a loan and go for it."

"All right. Draw up the papers."

That was the best financial decision I ever made. At the time, though, I didn't think it would amount to much.

Chapter Five

I was accepted into grad school at the University of Washington in English. I wanted to be an English professor and write books and stories, not treatises on the use and misuse of the word *whom*. English seemed the right way to go, so I planned to eventually get a PhD.

I came to Seattle to look for a room and a job before school started. I went to Barbie's place and asked her to put me up for a few days. I had another reason, but only my subconscious knew it at the time.

She lived in an older, small, crappy house in Wallingford with yellowed paper in some of the rooms. She was an artist and didn't want to remove the paper. What being an artist had to do with it, I didn't know. It was classic and needed to be decorated around. To me, what wasn't gaudy was dull.

She also had weird antiques like umbrella stands with canes in them and coat racks with hat racks on top. She had chamber pots made of beautiful porcelain, filled with rolled-up magazines, sitting beside the couches and chairs. Despite the fact that no coal had been burned in the furnace for forty years, her house still smelled faintly of coal.

I walked up the old concrete walk with cracks in it, up from the concrete sidewalk with more cracks, seeing how the lines all bulged in irregular ways. The place depressed me, but so did Barbie. She was married for the second time to a man I'd met only once, at their wedding. He was an automobile tire salesman who drank too much in public, smiled too much, laughed at everything, and seemed to be trying too hard to make people like him by being a clown. I learned that was a lousy idea that never worked very well, but maybe it was good for a salesman. I didn't like salesmen much.

I rang the doorbell. When Barbie answered, she seemed surprised to see me, though I said I was coming. She was just twenty-two, while I was twenty-six, but she looked an ill-kempt forty, with lines around her mouth from chain smoking. Her dark hair looked unwashed and hung down unbrushed. She wore sweat pants and a floppy, long-sleeved shirt splattered with paint.

"Bobby!" she said with light enthusiasm. "Come in. Hug me. What brings you here?"

I wrote that in the letter, too. "I'm going to the University of Washington."

"I thought you graduated from college."

"I did. This is grad school."

"Oh. Good for you. You were always so smart."

I sat down, as she lit a cigarette. The room was filled with ashtrays overflowing with snubbed-out butts that seemed too long.

"Let's have a drink," she said.

"I don't want one. It's a bit too early for me. It's only two o'clock." I looked at my watch.

"Not for me, Big Brother." She sang as she walked into the kitchen. I heard ice tinkle in a glass. "Do you want anything, Bobby?"

"Sure. Coffee."

A few minutes later, she handed me a cup of instant coffee that was so strong, I suspected it would've dissolved a nail. I saw sugar cubes in the saucer and added three. That helped.

"Tell me about you, Bobby. Do you have a girlfriend?"

I nodded and sipped.

"What's her name? Do I know her?"

I didn't see how she could. "Nope. Her name's Joann. She's from Walla Walla, the town, not the penitentiary."

She laughed, tipping back her head to finish off her drink and rattling the ice cubes. She walked toward the kitchen for another. "I'm sure she's very nice."

Why in hell...? I wondered. "How are you, Barbie?"

"Oh, I'm fine. I even sell my paintings. Can you imagine?"

I couldn't. They didn't look like anything to me. They were blobs I assumed were painted with her elbows. "That's nice," I said sincerely. "How's your health? I mean, how are you getting along?"

"You mean, am I still nuts?"

"I never thought you were nuts." I squirmed in my seat.

"Yes, you did, and I was." She wore an inappropriate smile that seemed painted on, like she was a tragic doll. "I'm not anymore. I see a shrink twice a week. He gives me Elanil. He likes to talk about sex a lot. Either he's Freud all over, or he wants to fuck me. Maybe both." She set down her glass to light another cigarette.

The alcohol was affecting her. She squirmed in her seat, wiping her brow with the back of her hand.

"It's hot in here," she said.

"Barbie, what do you remember about it?"

"What?"

"You know what."

She froze, as if she were transfixed. "You mean Otis?"

"Yes."

"I don't remember anything. I was five."

"You were seven."

"Yes."

"He was on his bicycle playing around, holding onto a fender."

She looked at the ceiling and walls, anywhere but me. She polished off her glass of vodka and rose to get another.

"Hold off on those, Barbie, please."

"You think I can't handle it?"

I wasn't sure she meant just the booze. "It's only three o'clock."

She looked like she'd been insulted. "What happened?"

"You know what happened. His bicycle tipped over, and he fell under the wheel."

She cried, and I let her.

"His bicycle tipped over, because...because he ran over my goddamn tetherball! Our father hovered over him, screaming."

"I remember."

She cried more. I just felt drained. It had been a long time, but I couldn't cry about it anymore.

"It wasn't your fault," I said. "It could've been my ball. It was an accident, a shitty, tragic, meaningless accident. They happened. They aren't caused on purpose."

"God…."

"Even with God, there are accidents. Two-headed babies are born, little children are burned, and trees fall on people. Those are accidents. All of us develop a place in our minds so we don't carry around a lot of pointless, self-destructive, unwanted thoughts. It wasn't your fault. It was an accident."

She cried pitifully. "I don't remember anything else until the funeral."

"Neither do I."

"I was in a daze."

"So was I."

"Father was never the same, was he?"

"No, he wasn't."

"He was their favorite."

"He was the firstborn son. That happens."

We sat, not looking at each other, let alone touching, while time drifted past on sneaky wings. I wasn't sure anymore why I came. I forgot about asking her to put me up for a few days.

"I have to go," I said gently.

"Won't you stay for dinner? Gerry will be home soon."

"No. I have an appointment," I lied. As I walked to the door, Barbie just sat there. "Good-bye, Sis."

"Keep in touch, Bobby. Thanks for coming."

I walked out to my car, got in, and drove to the university where I belonged.

I inquired about an apartment at the student-housing department. As a grad student, I didn't belong in a dorm. There was a list of available apartments on the wall, and I noticed one right away.

> WANTED: Roommate to share
> apartment with two others very near
> university library. Split rent three ways.
> Three bedrooms, two baths.

The address and phone were given at the bottom. The last part about bedrooms and baths seemed like an afterthought.

I called. When no one answered, I went to the address. I'd just entered the building when a smiling, nicely proportioned woman of twenty, wearing jeans, a purple blouse, violet sweater, and white running shoes, followed me up the stairs. She carried groceries in a knit bag.

"Hello," I said.

"Hello, Yourself," she said in a cute way.

We walked up two flights, and I realized we were moving toward the same door.

"Have I got it right?" I asked. "I was looking for the people who advertised at the university for boarders."

"Yep." She looked me up and down. "Not boarders, though—a roommate. You interested?"

"I think so."

She opened the door without using a key, and I followed her in. I saw a small kitchen with an electric stove, refrigerator, sink, and drain boards. Everything looked white and clean.

"Who are you?" she asked with a grin. "BS, MS—more of the same, or PhD—piled higher and deeper? Old joke."

"Excuse me? I want to be an English professor and write books. I mean, stories."

"Can you cook?"

"As a matter of fact, I can. I've been working as a cook on fishing boats in the summer, and I worked at the commissary at State. I also fried burgers at Burgerville."

"You were busy."

"Yeah. I was the laundry man for my dorm, too. I got twenty percent."

"Not much time for a social life."

"You got that right."

"Have you got a girlfriend?"

"Kind of, I guess."

"That means one or the other of you is cold to the idea."

"You're very wise. I don't know your name."

"Annette Sands. Hello, Bobby."

"How'd you come up with Bobby?"

"You look like a Bobby."

"You look like an Annette."

"The rent's nine hundred a month, but everything is included, even garbage. That's three hundred a month apiece. That's awfully good this close to the U."

"Yes, it is. I accept if you do."

"You haven't met Dick."

"Dick?"

"He lives here, too, with me. He's a drama major, but don't hold that against him. He's as straight as an arrow. I accept."

"How about Dick?"

"He goes by my good judgment, and I judge you good."

"Thank you."

"Even if you have the same color hair as Thomas Jefferson and wear those little wire-rim glasses."

"I need them to see."

"They aren't exactly designer frames. You look like an English professor."

We laughed. Something good was happening.

"Throw your gear aboard," she said in a pseudo deep, rough voice. "Isn't that what fishermen say?"

"Yes, but how'd you know?"

"My father and brothers are fishermen from Ballard. They fish halibut."

"I don't know any halibut fishermen. I fished salmon."

"Do you like to eat salmon?"

"No."

"Why? 'Cause you had to eat it so much?"

"That's right."

"Too bad. I like salmon, and it's the only thing I know how to cook."

I went and got my gear and threw it into the little bedroom. Dick came home, and I immediately liked him. He was friendly and charming to me and did his best to make me feel welcome. He loved to talk on any subject, though it always turned toward theater.

That's how it's supposed to be, I thought. *He really likes what he's doing. He and Annette go together so well.*

We had good times, and the rent was cheap.

Chapter Six

I got a job as cook and what they called a *yardman* at Ivar's Restaurant on the waterfront, working most evenings, though I was really on call. I worked Saturdays and Sundays, sometimes all day. It was a good job in many ways. The pay was horrible, but I had a loose schedule. They never refused me time off if I really needed it.

I took home a lot of untouched leftovers—shrimp and oysters, fish, and even some clam chowder. The best thing was, people drank only part of their wine. I happily took home the rest. We had lots of parties with acting students and artsy folk. When I could attend, I stayed, watching the drama students try to impress each other. Some were very entertaining. Some were just affected and full of themselves. They were a curiosity to me, and I was to them.

Dick was in production a lot of the time, so Annette and I hung around together, particularly if the party was held at someone else's place. One party I remembered was at a student folk house on the shore of Lake Washington. Many of the actors and actresses had good voices, and I liked hearing them sing show tunes. There is nothing like a party filled with theater people.

Annette and I got drunk on the white wine I brought and stood on a small veranda while an African American woman sang, "I loves you, Porgy, don't let him take me...."

Annette became misty-eyed and held my hand palm to palm. My heart felt like it was opening up. Then she turned, put up her chin, and kissed me with her sweet lips. I held her, and something stirred within me.

On the way home, she put her head on my shoulder with my arm around her. I wanted to kiss her again, but I didn't.

Inside, Dick was home. They went to bed with barely a good night to me.

We had a lot of fun. I learned to play guitar and even let my hair grow long, but I couldn't stand the idea of a ponytail, and my beard would've been red. We ate like the rich and spoiled, using the food and wine I brought home from Ivar's.

Dick was a fine guy who attracted people. Besides being handsome, he was bright, quick, and friendly. He had the lead in almost every play he tried out for. Sometimes, I wished I were like him. Everyone knew he would succeed, particularly Annette. She thought Dick could do anything he set out to do.

It seemed faith in each other was a part of love.

Chapter Seven

Joann called from Pullman excitedly to say she was coming over for the weekend and would arrive Friday night. I was glad. It would be nice to see her. She was a great friend and good girlfriend during my last year at Washington State University. She was a junior and had one year left.

I didn't have a lot of money or time. I carried sixteen hours of classes each week and fried hamburgers for another thirty-six. I liked Joann, and she liked me, and we found time to do things, but we usually ended up parked behind the student union in the dark, kissing and doing other things.

It wasn't until just before I left—I attended summer school to finish my English degree—that we finally made love in the back seat on a hot night in late summer. We said we loved each other, but I didn't mean it. I wasn't sure, but I felt she did. I'd long since learned to hold back on such serious statements. I didn't want her to feel like a slut.

Anyhow, after we finished worrying about her next period, we made love until the night I left. We talked on the phone two or three times a week, and she usually said, "I love you," at the end. I answered with, "Me, too."

I would be glad to see her.

Her parents ran a big dairy farm near Walla Walla. She had big shoulders and arms from carrying milk cans. She had pretty breasts, with soft, pink, plump nipples that pointed out proudly. They jiggled just right as she walked, like they were trying to get out. She knew what to wear, too.

I was proud to be with her, because of the way guys looked at her. She had the nicest smile that lit up her round face and accented the dimple in her right cheek. She laughed well, with her mouth wide open and white teeth flashing. I saved her eyes for last, because they always held my attention, with tiny crow's feet and expressive muscles shining at me.

It sounded like I loved her, but I didn't know. I wanted to.

I had the week off from the restaurant, so I planned a good time. I had twelve half-full wine bottles, most of them white Chardonnay that sold for twenty dollars a bottle. I put six in the fridge and bought a bucket of fried chicken from KFC, coleslaw, biscuits, and barbecued beans. Dick was in a play that Annette and I saw a couple times, so Annette and I were at home, sitting in the parlor, talking, when Joanna buzzed us and came up to the door I held open.

I took her overnight bag and kissed her. Her eyes were closed as we kissed. She bounced into the room where Annette stood with a welcoming smile.

"Joann," I said, "this is Annette. Annette, this is Joann."

They hugged like girls do, which I never understood, and I brought out some wine. We toasted, sipped, and drank happily, talking about a lot of things. It was a fun time.

"My boyfriend's Dick," Annette said, who always acted as if people wanted to know all about her. "He's an actor, a good one, and he wants to be a director someday. It rains a lot in Seattle, but that doesn't matter, because I have a good umbrella. I go to school only part time and work as a hostess, a waitress, really.

"I love to go to the theater, especially musicals. In high school, I sang in those. Isn't that funny? I don't sing that well. My feet hurt. Do you like high heels? Me, neither, but I wear them, because I have to. I'm hungry. Let's eat, for Christ's sake."

Joann replied with one-word answers and short expressions of amusement, likes, dislikes, humorous stories of her own, and lit up the room with her laughter. We got a little drunk, but it was just right—very mellow, and our faces feeling warm.

Annette went to her room early for bed. I had the feeling she did that deliberately.

"How is it here, Bobby?" Joann asked.

"It's all right. It rains a lot, but I grew up here, so that doesn't matter."

"That's not what I mean."

"The university's good. Being a grad student has its good points. I get paid to teach English 101."

"That's not what I meant, either."

"I guess I don't know what you mean."

"Living with Annette."

"I live with Dick, too. They're an item." I felt strangely defensive.

"He's gone a lot."

"So am I. I work at Ivar's down on the bay. I don't think I know what you're getting at."

"I'm not getting at anything. It's just awfully...Bohemian. Close."

"We watch our modesty." I laughed, but I recalled seeing Annette in a towel or her bra and panties occasionally. I blushed, and my eyes drifted away from hers. It was a dead giveaway, and I knew it.

"You like her. I can tell by the way you're around here. Around her, I mean."

"I like Dick, too."

"That's nice."

"Hey, you're making me feel defensive." She was showing me a side of her I'd never seen before, and I didn't like it one bit. "I'm here, because...because we split the rent three ways. It's close to the university."

She shrugged. "Oh, Bobby, I didn't come here to fight."

"I didn't know we were fighting about anything."

"Where's the bathroom. I want to shower and get all pink and clean for bed." She smiled widely.

"All right, but let's finish the wine." I smiled back.

We finished most of the Chardonnay. She was mellow and giggly as she took her bag and went into the bathroom. I heard her singing in the shower.

I sat at the table and finished another glass. When I heard bedsprings squeak, I went in, undressed, and climbed into the shower. I didn't sing.

"Hurry up, Bobby."

I dried off, sprinkled Old Spice on myself, turned off the lights, and crawled into bed.

"Bobby, I missed you terribly."

"I missed you, too."

She snuggled her naked body seductively against me. "I love you, Bobby."

I said nothing. I tried. I kissed her, stroking her breasts and running my fingers through her hair. I did everything, but it didn't help. Nothing happened.

After a while, I felt rotten. I didn't fall asleep until the early hours of the morning, and then not deeply. She got up and dressed. I lay in bed until I heard her leave the bedroom.

"Joann?"

"Yes."

"Where are you going?"

"Home."

"I thought you were staying the weekend." I pulled on my shorts and followed her to the living room.

"It isn't any good, is it?" she asked.

"Joann, I…."

"Bobby, you don't love me." She cried quietly.

I didn't deny it. "I'm so sorry."

"You love her, Bobby."

"No."

"Yes. It's obvious, Bobby, subtle but obvious."

I went to her and held her. She relaxed for a moment, her shoulders shaking, then she pulled away.

"Good-bye, Bobby." She hurried out the door.

"Joann," I pleaded, though I didn't follow her.

I sat and put my face in my hands. My cheeks were wet, and my eyes swam. Inside, I ached.

Annette came in, looking for me. "Bobby?"

I didn't answer. She sat and put her arm around my shoulder.

"What?" she asked kindly. "Where's Joann?"

"She left."

"She did? I'm so sorry."

"I didn't want to hurt her. I can't stand the thought of hurting her. She's kind and vulnerable, so nice." I began crying.

"Bobby, listen to me." She put her hands on my wet cheeks. "You're a nice guy."

"I didn't want to hurt her."

"I know you didn't, and she knows, too. There's no fault in these things. You can't blame yourself, because you couldn't pretend to love her. Come on. Dry your eyes. Get up. Get dressed, for heaven's sake." She kissed my forehead.

I felt like a little kid. I slowly stood, showered, and dressed in jeans, a white shirt, Hush Puppies, and a necktie. I went to the university, forgetting it was Saturday, and there was no eight o'clock class.

As usual, it rained.

Chapter Eight

Teaching English 101 and 102 and American Literature was demanding but fun. I had very little patience with young folk who didn't care if they learned anything or not. I always started my new classes in a certain way, and, by the end of the semester, we were either friends, or they were gone.

"How many of you are English majors?" I asked.

No one held up a hand.

"How many of you are here, because this is a required class?"

A few liars raised their hands.

"Does anyone know when to use whom or who?"

One girl did.

"When?"

"Who is used for direct address, like *For Whom the Bell Tolls,* as opposed to *Who Do the Bells Toll For?*"

I didn't understand then, and I still don't. I smiled, and she got an A for her grade later.

"We're going to learn subject from predicate," I said, "nouns from verbs, adjectives from adverbs, subjective, reflexive, and point of view. We'll stay awake, because we'll all have a lot of coffee for breakfast."

I did my best to be funny. Sometimes, it worked. Sometimes, it didn't.

College girls wore miniskirts, but I thought the term should've been microskirts. They always sat in the front row and never kept their knees together. I felt like a dirty old man, but most of the time, I was just embarrassed. I became an expert on underpants, though some girls fooled me and stopped wearing them. I had my picture taken a couple times a day. I tried a lot of schemes to make the front row for men only, but nothing worked very well.

Finally, I decided my female students were going to hear the truth. I asked my assistant dean, a woman, to come to the class so she could witness my approach. She watched in abject horror as I addressed the problem.

No one laughed. From then on, girls only sat in the front row if they wore jeans, slacks, or shorts. Sure enough, one microskirted, fat hussy put in a sexual-harassment complaint. The assistant dean came to my defense, and it ended there. The girl was transferred to another 101 class. I was pleased to learn later that she flunked English 101.

I enjoyed teaching literature. Many times, I met the class in the student union, where we could have Cokes and coffee to discuss what made good writing or what made classic literature classic. It wasn't just because it was old. Because people read Erskin Caldwell, Mickey Spillane, or Louis Lamour, did that make it good literature? I wasn't sure, but, if people didn't want to read something written, it wasn't any good, either.

I liked classes we held outside in picnic areas on nice days. My students paid more attention and seemed more cheerful. Maybe *I* was the one who was more cheerful. I liked having them write essays that I insisted be kept to two pages, and the quality of the writing was a pleasant surprise, as well as the thought the students put into them. As the class progressed, those essays became better—usually.

I didn't want to pick on the athletes. Many were fine people and sincere students. Sometimes, however, they expected special treatment and wanted something for nothing. They got nothing for nothing from me.

As a former student, I knew about the underground library of essays and term papers. They were available on the Web, too. Sometimes, a mediocre student handed in an essay that seemed above his skill level. If it was a rare incident, I ignored it and gave the student a C+.

However, one football star made a big mistake. He handed in a wonderful essay entitled, *The Suffering of Innocents*. I really liked it, mostly because it was one of my best pieces, for which I'd been given an A.

I wrote on his paper, *Plagiarism gets an F. You flunk.* When I handed the papers back, he read the note and shouted, "What the fuck?" and stormed out the door. Most of the other students seemed to know what happened.

The following day, the coach, dressed in baggy pants with a sweatshirt and baseball cap, was waiting when I arrived at the classroom.

"Professor…."

"I'm not a professor. Who are you?" I knew, but I didn't like his tone.

"I'm Coach Lange!"

I didn't reply.

"You have Sam Mickalitz in your class." It was a statement, not a question.

When I didn't answer, he added, "He says you flunked him."

"That's right."

"God, he's the star on our football team! He'll start varsity fullback next year, for Christ's sake."

"For whose sake?" I asked.

"Come on, Professor. You shouldn't…."

"I'm not a professor."

"Give the kid a break. He's a really nice kid. There's no need to land on him like that. He's a nice guy, and we need him. Can't you just give him a C and move him along? He'll be out on his ass, you know."

"I have nice kids in my class who do honest work for a C."

"I know, but can't you, you know, skip a page this time?" He tried to pat my back.

I shook him off. "All right. Tell you what?"

He smiled, congratulating himself.

"You put Danny Loop on the team. He's a bit skinny and weak, but God, he's a nice guy, a really fine fellow, and I'll give your boy a C."

He stopped smiling. "You're a real smartass, Professor."

"You'd a dumb ass, and I'm not a professor."

"I'm going to the head of the department!" he shouted.

"Go to the fucking dean." I closed the door.

Dr. Avery, the head of the department, called that afternoon. "What did you tell that Neanderthal?" He laughed.

"I told him to appeal to the fucking dean if he wanted, but the flunk stands."

There was a long silence. "Good. Come over before the next department meeting. I'd like to see you again face-to-face. Nice having you on the staff."

"Thank you, Professor."

"I'm not a professor yet, but I *am* a doctor. I have a PhD in English, for what it's worth." He hung up, still laughing.

Chapter Nine

Dick was at the top of his class in professional actor's school. He was dedicated to his craft and continued to redefine *stage struck*. In a way, he was always onstage with those who watched him.

He alienated some people, though not many. He was the most-likable person I ever met. Of course, as a geek and English major, I didn't have many friends. Dick's biggest ambition was to become a film director.

I came home early one afternoon to find Dick already there, anxious and excited. He was waiting for a phone call. It rang just as I arrived.

He was in the bedroom, so I heard only bits and pieces. I heard lots of, "Thank you," "Yes. Yes, I'd really be interested," and, at the end, "I could come right away. Tomorrow. Yes. School's out."

Dick's excitement was obvious in his voice. He ran into the room and nodded vigorously. "By God, Bobby, that was Stewart Hollingworth from Hollywood, USA! He offered me second assistant director on his new film. I can hardly believe it, Man. He read my recommendations and résumé, and he's going to hire me!"

"That's really great, Dick. Congratulations, my friend."

We shook hands.

"I have to be there the day after tomorrow. I have to drive my Bug. I hope it makes it."

"It will."

"I'll be out of here in an hour, then I'm on my way." He raced back into the bedroom.

"You can have my suitcase!" I yelled.

"Thanks. I need it."

In a while, he came out lugging two suitcases and a handful of clothing on a hanger. "Bobby, could you? Would you?" His eyes asked a question.

"Fine, Dick. Here's $200."

"Thanks. I'll pay you back when I can."

"I know you will."

"I love ya, Man."

"Me, too. Congratulations again." He was at the door when I asked, "What about Annette?"

He stopped for a second and glanced back. "Explain, will you? Tell her I'll call as soon as I can."

"Good-bye."

"Good-bye."

He was gone, and the first empty space was there.

Chapter Ten

I worked late at the restaurant that night. There were plenty of graduation parties, so the restaurant was busy until one o'clock that morning.

When I came home, Annette was already sleeping. I brought home a good supply of half-empty wine bottles, setting them on the table as I glanced into her room. She snored relentlessly, so I went to bed.

The following morning, she had to work early, so I didn't wake up until I heard the door close. We'd both be home that afternoon.

She was there when I returned home. The room felt as icy as when my dad died. My cheerful, "Howdy do," was met by only a nod by the young woman with her legs curled under her on the yellow, threadbare couch. I looked away and went into the kitchen to set down my things and take off my coat.

Knowing the answer, I asked gently, "Did he call?"

"Uh-uh."

I sat beside her. She'd been crying, but she wasn't crying then, just looking beyond sad.

"Annette, listen. He loves you. It's been only a few days."

"If he loved me, he would've called."

"Maybe he doesn't want to call until he finds out if he really got the job. Maybe he wants to be sure. If he didn't get it, he might be embarrassed or upset. He has a lot of pride."

She smiled weakly and put her hand on my arm. I wished she'd leave it there. It felt….

"You're trying to make me feel better, Bobby. You're the incest, sweetest person I ever knew."

"For a redhead," I quipped.

"For any colored hair, you boob." She smiled again, but it seemed real that time.

God, she looked so beautiful with wet cheeks and watery eyes. I wanted to hold her and tell her I loved her. The thought left a lump in my throat, and I couldn't say it.

She stood and put on a tape she immediately began to sing and hum along with. "There was love all around, but I never heard it singing…."

To me, she sounded like an angel. When she sat down, she looked right at me and sang to me. I wondered if she imagined me as Dick, but I didn't really want to know.

I brought in a cold bottle of Chardonnay, poured two glasses, and sat beside her again. I sipped mine. It was good. She gulped half her glass and looked at me.

"Nice," she said.

It was hard to say later where the afternoon went. Eventually, it faded into evening shadows, and the room became dim. I couldn't remember what we talked about so much, but we talked earnestly, quietly, loudly, seriously, hilariously—and together.

I warmed a delicious quiche with stir-fry veggies from the restaurant, and we washed it down with wine we could never have afforded to buy. We ate by candlelight without speaking.

She put our dishes in the sink. When she returned, I was on the couch. I raised my arm, and she settled under it, looking at me with searching wonder. I kissed her tenderly and deeply. She put her hand behind my neck and pulled me close. I couldn't stop kissing her, and she welcomed it eagerly. My heart pounded against her soft breast.

"Hold me, sweet Bobby," she whispered.

She stood slowly. Her eyes on mine, she took my hand and led me to my bed. "I want you to hold me all night."

"I love you, Annette."

She wore shorts and a T-shirt. She pulled the T-shirt over her head and removed her bra. I kissed her, holding her close as I unbuttoned her shorts so she could slide out of them, along with her ruffled panties. Somehow, I removed my own clothes. She helped. We folded together as one onto the sweet-smelling, soft bed.

Tender kisses began, then deeper ones filled with tingling tongues and passion. Her tiny breasts with rosebud nipples filled my mouth, as they responded to my eager lips. Gently, she pressed my head down until my tongue explored and tasted her clitoris, protected by pebble-like leaves of silky skin. She arched and moved, turning under me until she gave a soft cry like a sweet-sounding bird before pulling me to her chest and giving herself to me in full surrender.

I kissed her continuously as we made love. When my orgasm came, so did hers. I felt her wetness on my thighs and smelled her scent in the air. We held each other with arms and legs.

"Annette…." I had to say it. Fear came, a pulling, relentless sensation in my throat. "Annette, I love you." I looked into her beautiful face.

"I know you do, my sweet Bobby. Hold me. Love me again." She pulled me to her soft, shiny, sweet-smelling body.

In the morning, I slept soundly in a mythical place full of sunshine, music, and warm softness. Distantly, I heard the phone ringing in the kitchen. Annette was up, answering it quickly.

"Dick! Dick!"

It became difficult to listen. I gathered my clothes and went into my bathroom to shower and dress. I felt sullen acceptance of something I couldn't change no matter how I might wish otherwise. I was on my way out the door when she hurried up and talked so excitedly, it sounded like jabbering. I'd once thought that charming and cute.

She took my elbow. "Dick got the job. He's assistant to the assistant director of a TV series. He's so happy, and so am I. He has an apartment by the studio, and he wants me to come down. He said he wants to marry me now that he has a future.

"Oh, Bobby," she said with a giggle. "I have to pack. The bus leaves at three. Bobby, could you loan me some money?"

I didn't answer. I had two $100 bills in my wallet, which I gave to her without a word and without looking at her face. If she knew how I felt, she didn't show it.

"Bobby, you're so sweet and wonderful. You're a wonderful friend. Thank you."

"You're welcome." Without looking at her, I walked out into the rain.

"We'll write," she said, as I closed the door behind me.

I walked around the rear of the building and found a wet bench in the park. With my hands in my coat pockets, I stared at my shoes. I wished many things, but the main one was that I'd never let myself be so unprotected and vulnerable again. I was angry only at myself.

Anger eventually gave way to the greatest disappointment I ever felt. Even with that, I pledged to—to what? I felt like I'd been climbing many peaks, to being a PhD, a college professor, and an author of meaningful work that people would want to read. Before, I felt like I was going up. It would take time, but I realized I'd feel that way again, or was I just being a pouty little boy?

Thoughts like *Not fair*, went through my mind. *What does that mean? What in the world is fair? Does fair mean equal, where everyone gets the same thing, the same amount, and the same treatment?*

The world isn't that way. Did everyone deserve the same? Hell, who knew? Maybe I just paid $200 for…a nice piece? If that was the case, it was worth it. I chuckled and almost laughed, but I was still wiping my eyes.

God, does she even know how I feel? I wondered. I remembered telling her I loved. She replied, "I know you do, Dear…."

For some reason, I thought of Joann Clark. Had I hurt her that way? Was it my turn? God, I hadn't wanted to hurt her.

Come on, Man. Buck up. You'll live. Someday, you'll laugh about this, but now, it hurts.

"Sometimes we just have to be glad we had some time to spend together…."

I never liked that song.

Chapter Eleven

After a while, I stood, pulled my raincoat around me, and began walking. I walked around campus, thinking of a lot of things—what I really wanted from life, what I regretted, what I understood, and what I didn't understand. I felt like I was in a game where no one explained the rules, or the rules could change suddenly, making all the difference.

The campus was mostly deserted, with only an occasional student, teacher, or janitor passing by. It was a cold, gray, rainy morning. I felt like it was raining in my heart.

I walked to the avenue and looked into store windows. Most were just opening, and the usual traffic jammed at the lights. All the parking places on the street were filled. People and vehicles buzzed around with purpose. What was my purpose? I wasn't sure.

When I began shivering, I returned to the apartment. It was late afternoon. The door wasn't locked, and it was cold inside, so I turned up the heat and looked around.

The place looked and felt hollow, a room filled with corners. Annette's easel was propped against the wall in one corner with her cast-off, used brushes scattered on the floor. It was as if someone took down a lighted Christmas tree and left tinsel on the rug and an empty space against the wall.

I dumped my wet clothes on the floor and went into the kitchen in my shorts to sit on a wooden chair with uneven legs. I tried to drink some wine, but it wasn't very good.

I took a hot shower, pulled on sweat pants and shirt, and flopped on my rumpled, soft bed. Annette's sleeveless shirt lay under the covers. I smelled her faint perfume. When I closed my eyes, I felt her presence for a moment and saw her face.

I buried myself under the down comforter and eventually slept.

I dreamed I was grabbing chickens, and they kept shitting on my arms.

It was difficult to tell what I did for the following four years. I took up tennis and golf. I bought a bicycle and joined a bicycle club. I did a lot of things in my spare time, and I met plenty of women and found I could love them all cheerfully—for a while, in a way.

Dick and Annette wrote at first. They were married immediately. Two months later, I received a little blue-and-red note about a blessed event on its way. That ended something for me, and I found I was happier.

Dick did well in the TV movie business. I began seeing his name as assistant director, then director, and then associate producer. I always liked him, and I was happy for him. I thought I was happy for Annette, too. Sometimes, they called and talked to me. We always ended up happily saying we'd get together soon. No one mentioned the $200.

I became friends with a physical education teacher who was smart as a whip. He was a laughing, easygoing guy with a perpetual smile and a ready slap on the back. He got me interested in boxing and judo. I began weightlifting and working out at the gym. I knew it was good for me.

I gained weight. My shirtsleeves grew tight on my arms, and my pant legs became tight against my thighs. I was able to run five miles. Some of the women I met were through him. Some looked delicate until they threw me on my ass.

When it was time for me to receive my PhD, I sent an invitation to Dick and Annette. They called when I was out and left a message saying they couldn't make it to the graduation, but they were proud of me and wished me well.

Afterward, I had the damnedest surprise of my life when Karen, Anton's daughter, called.

"Hello, Bobby."

"Hello. How are you?"

"We're fine. You're finished with school now, aren't you?"

"Yes."

"It's time to discuss the will."

"Oh, yeah."

"Have you been reading the reports, the ones we send every quarter?"

"No, I guess not." I looked down at an entire drawer filled with unopened letters.

"Can we come over tomorrow? We need to talk."

"Sure. When?"

"We'll be there at ten. Good-bye."

I glanced at the drawer, then left to go play at the gym.

The following morning exactly at ten, someone knocked on my door. I still had the same apartment, though I had it painted and added new furniture. Dick and Annette's room became a nice office.

I brought Karen and her husband into my office, because I saw they had a briefcase full of papers. They smiled, and I mean, they *smiled*. Their expressions lit up the room.

"Do you guys want coffee?" I asked. "I just made some."

"That would be nice in a minute or two, but first...." Karen spread a few pages on my desk. "What do you want to do with your share?"

"My share?"

"Of the development. Did you read anything?"

"I guess I should have."

"Yes, you should have." She pointed to figures on the paper. "That's the overall value. It's twelve million dollars."

I stared at the paper.

"This is how much we've put into your account so far." She pointed to $750,000. "That's half, minus our management fees and overhead so far. We kept $150,000 the last two years for our work. Is that fair to you?"

I nodded and mumbled an agreement. It seemed fair meant a lot of things. I stood with my arms hanging loosely, my expression gaping, as she continued.

"We built apartment houses." She showed me pictures. "There are six of them, with fifty units each. They're almost always full. Two more are being built along the lake, if you approve. Bobby, we can go either way. We can cash you out, or you can go on with us."

I didn't say a word.

"If you stay with us, we'll make more money for you."

I still didn't speak.

"You can draw $160,000 a year easy. What do you say?"

I finally found my voice. "I stick with you."

We shook hands.

"Let's have that coffee," Karen said.

"Wait. How'd you finance all this?"

"Don't you remember signing over the property to us? That took a lot of trust. We used that and the new apartments as collateral as they were finished."

"Oh."

After taking a leave of absence from my teaching position, I rented a cabin on Whidbey Island, a comfortable place overlooking Puget Sound. It had a big fireplace and was safe and snug from wind and rain.

I had an idea for a screenplay. I got a book for writers that explained how to write a screenplay and began with passion, working as often as I felt like—morning, afternoon, at night, or whenever. Between times, I walked on the beach or rode my bike on roads above the cliff around abandoned Fort Casey, with its gun emplacements left over from World War Two, haunting the place in their emptiness. I shot a cottontail occasionally for dinner, saving the skins and tanning them for the fun of it until they were soft and shiny.

My idea went slowly, and I kept rewriting bits of it. It was different from writing stories, and I found the process difficult at first, but it slowly came together.

It was about a guy and his girlfriend who went diving for sunken treasure in Indonesia, looking for lost Chinese vessels containing gold, jade, or priceless pottery. The story was full of suspense, danger, sharks, pirates, and plenty of narrow escapes, all wrapped around a love affair that ended in betrayal and greed. In other words, it was true to life.

When I finished, I didn't like the ending at first, but, the more I tried to rewrite it, the more it stayed the same.

I had a friend in Seattle edit it. When that was finished, I typed it and put it in a spiral notebook before trying to publish it. No one would read it, despite the number of query letters I sent to screen agents.

Then I realized I already knew a producer. I became excited when I thought of that. I dug out Dick and Annette's phone number and called early one morning. Annette answered. Even after five years, something lurched in my chest when I heard her voice. It wasn't easy forcing myself to speak casually to her.

"I have a screenplay," I said eventually. "I was wondering if Dick would consider looking at it."

"Of course he would." She got Dick on the phone, who seemed friendly and cheerful. He eagerly agreed.

I sent it to them. Two weeks later, at midnight, the phone woke me from a wine-induced slumber.

"Bobby, this is Dick."

"Who?"

"Dick, from LA, for Christ's sake."

"Sorry. I'm just waking up. How are you? Did you read my movie?"

"Yes, I did, and it's great. I mean, it's *really* great. It's a brand-new idea, Man. I've already got backing. I want to produce and direct it myself."

I heard Annette on the line.

"Bobby, you did a great job. I can't wait to give you a big kiss. This is just what Dick needs for his career, too."

"Bobby," Dick said, "I'll send you a contract—an agreement. It's on contingency, you understand."

"What does that mean?"

"Well, the bottom line is, I can't pay you anything up front. You get a cut of the picture proceeds. I don't have the bucks up front, but, like I said, I'm already getting backing for expenses. There's an old set on Catalina Island that'll work perfectly. We can shoot there and in Jakarta for pennies, relatively speaking."

"I'll leave that up to you."

"It's the contingency thing, all right. Ten percent of net?"

"Hell, I don't know. Whatever. I don't need the money. I just wanted people to read it. I mean, see it."

"If I'd known that, I would've made it five percent."

"That's all right if it helps us get going."

"Damn it, Bobby, you haven't changed a bit. It's net ten percent after expenses. You'd give away the store, you idiot. You could do a lot better, you know."

"Hell, I couldn't get anyone to read it before you guys."

"I read it, and so did some finance guys," Annette said.

Annette and Dick seemed delighted with the proposal and said, "It's a go."

When the agreement arrived, I signed it, had it notarized and witnessed, and returned it.

One month later, at midnight, Dick and Annette called again.

"We've got the principals cast," Dick said.

"That didn't take long. Anyone I know?"

"Not unless you watch TV soap operas. They've got real talent, but they aren't big names. We do have big-name publicity people, though. That costs big bucks, but it's necessary. We're using the *new writer, new talent* theme."

"I guess."

"Bobby," Annette said, "we're having a big party with the cast. You need to come down to meet them. It's in two weeks, right before we shoot. Can you come?"

"Sure."

"It'll be nice for you and us to see each other again."

Plans were made. Three weeks later, not two, because nothing was on time in Hollywood, I was in LA in a Motel 6 near Hollywood and Vine, driving a red Honda Civic I rented at LAX.

The afternoon of the party, I called and got directions to the house.

They laughed when I said I was at Hollywood and Vine. Of course, they invited me to their house, but I wasn't ready for that. I said I had other business in the city, and they didn't press me for details.

After getting lost several times, I found their house on the outskirts of town. They had a circular driveway filled with cars, so I parked in an uncomfortable, cramped spot that stuck out into the road a bit. I walked slowly to the door, wondering if I was dressed properly—new suit off the rack, shiny black shoes, and a haircut from a salon, not a barbershop. I even had designer glasses that were in style.

My palms were sweaty, and I heard myself breathing loudly as I rang the bell. For a long time, no one answered, then a short guy with a crew cut and bright shirt opened the door.

"Come the fuck in, Dude." He walked away.

I stepped in, closed the door behind me, and walked down the hall to the living room.

Theater people know how to party. There were fifteen people in the room, each acting like he or she was the center of attention. They laughed too loudly, moved too much, and seemed able to smile with their entire bodies. Only one guy wasn't doing that. He stared out the window at nothing. I caught an odd smell, like burning grass. It seemed most of the smell came from his direction. He wore green Bermuda shorts, a yellow, short-sleeved shirt that was too big, loafers, and no socks.

I wondered if he smoked his socks. Later, I learned he was a notable artistic director. In a few seconds, I realized I was the only one in a suit. Everyone else had clothes that redefined the word *casual.* One woman had on a one-piece outfit like Jane from the Tarzan movies, except hers was scarlet red. I was red, too, as I looked down her cleavage. I had the urge to drop something on the floor to make her bend over and pick it up.

No one paid me any attention, so I just stood there. Finally, Dick and Annette came from the kitchen with glasses of drinks and something to eat. I went to say hello, but they saw me coming, set down their burdens, and raced over.

I remembered how Annette could smile. Perhaps it was just me, but I felt her smile lit up the room. As I welcomed her hug, old feelings rekindled in me.

"Bobby, it's so nice to see you!" she said.

"Thank you, Annette." *I still love you,* I thought.

"You look great, Bobby." Dick squeezed my hand and patted my shoulder.

"Thanks. So do you." *You lucky son of a bitch.*

"Attention, Everyone!" Annette called. "This is Dr. Robert Abbott, the brilliant writer who's responsible for your being here."

They stopped showing off to each other and applauded enthusiastically, whistling, shouting, and calling hello.

Annette grabbed the Tarzan woman and brought her over. "This is Jean Paulo, our leading lady."

She kissed my cheeks, held my face in her hands, and looked into my eyes dramatically. "You're brilliant." She had a cute accent. She gave me an unexpected kiss on the lips.

I smiled, and everyone laughed at my embarrassment. A young, very handsome guy in a ponytail came over to grab my hand.

"You do great work. I'm Ronnie Dunn, your leading man."

"Nice to meet you. I think the casting director did well with both of you. You look just like I imagined. Thanks for taking the parts."

People thought I was being charming and applauded again. Maybe I *was* charming, but I meant it, too.

Dick and Annette handed me a scotch. We stood and talked about the old days in our shared apartment, the music, parties, friends, my endless supply of wine, their success, and my PhD. For some reason, I didn't mention my money. Perhaps I wanted them to still think of me as a struggling student—or a bit of a martyr.

Dick excused himself, and Annette said with a serious smile, "Come with me, Bobby." She pulled my hand and led me to a child's bedroom, where a little redheaded, blue-eyed girl listened to a story being read to her by a serious-looking college student with thick glasses and a smile painted on her face. Without a word, the reader left as we entered the room.

"Bobby," Annette said proudly, "this is our little Lucy Lou."

The little girl looked up at me and smiled. I knew that smile. I sat on the sofa beside her, and she immediately climbed into my lap, looking at me quizzically.

There was something familiar about her, something that, as the

Italians said, made my "heart whistle." I looked into her eyes, and she stared into mine without blinking.

"I'm Bobby, you cute little thing," I finally managed.

"I know. Mama says you're very special and nice."

"She does?"

"Yeah. Will you wipe my nose?"

"Sure."

Annette giggled and handed me a Kleenex. Lucy Lou honked into the Kleenex, and Annette and I laughed, though Lucy didn't see what was so funny.

I don't remember how long I stayed there. After a while, Annette excused herself. When she finally returned, Lucy was still on my lap, and we were laughing about something. I don't remember what it was.

"Lucy has to go to bed now," Annette said.

"See ya," the darling little girl said, kissing my cheek. She followed her babysitter, who reappeared from nowhere, into her sleeping quarters.

Before she left, Lucy looked back at me with a pleasant, puzzled look. It was the same way I looked at her.

"Come outside onto the patio," Annette said, taking my hand and leading me beyond sliding doors to stand by the gate around the swimming pool.

She was quiet for a few minutes, and so was I. She wouldn't release my hand. I felt her heart beating in her fingertips.

"Do you want another drink?"

"No."

There was another long pause. I felt—I wasn't sure. Mean or vindictive wasn't quite right. Perhaps a little betrayed or angry.

"Are you and Dick going to have more children?" I asked quietly. My tone wasn't kind.

Annette wouldn't look at me. "We can't. He's sterile. He had mumps when he was an adolescent."

"Lucy?"

"She's yours, Bobby."

That stopped me cold. I knew, but hearing it…. "Dick?"

"It's all right, Bobby. Everything is…all right."

She looked at me with great kindness. I think I knew the moment I saw Lucy. Dick had brown hair and black eyes, but sometimes, we know things without knowing how.

"Bobby." She wrapped her arms around my neck and cried quietly. I felt tears on my cheeks. Were they hers or mine?

"I loved you," I said softly. "I think…I still do."

"I loved you that night, Bobby. I really did. There was so much between us. It wasn't just…a thing. It was real."

"Why couldn't it be with me, or…?" I didn't finish.

There was a long silence.

"It just didn't happen that way," she said. "Please believe me when I tell you that I'll always love you like I did that night."

I took her arms from around my neck and held them at her side. "Thank you, Annette. Thank you for telling me that." I kissed her forehead, released her, and walked out of the house to my car.

I felt like I was saying good-bye. We have to receive and accept love and gratification in whatever way they are packaged at the time. Otherwise, life can be like grabbin' chickens. Sometimes, you get shit on your arms, and sometimes, you get a drumstick for lunch.

Youngblood Of The Gran Rhon

Chapter One

I turned off the well-worn road of ancient, cracked concrete repaired with dried-out tar onto a smooth dirt road running alongside a group of buildings labeled *Grand Rhon Center* on a cracked, worn, roadside sign made of pine boards.

The buildings were old but well kept—a gas station, quick stop-start combination, that also advertised a fly shop. A very old blacksmith's shop with open front and no sign of recent activity was nearby. There was a separate veterinarian's office for large and small animals that had a corral behind it, a hideously green motel with four doors and a sign that read *Inquire at Store,* and a small, white brick building with a sign that read *Medical Clinic Open Tuesday and Thursday 9 till Noon.* I wondered what people did if they became ill on Wednesday at three o'clock.

The dirt road was an improvement over the concrete, but I had to slow down due to the dust. In a quarter mile, I came to a big, heavy, black-iron cattle gate with the welds still showing. A sign was wired to the gate. *Welcome. If you don't close the gate behind you, we'll shoot you.*

The ranch house was made of logs that looked like they came from the surrounding forest. All were uniformly one foot in diameter and seemed freshly oiled. The large front porch was painted light blue, as were the window frames. The roof was bright-red corrugated metal.

I drove past a well-kept, orderly garden filled with sweet corn, potatoes, onions, carrots, peppers, cabbages, and lettuce. Beside the lettuce were hills of beans, squash, and cucumbers. The built-in sprinkler system went off just as I drove past.

At least six lilac bushes bloomed around the yard, interspersed with rosebushes. On each side of the house stood carefully pruned fruit trees. A white horse, brown horse, and two ugly black mules that were past their prime chomped grass in a fenced pasture.

As I left the car, I heard the Gran Rhon River nearby mingling with the calls of crows circling overhead. They always seemed angry with each other, the world, or both. Mr. Youngblood sat on his porch puffing a homemade corncob pipe. Rather, it was Dr. Youngblood, a veterinarian.

He stood and yelled a big, dog that was sizing me up for lunch. The damn thing looked like a cross between an Airedale and a Great Dane—later, I learned I was right.

"Buddy!" he shouted.

The dog, looking ashamed, approached me apologetically, his tail wagging. Big dogs frightened me, but I managed to pat his head. He looked grateful and licked my hand with a tongue the size of a necktie and as wet as a mop.

"Dr. Youngblood, I'm Howard Singer. It looks like I bought your property. I'm glad to finally meet you."

"Come up and sit." The old man gestured.

I looked him over. I knew he was in his nineties, but he stood straight and moved quickly. His red face was clean-shaven, and his many wrinkles weren't that deep. His bright-blue eyes were alert, and he sported a full head of hair that was mostly gray with strands of red in it. His clothes were clean and colorful, and he wore a pair of shiny cordovan boots. If he was looking me over, he didn't let on. He smiled and invited me to sit in a swinging chair.

"You want a drink?" he asked.

"Sure."

"Water, pop, or buttermilk?"

"Water, please. That would be nice."

"Good water here." He went inside and returned in a moment. "It comes from a well that's 500 feet deep, cold and pure."

It was good, and I downed the whole glass. "Thanks. What do they call you?"

"Bucky, Doc, or *Guapo.*"

"*Guapo?*"

"That's Spanish for handsome." He chuckled as he sat down and put up his feet.

"People call me Howie. That's a nice set of boots, *Guapo.*"

He chuckled. "Yeah. A patient brought them up from Mexico for me. Rather, it was a patient's owner. The patient was a horse. He took a bunch of measurements of my feet. These boots fit like a glove when I first put 'em on. People make a mistake when they buy boots that ain't comfortable from the get-go."

"What can you tell me about yourself and the ranch?" I asked respectfully.

"I can tell you everything about both if you want to listen. I'm a long-winded son of a bitch and a first-class storyteller. Where to begin?"

"How'd an Anglo like you get a Native American name?"

"That's a long story. It's kinda complicated." He sat back in his chair and lit a pipe. It smelled like he smoked old barn straw, and he produced the bluest smoke I ever saw.

I became aware of two things. He was lonesome as hell, and he wanted to tell his life story. I was glad. I took mental notes and wrote them down as soon as I could. My memory surprised me. He spun a tale that caught my attention.

My mother showed up in Asotin when I was about six years old. She was with some galoot who wasn't her husband, and nobody thought much of either of 'em. He got a job in a garage, working on cars. He was dirty all the time, with grease tattooed into the cracks in his hands and under his fingernails.

My mother called herself Brenda Bumpf. She wore flowery dresses that were too short and always had a big bow in her hair. Her lipstick was too red and was a little smeared. When she could, she chain-smoked. She worked as a waitress and bar hop at the Little Nickel Bar and Grill in Asotin.

I don't know exactly why, but the geezer she hung out with was arrested and carried off to jail in Walla Walla. It must've been bad, because he was sentenced to five years. Off he went, leaving my mother and me on our own.

I don't remember her being mean to me, but I was left alone while she was at work and had to fend for myself while she dolled herself up and went out to bars at night. Sometimes, she sneaked a guy in. We always ate better for a while after that. That was when my dad, Emerson Youngblood, came into the picture.

My mother got sick with the flu and pneumonia and couldn't work. We quickly became destitute. Emerson was involved in some kind of welfare job. I think he was supposed to just look after the Native Americans, but he drew no barriers, and he became involved in her plight.

He brought us to his home, where she lived for five years. They had some sort of agreement, and they got along well. I remember him going to her bedroom for an hour or so, then coming out carrying his clothes on the way to his own room. As young as I was, I knew that was odd, but they got along.

Sometimes, he got angry drunk when she went to town and came back early in the morning smelling of booze and cigarettes and still drunk. He always let her sleep in the following day as long as she wanted, and that smoothed things over. Sometimes, she left for a few days, claiming she was visiting family in Oklahoma. I knew she went to Walla Walla to visit her prisoner lover.

Emerson Youngblood was a full-blooded Nez Perce from the Oregon side of the Snake River. His father raised him on a ranch, along with his two brothers, after his mother died of consumption. I never knew his brothers, but he was a leader of men, a descendent of Chief Joseph, an educated man who knew the value of education and sent his boys off to high school in mission schools.

He must've been a hell of a man, because Emerson was a hell of a man. He was a smart, kindhearted, hardworking, wise man who earned respect from anyone who knew him and care from most. He taught himself to be a farrier and blacksmith. He bought books on it and worked for the good ones in the area. He ran the shop back on the road.

It's a real mystery how he acquired this 600-acre ranch and the river, but somehow, he owned them outright. I saw the title. It had something to do with the Hudson Bay Company years ago, but I don't know and never asked.

Grand Rhon means Grand Rendezvous, a meeting place for the old mountain men and trappers who named it. He owned the part down the river where the Gran Rhon meets the Snake, as well as this meadow. I saw the survey and the deed.

Being a Native American was serious business for him. He talked about the Nez Perce and their horses. Once, the US Army, in all its benevolent wisdom, shot 500 Appaloosa horses just to subjugate the Native Americans. He knew the entire history of the Nez Perce war and told anyone who would listen.

If it hadn't been for the Nez Perce, Lewis and Clark and his whole bunch would've been wiped out, starved, or killed. The Nez Perce had good trade relations with the French and British. They even helped the American immigrants at the end of the Oregon Trail. They went to their reservation quietly, because old Chief Joseph knew what was coming would be inevitable. He understood that war would be futile.

The land the Nez Perce were originally given was beautiful rolling grassland and fertile valleys. They adapted well, but it didn't last. The whites wanted it, too. They coveted it, so they took it. A couple young bucks killed an American trader who was a well-known ne'er-do-well and crooked cheater. That was all it took.

Then came the great American cavalry. The whole damn tribe left—women, children, old folks, dogs, and horses. They went across Lo Lo pass, if you can believe that, with the soldiers nipping at their heels like dogs. For 1,000 miles, they kept ahead of the finest cavalry in the world. Other tribes, like the Blackfoot, betrayed them, or they would've reached Canada. They stopped twenty miles from the border, because they thought they were across. The army surrounded them and had a grand time taking potshots at them from a distance.

Looking Glass was their war chief. Joseph was the peacemaker when they surrendered. Chief Joseph wasn't allowed to go home until he was dead. He's buried over by Walla Walla somewhere. They locked him in the Native American reservation at Colville, Washington.

Like a lot of Nez Perce, Emerson was big and strong, over six feet tall and not an ounce of fat. He never smoked, but he almost always had a chew of Star plug in his cheek. Unlike others Native Americans, he didn't drink and wouldn't allow alcohol on his property or near him. He saw what it did to his people and understood that Native Americans couldn't drink the stuff.

I knew about alcohol firsthand, having been forced, shall we say, to study it. In some people, though not all, it's converted to a substance in the brain that's no different from heroine. That enzyme is responsible for the euphoria and craving. Alcohol is denatured, or metabolized, in the liver.

Some nationalities have more enzymes than others. The ones that have little get drunk earlier and harder and stay drunk longer. The enzymes in their brains make them higher, more euphoric, and they stay drunk easier. Native Americans have the wretched enzyme in their brains and lack the ones in the liver. They lose all around.

There's another thing—alcohol fits into Native American society and attitudes too well. They feel like, "The hell with tomorrow! Let's party!"

Emerson knew those things, but he had his religion, too. It's hard to explain. He wouldn't attend a white man's church after leaving the mission school, though he prayed a lot, always in his native language with his eyes closed for a few seconds. Sometimes, it was a few minutes. He had no use for all the dress and sex hang-ups we live with. Though he was honest, he loved tricking people with trades like horses and guns. It was a game to him.

He didn't take to me right off. I was blond, blue-eyed, and cried a lot. I was pretty small and thin, too. The way he fed me, though, I started growing. He bought a milk cow that I suspected was just for me.

One day, there was a breakthrough. I scraped my knees and elbows pretty bad when I fell into a prickly pear cactus. Though I'd just turned seven, I didn't cry.

"Damn dirty shit!" I shouted, copying Emerson's language.

I'll always remember how he looked at me. He patted my head and shook my shoulder.

One day, he said, "Let's make a couple of slingshots."

I thought that was a swell idea. He found a couple trees with the right forks, cut them, and let me whittle 'em smooth. I got an old rubber inner tube from the garage and cut strips just the right size to pull and stretch. He cut the tongue from an old pair of boots to make the pouches. When we put all the parts together, we had two fine slingshots.

Then we took a handful of marbles from a bag he had in the garage. "I was the marble champion of the reservation," he said with a huge grin.

Man, we had a great time. We shot at squirrels, birds, rabbits, fence posts, and leaves. I don't remember ever hitting an animal or bird, but it was fun. We got to be friends. I followed him everywhere and started walking and acting like him. Hell, I still do. I stand with the weight on one leg, the other knee bent a little, my hip slouched forward. All cowboys do that.

He always stuck his thumbs in his belt when he spoke to people, and I did that, too. He never removed his hat unless he was going into a house, and sometimes, not even then. I never saw him eat with it on. I see cowboys—I guess that's what they are—eating in restaurants with their hats on. A few old-timers still do that, but he didn't, and neither do I.

He gave me one of his old felt hats that was way too big for me. He put it in boiling water and let it dry in the sun. That didn't work very well, so he stuffed the inside with toilet paper. At least it stayed on my little head. He made me a stampede strap that went under my chin to hold the hat on.

When school started, he took me and got me enrolled. It wasn't my ma. Grades one through six were in two rooms. The schoolhouse was across the street from the blacksmith's shop. It's gone, burned down after World War Two by some kids playing with matches.

I liked school. If you'll pardon me for saying so, I was smart. Somehow, being bashful as hell was interpreted by the teacher as being polite. Anyway, they all liked me and gave me extra attention and extra work. I think I was the only second grader who had homework. As luck would have it, the only boys in the school were older than I was, and I wasn't about to play with girls.

I liked jumping rope, though, and I got good at it, doing the double dip. At lunch, I crossed the street to the blacksmith's shop and ate with Emerson. Eventually, thanks be to God, I called him Dad. Before that, it was Emerson.

"How'd you start calling him Dad?" I asked.
He leaned back and smiled as he tamped out his pipe.
"I'll get to that." He winked.

After school, I watched that big Injun pound iron. He had me pump the bellows for him. Other times, he had a small job for me to do, saying it was a task. I could hardly lift that mallet at first, but, with time, I learned how to make buckles and rosettes for harnesses and bridles that passed his inspection.

By the time I was in high school, I was shaping horseshoes out of bars of steel, and he let me shoe a few of the easier animals. The rough ones he took, making me hold their noses with a twitch. Sometimes, he rigged up ropes and threw an animal down, while I sat on its head. He always said, "If I wanted to take all day, I'd have them stand still for me, but I can't spare the time to baby 'em."

You should've seen him handle horses. He and his friend drove a dozen wild horses in during late summer, usually yearlings, year-olds, and older mares. The mares he turned loose again. It took a week or more for 'em to run off, because their damn colts were still suckling. When they went dry, they left over the hills a couple at a time, moving toward Rattlesnake Ridge.

Breaking them was a fall and winter job with the idea of selling them as saddle horses and cow ponies come spring. He trained them in groups in that big round corral.

He pointed at the round corral, made of foot-thick logs notched at the ends like Lincoln logs. There was a snubbing post in the center.

He had a way with horses he tried to teach me, but I learned only part of it. Later, if I had a problem pony, I left him for a week, and he would fix it. He got a halter on 'em by following 'em around and talking to 'em in his own language. He whispered and blew in his lips.

I asked what he was saying to the horses.

"Stand still, you stupid bastard, or I'll kill you."

That made me laugh.

When he got halters on, they were a special kind with a bosal around the horse's nose. He tied up one hind foot with a loop through the bosal and the end of the rope on the ground. Those were called sidelines. If an animal stepped on its own rope while jumping around, it threw itself.

After being tied up like that for a day or two, they stood still or walked very slowly to their water and hay. Next, he taught them to lead, working with one or two at a time.

He took a thick cotton rope, tied a bowline around the horse's withers so it wouldn't tighten, brought the end through the bosal, and fastened it to a truck tire. When the animal backed away, it thought the tire was chasing it. The horses kicked and squealed, dragging that tire around for half a day before they learned how to move with it.

After that, they were just fine. He would do what was called, *sack 'em out,* by waving blankets at them, then he'd handle their feet, trim their hooves, touch 'em all over, pull their tails, trim their locks, comb their manes and tails, and wash 'em with a hose. Finally, he put a saddle on them. He didn't want them to buck even once. He kept their heads up high, which stopped 'em from bucking.

He climbed on and off, from the right or left, over the shoulders and off the rump, until the horse was bored with it all. Somehow, he knew when it was enough.

"How do I know when it's enough?" I asked once.

"You'll know."

He was right. That damned guy held the horse's head and spoke to it in his language, gave it sugar lumps, and blew his breath into its nostrils, until it stood still. That's a horse's way of making friends.

I never saw a single one of his horses buck. The real buckers were six-year-olds off the reservation. When I was in high school, I rode some of those horses for sport and rodeo competition. I was good at it, particularly bareback broncos.

"Want some more good water?" he asked.

"Yes, thanks."

He came back with a glass in each hand. "Where was I?" he asked, sitting down.

"You were a boy in grade school, following a Native American around."

"Oh, yeah."

When I was ten years old, he bought me a single-shot Sears and Roebuck .22 rifle for my birthday. We took it out behind the barn and set some bottles against the side of a hill. At first, I couldn't hit a thing. He watched me try awhile, the barrel waving around, and said, "Brady, let me teach you something. Your eyes are going from the sight to the can and back. No one can hold a gun steady when he does that. Focus on the target. Line up the sight in your mind's eye. Practice that."

I did. In a few shots, I hit the mark every time. The same principle applied to pistols, shotguns, bows and arrows, and slingshots. I never miss. I got so I carried that rifle everywhere. There were lots of blue grouse in those days. I could shoot off their heads. We ate a lot of grouse.

One day, I was heading out the door with my rifle when Bucky said, "Let's have beefsteak for dinner."

I got the message. I shot a lot of cottontails for a while before I was nudged back to beef steak.

He slapped his knee and laughed.

"How about steelhead and salmon and trout?" I asked. "There's a river right here. People come from other states just to fish the Gran Rhon. That's how I ended up here."

"Ended up? Is this your last stop?"

"I don't know."

"Good. A man should never know where he's ended up. It kills the imagination."

His philosophy spoke, which he showed no evidence of living himself. He paused to stare at the trees.

I let him do that awhile, but finally, I asked, "Where was your mother in all this?"

He resumed his story.

When she wasn't gone to town or elsewhere, she sat around, drinking beer, smoking cigarettes, reading magazines in her slip, and doing nothing. She cooked sometimes, I guess, and kept the place clean. She washed the clothes and painted the house several times, inside and out. At night, she let Brady have a poke when he wished, though I saw he wanted it less and less.

One day while Bucky, or Emerson, and I were out shoeing horses and mules for rangers, she up and left, taking all her things. She didn't even leave a note.

It turned out they let that dude out of jail, and he came looking for her, so she left. We didn't give a rat's ass, but Bucky became serious and said he'd be away for a few days.

He went to a lawyer and drew up papers to adopt me. He learned that my ma and that dude were outside Asotin, and she was served with papers commanding her to appear in court. I had to go, too.

We arrived an hour early. When she came in with the dude, Bucky ran up and took her aside. He looked at that dude, and he didn't budge an inch. I saw the two of them talking and arguing, though they kept their voices down. Then he handed her an envelope.

She took it, glanced at me, then went in with the dude. She signed the adoption papers without even looking at me. I cried without knowing why. A guy should have a mother, but hell, she was no mother except that she washed my clothes, made my lunch, put cold rags on my head when I had a fever, and sometimes kissed me good night, leaving the scent of her perfume on my nightshirt and a smear of lipstick on my forehead. For a few years after she left, she sent me a birthday card or Christmas card from California with five dollars in it.

After a while, that stopped, and I never saw her again. Many years later, Emerson told me he gave her $5,000 he saved from Native American money over the years. I'd been sold and bought for five grand. That was more than anyone could get for me today. He loved his joke, but it made me sad, though I never detected any sadness on his part.

You asked about fishing the Gran Rhon. It's as good as ever despite what the bunny huggers say. At least the Rhon is. I don't know about anywhere else on the Snake. There are big years and not-so-big years.

Thing is, people around here go when the fish are in. We don't wait out time, beating the water before the run starts or after it's over. We always had lots of fish, all we could use or give away. We had it fried, barbecued, Indian smoked, stewed, baked, and boiled. Dad had a way of cooking it I really liked. He boiled saltwater with onion and pickling spices and threw in the fish. We ate it cold on pita bread with mayonnaise.

"Sounds good," I said. "You just called him Dad."

"Yeah. I couldn't call him Dad around you until I got to know you."

You don't know me at all, for Christ's sake.

When the judge handed Emerson the adoption papers, it sure was easy back then.

"Now you can call Emerson Youngblood your dad, Young Man," he told me. "He's one of the finest men I ever knew. See that you deserve it."

Emerson looked at the judge, sitting there like a potentate in his black robes, and said, "He deserves it, because he's himself, and I love him."

The old man choked up a bit on that last part, but he didn't have time to do anything about it, because I said, "I love him, too."

I stared at my shoes.

When I was eighteen, I legally changed my name to Youngblood. From that day in court, that's what I called myself.

Dad and I broke a lot of horses. The ones we thought useless, we sent into Clarkston to the butcher's. We got fifty cents a pound sometimes. Because we weeded out the bad ones, we got a name for first-class saddle horses and cow ponies. People came from all over to buy them. We went to a horse auction in Clarkston once. Emerson saw a young Arabian stallion that he had to have. He paid $1,000 for it—a lot of money back then for a horse.

"What will we do with it?" I asked.

"We'll breed those Mustang mares with him."

"How?"

"Simple. We'll turn him loose with the herd and shoot all the males."

That was what we did. You have to understand that there were a lot of wild Mustangs back then, and they were eating up good cattle range. The offspring were the finest, prettiest, and nastiest critters you ever saw. Damn, they were hard to break.

Dad had a girlfriend from the reservation named Susan. She had a boy my age. I'm not sure who his father was, but it could've been Emerson. When I was twelve, they came to live with us. The boy's name was Russell Faloway.

We became the best brothers and best friends in the world. Susan smothered me with hugs and wet kisses constantly.

The three of them talked Native American all the time at first, but I didn't mind. I picked up a lot of words, and I taught them proper English—when they would listen. Russell had to attend the Native American school in Walla Walla, but he came home every Friday and stayed until Sunday. In high school, he was approved to attend high school with me in Asotin. That's another story. He was smart enough, but I helped him a lot with his homework. He was quite a bit behind at first.

Anyway, we had five of them half-Mustang, half-Arab three-year-olds to break. Russell was a hell of a good hand, especially with a rope, and together, we had that job. We went through all the stuff I told you before, but those shitheads still bucked. We tied their heads up high, climbed off and on until they were quiet, then we released them.

It was my turn to mount one when Russell decided to play a trick. He made a step loop in the tie-down rope that would pull out and release the pony when it pulled back. Rather than being tied tight, the horse had ten feet of slack.

I got on, the horse yanked back, the rope came loose, and the bronco exploded into the air, landing on all fours, twisting and snorting, rearing and sunfishing. With a loud crack, the horse dropped like he fell from an airplane, dead with a broken neck.

I sat on top as a tiny breeze came up, whirling dust here and there. A bird chirped something rude. Russell and I looked at each other.

"Emerson's going to be pissed," he said.

"Yeah. I'd better go tell him." That was the only time I was scared to face him. It was a beautiful horse, all pure black and shiny, and it would've been worth $500.

Emerson spanked me only once when I went swimming in the river when he said not to go. Sure enough, I got caught in the rapids and had to walk back a quarter mile, all bruised from rocks and cut in several places, not to mention barefoot. He whipped me with a canoe paddle. I screamed like hell, but it didn't hurt that much, and I didn't fool him. He shook my arm next. I knew he did it, because I'd done something dangerous.

"Damn it!" he shouted. "You could've been killed!" His voice quieted. "What would I do around here without you?"

That wasn't much of a spanking, but I never did that again.

I had to face him about the dead horse. He'd told us a hundred times not to let that rope be longer than one foot until the horse stopped itself tossing around. My feet plopped in the dust, and I wished I was on the moon.

I went to the door, and, for some damn reason, knocked instead of walking in. Dad came to the door. I opened it, and he stared at me, his brow wrinkled.

"What?" he asked.

"We killed that black mare," I blurted between sobs.

He looked at me for a long time. "Damn. I knew that was a no-good son of a bitch. If you got to kill 'em to break 'em, they ain't no good nohow." He said several things in his own language that I didn't need a translator to understand.

"Come on." He pulled on his boots, and we walked out to the Ford farm-all tractor. I climbed up on the side.

"No," he said. "You drive."

He opened the gate for me. I ground those gears pretty hard while he made a show of plugging his ears and closing his eyes. Off we went, with Dad walking behind. We removed the gear from that horse with our mouths wide open. It was really sad, and Russell and I cried a little.

"Quit your damn blubbering and tie that horse on by the neck," Dad said.

We ran to do it and collided like bowling pins falling.

"For the love of Pete!" He did it himself. As he pulled the horse to the ditch behind the barn, he looked back at us and said, "Quit for the day. Go swimmin' or something."

We gathered our gear.

"We'll get us a couple bears in a few days," he called.

I knew he noticed that the snubbing line was ten feet long. He started to say something, but he changed his mind for reasons only he knew.

Bears came after that carcass, all right, along with coyotes and buzzards.

Dad fixed a car headlight to an apple box and powered it with a car battery. It made a great nightlight. I have to confess, we skinned a deer sometimes when we ran out of meat. That time, we waited until we heard bears snapping bones.

We hid in the rocks. When we jumped up, we turned on the light, and Russell and I cut loose with our .30-.30s. We blew a lot of holes in the ground, but we got two nice bears. The worst part was skinning them, seeing them without their hides. They looked like two naked, dead people. That's the only time Native Americans won't look at bears.

If you ask me, bear meat's awful. There are big chunks of fat in it that are strange, to say the least. We cut all the meat into steaks and roasts. Susan cooked some, and we gave the rest away to her friends and family. She scraped and tanned the two hides, so we kidded her about being an Indian squaw. Native Americans cured hides by urinating on them, rubbing them with the brains, and chewing them. I don't know if she did all those things, but she did some. She sure had beautiful teeth.

She sent them to an old woman on the reservation who turned them into a beautiful pair of chaps for me. They damn near got me killed, too. If Russell hadn't been there, I would've been dead.

He and I were going for a ride, and I put on my chaps. When I went to mount my horse, he smelled the bear and went crazy. He reared and took off, and my right foot was caught in the stirrup. I tried to roll and get my foot loose, but I was dragged twenty feet until I came near Russell. He flew out of his saddle and caught my horse's reins with one finger. Somehow, he held on and stopped the horse, or I would've been used as bear bait.

Dad came running and chewed me out. "You can't just go at a green-broke horse lookin' and smellin' like a damn bear!"

He took the chaps and laid 'em across the saddle until the horse stood still, though it was shaking and sweating. Then he left the hides in the stall with my mount for a week. Finally, the horse ignored the chaps, treating them like a saddle blanket. It took a couple weeks. I made the horse walk around with the chaps on the saddle horn for a while before I got on him.

High school and junior high were in one building. I went to Pomroy for school. I was only thirteen, but I drove an old World War Two Jeep we had. Russell went to the Native American school in Walla Walla, but we saw each other every weekend.

There were two brothers in ninth grade, nonidentical twins, I think. They started out giving me a rough time and were as mean as coyotes. I was pushed and tripped. One day, for no reason, one slugged my face and gave me a black eye.

The teacher, Mr. Klevins, asked what happened, and I said I'd been hit by a tetherball. I was a tough guy, but I was also self-conscious and insecure starting junior high. I knew he didn't believe me, but he asked no more questions. After putting ice on it, I was told to sit down awhile.

When I came home, Dad looked at me and asked, "What happened?"

I cried a little, partly because I'd been holding it back all day, and blurted out the story. He didn't look angry, just determined.

After dinner and chores, he brought out a boxing glove and put it on his hand. "I used to box in amateur matches. I was the champion of the whole tribe—Nez Perce, Yakima, Cayuse, and Palouse. Let me teach you a few things."

I nodded.

"Let's see you hit the glove as hard as you can."

I swung and missed, because he pulled back half an inch.

"See? When you swing like that, it's no good. There's no force behind it, and it's too easy to dodge. Hit straight out like this." He demonstrated. "Shoot your fist out from your shoulder, driving it. It's like shooting a gun. Keep your eyes on the target. Whatever you do, keep your chin to your chest. Make your fist as tight as you can."

We messed around for an hour, with my hitting the glove with both hands. I'm ambidextrous. Over the next few days, he taught me how to hit the belly right under the xyphoid—the solar plexus. I was a natural boxer, though I never liked the sport.

The next week at school, sure enough, they came at me again. I carried my lunch in an old, wrinkled paper bag that embarrassed me. It seemed like all the other kids had nice, new paper bags or lunchboxes with thermoses in 'em. The guys started poking fun at me about my bag, and one of 'em slapped it from my hands to the ground.

Emerson told me another thing—hit someone square as you can right on the nose. That makes their eyes water like hell, and usually, the nose bleeds like a hose. My left fist came out like a piston, followed by my right, before I could think about it.

I spun and pasted the other guy the same way. Blood and spit flew everywhere. Klevins, the teacher, saw it and hauled those two jerks with their broken noses into the office, where a nurse was on duty. I picked up my lunch and ate it right there.

I learned something big from that. You know what it was? Revenge can be good for someone, damn good. Despite what the psalm singers say, it can be therapeutic.

The daddy of those boys was a deputy sheriff. He came into the school, the red light whirling on his car, but I wasn't frightened or intimidated. I just followed him into the office, where Klevins was just hanging up the phone.

"Who beat up my boys?" the cop shouted. "I'm taking them in!"

"Well, now, Deputy. There was no *them*. It was just him." He pointed at me, standing by the door, a skinny kid five-feet-four-inches tall with freckles and spots of blood on my face.

The deputy stared at me, unable to believe it.

"They started it," Klevins added. "They were picking on him and pushing him around. It wasn't the first time, either. I saw the whole thing and spoke with the superintendent. One more fight from your boys, and they're both expelled. As of now, they've been suspended for the week.

"I suggest you take them to a doctor. Their noses are broken. By the way, I spoke to your boss, the sheriff. He agrees with me. He wants to see you."

I never had to fight again until college, but that's another story.

I started hanging around with a kid named Charley Artez. His dad was a rodeo star around these parts. In those days, cowboys did it all—bulldozing, roping, saddle bronc, and bareback bronc riding. Brahma bulls came later. He was called Tucker Artez. You probably heard of him.

He was the biggest star and all-around cowboy at the Pendleton Stampede four years running. Charley and I had him as a teacher and coach. I took to bareback bronc right off. When Russell was home, he went with me, and Tucker taught him all he knew about roping, which was plenty.

The funny thing was, his own kid wasn't interested at all. He spent his time tinkering with old motorcycles and car engines. At fifteen, he could fix anything. I remember he had a collection of three Jeeps he was always working on.

Tucker laughed at him. "I'll bet someday, they have a Jeep rodeo." He was right, too.

Charley took two of those Jeeps apart and welded them together, so they had an engine on both ends. Russell said it would drive him nuts to think that Charley could go two ways simultaneously.

Charley painted that contraption blue with pink polka dots, added whistles, bells, and smoke bombs, and took it to rodeos as the clown. He'd drive in with a clothesline of bloomers on it, like he'd just gone through somebody's yard. A bunch of fat ladies in their underwear chased after him, and he could escape by going forward or backward in his trick car.

By the time he was eighteen, he quit school and went to fairs and rodeos all over the country, making good money.

I got my first girlfriend toward the end of my third year of high school. Before that, I was too busy. That's a lie. I was scared of girls.

Anyway, at a barn dance over at the grange hall, a girl asked me to dance during ladies' choice. I didn't know how to dance, but she was a good teacher. Her name was Geraldine. She was kind of fat, with a round, cute face and tits too big for her. We danced a few times, slow and fast, drank too many Cokes, laughed at each other's attempts to tell jokes, and held hands a lot.

When it was time to go home, I walked her to her dad's car. When he wasn't looking, she kissed me full on the mouth. I felt as if my feet were off the ground the entire way home.

She was in my school but one year behind me. We hung around at school a bit, but mostly we ignored each other until Friday or Saturday night, when I drove over to pick her up in my Jeep. We usually went to town for a hamburger or hung around the hamburger shop with other kids.

On the way home, we parked, kissing and squirming in the front of the Jeep. Petting started pretty fast, and I had her shirt off and her big tits out. Then I started fumbling under her skirt. Those silky hairs drove me nuts—her, too. She held onto my arm but never pulled away. Her eyes were always closed.

One time after half an hour with my hand under her dress, she suddenly released my arm and reached down with both hands to remove her panties. She had my dick in her other hand, and I was ready to go.

Try to find a position in a Jeep. It didn't matter, because I bounced off her a couple times and covered her silkies with semen. She screeched, pulled up her panties and her dress down, and stayed on her side of the car. She became distant. When we got to her house, she said good-bye and ran inside.

She wouldn't look at me at school after that. It hurt my feelings, not to mention my crippled manly pride. I was glad when she moved to Lewiston.

Russell, Charley, and I loved to fish the Gran Rhon. It was a small, beautiful river cutting through hills and paths. The water was a little blue and almost clear. Charley had a boat he made from huge truck inner tubes and four-by-three-quarter boards held together by thin ropes through holes in the wood. He was smart, because a flat sheet of plywood wouldn't have moved like our deck did. The planks bent as the inner tubes shifted in the rough water.

We often left the truck at the mouth of the Snake and drifted from the highway down, dragging an anchor to go slow enough to fish. We caught some beautiful bright silvers and springs, as shiny as new bumpers. We also caught steelhead that fought like fury. The red stripe on their sides was visible in the water.

Once the anchor was secured and everything was quiet, we brought the fish alongside so Charley could photograph them with his Brownie. Then we cut the line at the hook and released it. We always used hooks that would dissolve in the fishes' mouths.

Canoeing down the river, we sometimes lost control and spun, whooping and hollering. Once we ended up in a back eddy, bumping against the shore. We sat there, laughing at ourselves, eating our lunch and drinking Rainier beer we kept in a sack alongside the raft.

"What's that smell?" Charley asked.

Russell sniffed. "Not flowers."

"I smell it, too," I said. "Let's go see."

We tied up the raft and climbed out on shore. The sweet smell was easy enough to follow. We moved cautiously through the woods until we saw an open spot ahead. Two big vats with propane burners going under them were the source of the smell. Fluid moved through old automobile radiators.

"My God," Charley whispered. "It's a still."

"Yeah," Russell said. "It sure is."

"Let's get out of here," I said.

We'd heard of people getting shot when they stumbled onto stills. Lightning killed people in more ways than one.

I noticed a man with a keg and scruffy beard moving around, checking things, and we slowly backed away until we could hightail it to our boat and get out of there.

The county health nurse was a friend of Emerson's. I heard her talking to him when she stopped at the blacksmith's shop.

"Something weird's going on down the river here and in town," she said. "People are getting sick as all get out, and it turned out to be lead poisoning." She clucked her tongue.

I immediately thought of the moonshine still, because the core of automobile radiators was lead. Somewhere, I'd read that moonshiners in the South were killing people with their moonshine, because they used automobile radiators as condenser coils.

I didn't care if someone wanted to make whiskey, but poison was something else. I was out of high school at the time, right before I started college. Russell and Charley weren't there, so I went to the sheriff's office alone.

I explained what I knew to the sheriff, and he was interested and alarmed. He called in his deputy. "Listen to this," he said.

I explained it again. By then, there were two deputies.

"Where's this still?" Sid, the father of the twins I once beat up, demanded.

"Listen, Deputy," I said, looking him in the eye, "it's not my still."

"Hold on, Son," the sheriff said. "I'll get a map."

When he brought it out, I studied it carefully. "I can't be sure where it is on the river. We were floating it, fishing."

I found a small road that ran off the river road toward the river. "It must be at the end of this road."

"That's not much more than a trail," a deputy said. "It's all overgrown, and there's an iron gate across it. I was just down there. There are signs that the gate's been opened and closed a few times, though."

The sheriff looked up from the map into my eyes. "Can you find the place from a boat in the river?"

"Yes. I think so."

"OK. We'll set it up for tomorrow. Sid, you take…. What's your name?"

"Brady Youngblood."

"Take Mr. Youngblood down the river in the boat. We'll come in from the road."

Sid wasn't pleased.

"Sid, I know you can manage the float boat, so you do it."

Sid nodded. I would meet him at the launching ramp at six o'clock the following morning. I estimated it would take forty-five minutes to reach the spot, so the other men would come in from the road.

When I reached the ramp that morning, the boat was already in the water, and Deputy Sid was waiting impatiently. I said, "Hello," but he didn't answer, the asshole.

We got downriver to the spot in half an hour, tied up the boat, and went quietly through the woods to where we found the clearing.

Sid smiled when he saw the still. A big man poked in the vats with a paddle.

He stopped and stared down the road. Suddenly, he dropped his paddle and ran to a tire, where a single-shot shotgun stood. He lifted it and walked toward the road.

Sid stepped out in the open. I was right behind him.

"Halt and stay put! You're under arrest. Put down the gun." He hadn't drawn his pistol.

The man turned and fired. Sid gave a half-scream and slumped forward. Something tore through the side of my coat, and my skin stung.

The moonshiner frantically opened his shotgun to load another shell, but his hand shook, so he had trouble. Sid was bent over double on the ground.

Without thinking, I pulled the big revolver from his holster and cocked the hammer. Neither of us spoke. The man finished reloading and smirked as he raised the barrel toward me.

I shot him square in the chest, breaking the shotgun as the bullet passed through it. He stared in disbelief, then fell over backward. Another guy with a bushy beard ran out of a tent with a .30-.30 carbine in his hands, his eyes wide.

When he saw me with the pistol, and his partner lying face-up on the ground, he dropped the rifle and raised his hands. "Don't shoot!"

Hell, I was shaking so bad, I couldn't have hit the broad side of a barn. The sheriff and the other deputy ran down the road. While the deputy handcuffed the bushy-faced moonshiner, the sheriff came up to Sid, who moaned and lay on his side.

We rolled him onto his back. There were four holes in his shirt in a line from above his belt up to his chest.

"Damn," the sheriff said. "That's two-oh buckshot. You hurt, Son?"

I almost said, "I ain't your son," but thought better of it. Instead, I lifted my coat and shirt to reveal a bleeding crease on my side. I pressed a bandanna against it. "Didn't go in," I said.

"What the hell happened?"

I told him, and he looked annoyed.

"You shot him?" He nodded toward the dead man.

"Yes. He was about to shoot me."

He didn't say anything. "Damn it, Karl, get the car in here now! Let's get Sid to the hospital."

"What about *him?*" he asked.

"Fuck him." He handcuffed the bushy-faced man to a tree. "Let's go."

"That's about the end of that story," he said. "Look at this scar." He pulled up his shirt. "It's a good one, all right. After a lot of pictures were taken, the still was dismantled, and the lead poisoning stopped." He seemed to be enjoying a private joke. "Deputy Sid's been nice to me ever since."

"I'd better get out of your hair. I just wanted to meet you and talk to you." I started to rise.

"You aren't in my hair. Stay for supper."

"What are we having?"

"Blue grouse and fried potatoes, with tomatoes and cucumbers from the garden."

"You talked me into it."

We talked a lot more. Eventually, I helped him light a fire in his woodstove and prepare supper.

"I don't drink," he said.

"Neither do I," I lied.

Instead, we had iced tea made in the sun, with lemon added. It was pretty good.

"See that ridge?" he asked, waving behind him.

"Yes."

"It's called Rattlesnake Ridge."

"It is?"

"Yep, and for good reason, too."

I felt another story coming.

When I was sixteen, I was up there cutting wood for our cookstove when I stepped over a log. *Wham!* I was hit in the leg. At first, it felt like someone hit me with a stick, then it began to tingle and burn. Then it hurt like the fires of hell.

I screamed, and Dad ran over. He knew immediately what happened and laid me on a soft, grassy spot.

"Don't move a muscle," he said.

He removed my belt and used it as a tourniquet just above my knee. The pain was so intense, I couldn't even scream. You know, it's not the poison from a rattlesnake that kills you, it's the shock from the pain.

Emerson ran to the truck and got his pistol. I thought he was going to kill the snake, but instead, he ripped open my pant leg with his knife, then he cut a piece of skin off where the snake bit me. I still have a scar there.

He blew away the poison. He sucked that wound fifty times and spat blood everywhere while I lay there, sweating and shivering. Lights and shooting stars were going off in my head. Even though I was panting, it was hard to breathe.

"Am I going to die?" I asked.

"Someday," he quipped. "Not today."

He released the tourniquet from time to time, and, at first, that made the pain worse. He made me lay there for a long time without moving. The theory is, that keeps the poison from being pumped through the body. Panic kills a lot of people who are snake bit. If the person who's sucking out the poison has an open sore in his mouth, the poison can get into his body and kill him. He knew that and rinsed out his mouth after every suck.

The funny thing about rattlesnake venom is that it's a very stable chemical. Boil or freeze it, it stays the same. People have gotten flat tires from snakes. When you kill a rattler, you're supposed to cut off the head and bury it. Once I saw a guy stick a piece of wood into a dead snake's head, and the mouth chomped down by itself.

Birds get at the heads, and it kills them. That's another reason to bury it. One time, Russell had a new pair of $65 boots. A snake struck one boot above the ankle without getting through, but he said he felt the boot getting all hot inside. Emerson pulled off the boot and tossed it in the campfire. I thought Russell would bust out crying, but, sooner or later, that poison would've killed him. It never goes away—never.

Antivenom used to be made from horse serum. Now, it's cows. Serum sickness killed more people than snakebites. I used it a lot on dogs, and they never got serum sickness. The funny thing is, pigs eat rattlesnakes. I don't know how they get away with it. Maybe if they get hit in the fat, the poison is absorbed so slow, it doesn't kill them.

I could tell he was enjoying talking, and I enjoyed listening.

"Stay away from Rattlesnake Ridge," he warned.

"I will."

"Part of it's on your property."

"I'll donate that part to the Catholic missions."

After dinner, we sat on the porch again, and he lit a homemade corncob pipe.

"You a veterinarian?" I asked.

"Sure am. I work half a day twice a week for some of my old friends. What do you do?"

"I'm an actor and writer."

He didn't bat an eye. The conversation was about him.

"Did you ever see a doctor or go to the hospital about your bite?"

"Nope. My leg swelled up, but it went down. In a while, I was as good as new."

"How'd you get to vet school?"

"Emerson asked what I wanted to do after high school, and I said I wanted to be a veterinarian."

"'So why don't you, then?' he asked.

"'It costs a lot of money.'

"'I have money for you. Indian money. I saved it all.'

"I was eighteen, and I'd been earning my own money for a while. 'That's your money.'

"'Nope. I saved it for you.'

"'What will you do for retirement?'

"'Hell, I'll never retire. If you want, I'll go back to the reservation.'

"That was a funny comment, but he was serious. I did all right in college and got along fine. Emerson paid for tuition and books, and I got a job in the commissary for room and board. Besides, some rich old cowboy offered a rodeo scholarship. It was the first of its kind. Since I was the best bronc rider around, I won. It wasn't much, but I always had a car and spending money.

"Russell had a full ride to school as a Native American. There are so many plans available for them, that some never get used. There are lots of reasons for that—none of them any good. He went to Oregon and studied farming agriculture. He won enough money roping in rodeos to have spending money."

"What about Charley?"

He squirmed as if suddenly uncomfortable. Finally, he said, "He was a hell of a guy. I told you how he was a rodeo clown, but he was also a guitar-playing, banjo-picking, yodeling, singing entertainer, too. He was good. You probably heard of him if you know anything about Western music. He called himself Charley Pine."

"I don't really like Western music."

"Why?"

"It's filled with clichés and lamenting about shit, like beer, divorce, jobs, and the ol' dog named Skip."

"It used to be that way. Now it's screaming and yelling that I can't understand." He paused. "You left out cheating and pickup trucks."

He settled in to tell another story.

Charley had a band, though he called it a group—Charley Pine and the Ridge Runners. They were successful in Washington, Oregon, Idaho, and into Montana and Wyoming. He wanted to go to Nashville in the worst way. Thanks to me, he did.

After the first year of college, I met a girl from Moses Lake named Linda Lou when I was at a rodeo party. We had great, boot-stampin' beer parties after a rodeo. They were really something. I looked forward to them more than competing.

Linda Lou sat up front alone, so I sat beside her.

"Can I buy you a beer?" I asked.

"No. I don't drink."

"You drink Coke?"

"Yes, that would be all right."

That meant she wasn't a Mormon, anyway. They didn't drink Coke in those days. Now they do, but it's only because they bought stock in it.

It didn't matter. I couldn't get a waitress over with that crowd, and I didn't want to leave that girl long enough to get to the bar. She said she was a student at Whitman in Walla Walla, studying music. She really wanted to be a singer.

"How'd you like to sing with the band that's playing right now?" I asked.

She looked at me with those big, blue eyes, and her dimples grew. I fell in love at that moment. "Yeah." She said it like it wasn't possible.

I took her hand and led her onstage to one side, waving Charley over when he finished his song.

"Charley, this is Linda Lou," I said. "She wants to sing with you."

He looked at her kindly. "You sing?"

"Yes."

"You any good?"

"I sure am."

"OK, Linda Lou, what do you know cold?"

"How about *I'm Lost in Love with You?*"

Well, she *was* good. She sang four songs, and something, Charley sang with her. They pleased and surprised everyone with *He Taught Me How to Yodel.* They sang that like they'd rehearsed it a hundred times. I was thrilled.

That summer, Linda and I spent all our free time together. She worked in a bank in Asotin and sang with the band on weekends. I went to as many shows as I could. When we were out of town, we stayed together. She was so affectionate. That's not the right word. She made love to me like she was singing her favorite song.

We said we loved each other, and I meant it. She did, too, at first. Then I saw trouble coming. She started putting me off, saying, "Let me sleep. I'm tired." "I have cramps." "Don't you think of anything else?"

I became desperate and ached for her. "Let's get married."

"Are you kidding?"

"No. I mean, soon."

"I don't want to get married. I want to go to Nashville with my own songs."

"I'll go with you."

"No."

"Just no?"

"I don't want to marry you."

That was plain, though it was hard for me to see, let alone accept. I felt physical pain in my chest.

The band, now called Lindy Lou and Charley's Ridge Runners, got a big gig at the Puyallup Fair in Seattle. They did well. I saw them when they arrived on the train at Clarkston. Linda was holding Charley's hand, and they kissed once in a while. I felt numb and desperate.

Charley saw me and ran over, leaving Linda to fuss with her purse self-consciously.

"Hey, Youngblood! What are you doing here?" he asked.

"I came to give you guys a ride," I mumbled.

"That's good of you, but I have my own car."

It became obvious that Linda was with him.

"We got a chance at Nashville," he said. "Can you believe it? It's Linda's songs."

She looked the other way as Charley ran over to take her hand.

"Congratulations." I turned and left. As I walked off, I knew I was leaving part of my heart behind, but I didn't look back.

He gazed into the distance. I squirmed in embarrassment, fearing he'd become more emotional than he already was. When he didn't, I was glad. Slowly, he put out his pipe and continued.

I returned to college at the end of summer and did well. When I came home for Christmas, we had a thirteen-year-old Native American girl named Daisy living with us. She was a Nez Perce from across the river, and her mother was Suzy's kid sister. Suzy's sister was all messed up with alcohol and pot and disappeared one night. No one ever saw her again.

Emerson suddenly had a daughter, and I had a little sister--sort of. She was a cute little shit with a round face, big black eyes, full pouty lips, shiny black hair, and one dimple. She seemed to giggle constantly, but I felt that was just because she was glad to be with us. Her drunken mother must've made her life hell.

That kid followed me around everywhere. She looked sad anytime I left, so I started taking her with me when I went fishing, to town, visiting, or even hunting. I gave her my old .22. She became a good shot.

She loved going to rodeo practice with me, which was three times a week. A guy gave me a wild little black Mustang, and Daisy and I trained it together. When the horse bucked her off, she got back on. She soon had that pony tamed into a fine riding horse. Emerson helped, though.

She rode bareback and said, "It's 'cause I'm an Indian." She rode that critter at least once a day, sometimes more.

I remember Suzy telling her to stop riding bareback with a dress on, because she was wearing out her underpants. She started developing breasts soon. She must've been a little behind because of poor nutrition until she came to live with us.

Anyhow, she became self-conscious and started walking with round shoulders. I thought it was funny at first, then I saw how sensitive she was. One day, I up and asked her, "Daisy, you know what? You've got the cutest little boobies in the world."

She didn't know whether to laugh or hit me. Suddenly, she smiled and hit me, anyway. That ended the problem.

When I returned to college at Washington State after Christmas and spring breaks, I realized Daisy was becoming a young lady in many ways, and not just the obvious physical ones. There were subtle things, too. She flirted with me in a way that was awkward at first, then became less so. She was fifteen going on twenty at times, then she'd become a silly little girl at others.

One day, she said, "I'm going to marry you."

I blushed like hell. I can't say I was flattered. It wasn't comfortable.

I got through vet school in two years. It takes four these days. I rode in lots of amateur rodeos to keep my amateur standing. I rode in college rodeos all over the West, sometimes as far as Oklahoma and Texas. I was good, and I knew it. I was on my way to being college bareback bronc champion, one of my big goals.

I still came home, because I liked seeing Dad, Susan, and Daisy. They seemed glad to see me, too, and the love they gave was easy to return. All three came to rodeos I was in if they could.

When he paused in his seat and twisted, I knew something uncomfortable was coming.

Daisy started running around with a bunch of kids from her high school that I didn't approve of. They were probably no worse than I'd been, but who knows? She started having less time for us in the family, and she was hardly ever home. She told Emerson she didn't want to be adopted, which hurt his feelings pretty bad, though I suspected it was because she didn't want to be my sister.

I didn't want her to, either, though I never would've admitted it. When she graduated from high school, she left to attend the university in San Francisco. She had a Native American scholarship and was given spending money from her aunt and uncle, as well as working a part-time job at the bank.

We missed her a lot. She wrote and called less and less. Maybe that's how it's supposed to be. Susan wrote her every week, which is how *that's* supposed to be, too. When Daisy called, she left us a number, but we could never reach her. She always sounded excited about a part in a play or musical or a TV commercial. That didn't surprise me. She'd always been an actress.

I had one more year left in vet school when the college rodeo championship came to Lewiston, Idaho. I was excited and ready. I had a girlfriend named Sandy, who was also the rodeo queen. We were close, but we were a long way from being in love. She'd been out to meet Emerson and Susan and liked them. They liked her, too. She kicked off her boots, asked for a sandwich if she was hungry, and made herself at home. They liked that.

The day came for my big ride. I called home that morning, and Susan answered.

"Are you coming to the rodeo?" I asked.

"I don't think so. Emerson isn't feeling well. He's got a bad cough, and his chest hurts."

"Does he have a fever?"

"I think so. He feels hot, but our thermometer broke."

"You should buy another one," I said sharply, feeling concerned. Emerson never fell ill.

"He's sleeping now. He was up coughing most of the night. I don't want to wake him. Why don't you call after the rodeo? Emerson's friend, Dr. Moffet, is coming by this afternoon."

"He's a horse doctor!"

"He treats a lot of people, too. He's delivered plenty of babies around here."

She sounded defensive, so I let it go.

"He'll probably fill Emerson up with penicillin."

"I guess that's all right," said, still worried. "Penicillin is penicillin, horse, dog, or man."

My ride came up late in the rodeo. I drew a big roan with one blue eye and one brown. He had a Roman nose, pig ears, and a constant sneer. He also had the big hindquarters I liked to see, but he was high in the withers, which I didn't like. To begin with, he was kicking hell out of the chute. It took three guys to get my bucking rig on him.

Sandy gave me a worried kiss before I lowered myself onto his back. The men tightened the bouncing strap around his haunches, and he went crazy.

I nodded. The gate flew open, and out we went. That nag lit on all fours, reared, bucked, twisted, snorted, climbed the air, sunfished, and hunkered down. I held on with all my strength, pulling ass down and leaning back as far as I could. I spurred his neck without stopping.

The horn sounded at eight seconds. I'd ridden him out and knew it was a hell of a ride, hopefully a championship ride. The pickup man rode up and unsnapped the bucking strap. It didn't seem to make much difference.

Then, without thinking, I waved away the pickup man and jumped off Indian style. I lit on my feet and went ass over teakettle in the dirt. Somehow, my damn hat stayed on, so I took it off and waved to the crowd.

People ran up from all over, slapping my back and calling me Champ. I almost broke my face smiling. I felt like a million bucks, and I don't mean all wrinkled and green.

That evening, they presented me with what I wanted more than anything at that time—a big, bold, silver belt buckle with gold inlay that read *Champion*. God, I was proud.

Before we went to the rodeo dance that evening, I called home and spoke with Emerson.

"How are you feeling?"

"Much better, except for a penicillin shot in the ass. That hurt more than my chest."

"Dad, should I come out? I have something to show you."

"I know—a belt buckle with *Champion* on it."

"How'd you know?"

"My God, I was on the phone with Sandy when you jumped off Indian style."

"Yeah, Dad. Indian style."

We were silent for a moment.

"I'm proud of you, Son," he said softly.

I choked up but managed to croak out, "I'm proud that you're my dad. I love you, you know."

"I know, and I love you, too."

As lightly as I could, I said, "I was afraid I'd have to come out there with a shovel."

"Naw. I'm better. You go dance with Sandy and have a good time."

"I'll come out first thing in the morning. Tell Susan hello. See you in the morning."

What a party and dance it was that night. There was plenty of fun, beer, and compliments. How many slaps on the back did I get? How many people calling me Champ? How many pretty girls I didn't even know kissed me?

Sandy and I had a good time. She wanted to stay with me, so I let her. Let her? Hell, I begged her.

I went out to the place at ten o'clock the following morning. My head still hurt. As I went through the door, I held the buckle in my hands.

Susan sat in a corner, rocking back and forth with a shawl over her head, making a quiet, high-pitched, whimpering sound. My heart broke into a million pieces.

We both wiped our eyes. Neither of us could look up for a while. Presently, he continued.

There were a lot of people at the funeral I didn't know. There were plenty of Native Americans and others. It seemed everyone he knew

came. I buried him with the big, silver belt buckle with the word
Champion around his waist.

I never rode in a rodeo again.

I graduated from vet school, passed my board exams, and set up
in town where you can still see my office. At first, mostly I did large
animals. I even had to show a few horses just to make a buck.

Susan returned to the reservation and lived there until she was
eighty-six. When she died, she told me she still loved Emerson.

"What happened to Daisy?" I asked.
"I'm getting to that," he said sharply.

Sandy married a lawyer from Lewiston who later became a judge.
She was happy, and I was happy for her. I could've....

Charley and Linda Lou did really well. They made records I still
hear on the radio today. The folk-music boom came at a good time for
them. They returned to Clarkston once. My God, that must've been
fifty years ago. We were all about forty-five then.

Charley looked fine. His wrinkles looked distinguished, and he
still had a full head of wavy hair that was in the process of changing
color. He had a small potbelly, a little extra chin, and he looked like he
spent a lot of time in the sun.

Linda looked like she'd smoked too many cigarettes. She had
wrinkles around her mouth, and her eyes looked like something
borrowed from a walnut. She'd gained at least fifty pounds, twenty of
which were in her tits, with the rest in her ass.

I'm not being very nice, am I? I probably didn't look that good,
either. It's funny how things work out.

"What about Daisy?" I asked.
"I'm getting there."

Russell got an agriculture degree and went to work for the Nez
Perce tribe down in the valley, where they got some of their land back.
We stayed good friends over the years. He died at eighty-seven, and I
still miss him. There's a park down in the Dalles with his name on it.
He was one damn good Native American.

"You want to know about Daisy, don't you?"

"I sure do."

He sat back in his chair and ran a hand through his ample white hair.

I was in practice here about three years, maybe more. Most of the work was driving to farms and ranches to take care of sick cows. I must've castrated about a million of 'em, I think, and horses, too. I never liked castrating horses.

Anyway, I came home one night and saw a new Volkswagen beetle parked at my front door. In those days, I never bothered to lock. Anyone could've kicked it in, anyway.

Someone was inside, waiting for me. She'd already made coffee, and I saw a lot of groceries on my kitchen table. She was in her old bedroom, too.

"Daisy?"

She came out of her bedroom, set down her coffee cup, and gave me the damnedest hug I ever had. She was crying softly, and I realized I'd never seen her cry before.

We held each other for a while. Feelings passed between us of life lived, pain, regret, sadness, disappointment, and some loneliness. They were tempered by accomplishment, but there was very little free-floating unencumbered happiness.

"Brady, do you ever think about me?" she asked.

"Every day."

"What do you think?"

"I think…I thought you were someone else, someone lost to me, like a page turned in a book. It wasn't just someone lost but something, like being young."

"Did you care?"

"It broke my heart. But then, a lot of things have done that. I was just waiting for it to heal."

"Did it?"

"No."

We separated, and she walked into the kitchen.

"Come," she said. "I brought steaks. I want to make your supper."

I was amused at her calling it supper, not dinner. That simple, down-home expression brought out a warm feeling of affection that hadn't been there for a long time.

I helped her peel and fry potatoes while she made coleslaw. She knew that was my favorite salad. I lit the charcoal barbecue on the porch. As usual, I used enough starter fluid to burn down a house. She laughed when I lit it and fell off the porch. It was good to hear her laugh, but I wondered what I looked like without any eyelashes.

After eating supper, we sat on the porch in the gathering dusk. The sunset was bright red and orange. Birds sang their bedtime serenade. It was time to talk.

She looked older, of course. Fine lines showed at the corners of her eyes, though she had few other wrinkles. The skin of her neck and face were darker but still smooth and tight. Her breasts were firm and pointed. I remembered them as little flowers and almost said something, then thought better of it and shut up. Her butt had more flesh to it, but, because of her slim waist, she looked awfully good.

"You know where I've been, Daisy. Where have you been?"

"You never got married?"

"No."

"Have you had lots of lady friends?"

"Yes, lots."

"Why didn't you get married?"

"I never found anyone who'd have me, I guess—anyone I also wanted, anyway. Have you been married?"

"No. Not really." It sounded like a lie.

"Why?"

"I never found anyone that I would have, who would have me." That sounded like another half-truth, but it seemed best not to pursue it.

"You did good acting. I saw you on TV a couple times. You were in a commercial for ponybras."

"Pantyhose."

"Panty something."

"I've done a lot of theater in California. I like live theater best. I never got to do any real movies."

"Real movies? Like porno?"

"No! Like *Lassie, Come Home.*"

"Oh."

"Anyway, I quit."

"You quit?"

"I just quit."

"Why?"

"It was a fast life—pot, booze, and rock and roll."

We both knew she left out the sex.

"I'm glad you're here," I said, ready to ask why, but she interrupted.

"I'm just recovering from an operation."

I waited.

"They took everything out, my uterus and ovaries. I had a pelvic abscess. My boyfriend, the one I was living with, brought it home to me."

She hadn't mentioned a live-in boyfriend. Strange, but I was slightly disappointed in her. Then again, it was none of my business.

"Now I take hormones and feel normal, as normal as I can, without…."

"So you left?"

"Yes."

"Are you really all right?"

"No." She started crying again.

I gathered her on my lap, and her tears ran down my neck. I kissed the top of her head and stroked her beautiful, shiny black hair. I kissed her forehead and cheeks, but I stopped short of her quivering lips, though I wanted to kiss them, too.

"Daisy, you can stay here as long as you want."

She did—for twenty-six years.

I guess I always knew I loved her from the day she was a little girl. When she said she would marry me and wouldn't let Emerson adopt her, I knew why. She didn't want to be my sister.

We got married one month later. Russell came up from Oregon

with Susan, and you know who else? Charley came, but he didn't bring Linda Lou. I never asked why, but I had the feeling I knew.

"That's about it. We adopted a boy and a girl. They're grown up and gone now. Emerson's an English professor at the University of Washington. Daisy, my daughter, hates her name, but that's what it is. She teaches kindergarten in Olympia. Both are happily married—I think. I have six grandchildren who come over and drive me nuts in the summer."

"Do you hear from your children?" I asked.

"Hell, yes. They drive me nuts, too. Why do people talk to older folks like they're kids?"

"I don't know, but you're right."

"God, they both check on me twice a week. I'd hate to pay their phone bills."

I knew he was proud of them, and he wouldn't mind having those bills. "Daisy?"

"She slipped over as she slept in a nursing home after she broke her hip. She was eighty-five."

"How long ago was that, Youngblood?"

"A hundred years."

It was dark out. He asked only my name and what I did, so I never said anything else. It was his story, not mine.

"Tell you what, Brady Youngblood," I said. "This one acre here, with the house and barn and all, I'll deed back to you to live on as long as you want."

"You mean until I die."

"Yes, I guess I do."

"It'll be another twenty years, you know."

"I know, but what the hell?"

"Yeah, what the hell? I accept."

www.ingramcontent.com/pod-product-compliance
Lightning Source LLC
Chambersburg PA
CBHW050522260626
47157CB00004B/1426